OTHER TITLES BY KATHRYN BERLA

THE KITTY COMMITTEE

Kathryn Berla

Amberjack Publishing

New York | Idaho

Amberjack Publishing
1472 E. Iron Eagle Drive
Eagle, Idaho 83616
http://amberjackpublishing.com

This book is a work of fiction. Any references to real places are used
fictitiously. Names, characters, fictitious places, and events are the products
of the author's imagination, and any resemblance to actual persons, living
or dead, places, or events is purely coincidental.

Publisher's Cataloging-in-Publication data
Names: Berla, Kathryn, 1952- author.
Title: The kitty committee / by Kathryn Berla.
Description: New York : Amberjack Publishing, 2018.
Identifiers: LCCN 2018000194 (print) | LCCN 2018003382 (ebook) |
ISBN 9781944995768 (eBook) | ISBN 9781944995751 (pbk. : alk. paper)
Subjects: LCSH: Friendship--Fiction. | Secrets--Fiction.
Classification: LCC PS3602.E75745 (ebook) | LCC PS3602.E75745
K58 2018 (print) | DDC 813/.6--dc23
LC record available at https://lccn.loc.gov/2018000194

Cover Design: Mimi Bark

"Whatever love we receive always comes as a form of grace."
—Magda Szabó

IF THIS WAS a horror movie, the screen of my laptop would fade to black. A grinning skull would materialize and burst into hideous peals of laughter before dissolving into the hacker's moniker. But this isn't just any horror movie. It's *my* horror movie, the one I'm living. There's no black screen, just the body of an email from an innocuous, seemingly untraceable sender.

I've been waiting for it—searching for it, if truth be told. Checking my spam just in case I missed it this year, always arriving at the same time, always with a subject that's just innocent enough to lull an unsuspecting reader into opening it and reading further. I'm not innocent. I'm not unsuspecting. I know it's coming. I know I could delete every email that arrives in late February to early March that isn't conclusively from someone I know. I know I could change my own email address and never look back. Close my old account.

But I won't.

The email will find me somehow.

Although I'm prepared for its contents, or at least its implied threat, a transfer of fluids causes my mouth to go suddenly dry and my palms to become suddenly wet. My heart squirms like a scared kitten trapped in a clutched hand. I bring my fingertips to my cheeks which feel thin, hollow, though I know they're not. The light is unbearably bright, my eyes unable to focus. Everything is virtual visual nonsense. I'm locked in a cell from which there's no apparent escape.

Maggie died only just yesterday? Is it possible it was only just yesterday?

Having no paper bag handy, I cup my hands over my nose and breathe slowly, feeling my stomach rise and fall.

Maggie.

Maggie.

Was that really you? They told me you could hear me, though I doubted it. Still I spoke to you, and, since no one else was in the room, I even sang to you. I doubt you would have enjoyed it if you actually *could* hear me.

How will I manage without you, Maggie? Your soft brown eyes that held me until the end. Wouldn't let me go until they closed the final time.

My carbon dioxide levels rise, pushing me from panic into pure sadness.

I reach for the phone and tap out a text to a number I should have lost long ago.

Did you get the email?

No response.

One minute.

Two minutes.

My phone rings.

"Hi, Grace. We really shouldn't text about this. Call next time if you need to talk."

"So, did you get the email?" I ask Carly.

"Yes."

"And?"

"And what?"

"What do you think?"

"What do I think? I deleted it like you should've. Didn't read it."

I hear the clattering of computer keys in the background, and I know Carly is working, only half listening to me. Placating in that way she does that makes me feel like an annoying child.

"Maggie died."

"Yes, I know."

"How did you know?"

"I called. Spoke to someone at the nursing station. They told me."

"I didn't know you were keeping in touch." These words are meant to punish. I know that. Carly will know that. And yet, it won't have the effect I intend it to have.

"Grace, she was my friend too. You're not the only one who'll miss her," she says in a way I want to believe is compassionate.

"It's just that . . . when was the last time you visited her?" I try again. It's futile, I know. Carly has an armor so thick that it can't be pierced. Especially by me. And yet I continue to fling my puny words against it.

"Grace . . ."

She's annoyed with me. I can tell by the way she speaks my name.

"It's not fair. She didn't deserve this."

"Who deserves death, Grace? And yet it comes to us all."

The clattering of computer keys continues in the background.

"Do you think," I start. "Do you *believe* there's something to it? To the email?"

"What email? I told you—I didn't read it."

"It said *'Vengeance is mine, I will repay, says the Lord.'*"

"Thanks, Grace. I just told you I deleted it because I didn't want to know what it said."

"Well, now you know."

"Now I know. Thanks to you." A phone rings nearby. "Grace, what is it you want me to say to you?"

Why did Maggie have to die? Why couldn't it have been Carly? Or me?

"There's no one else I can talk to," I say, aware of how pathetic that sounds.

"I don't get what you're saying. Do I think there's something to the email? You're the religious one. I don't believe in that mumbo jumbo. You tell me."

I lower my voice to barely above a whisper as though the walls themselves could capture and turn my words against me.

"I'm not religious anymore either, and you know it. But Maggie's cancer. Her anorexia. Do you ever wonder if—"

"Do I believe in fairy tales? No, Grace, I don't believe in fairy tales. There's no giant man in the sky who woke up yesterday and decided to turn his murderous attentions on Maggie. Don't be ridiculous."

"Forty is so young. To die."

"She had an aggressive form of breast cancer, and you should know about that stuff more than anyone. Lots of people die young. It's a cruel irony of life, among many others."

"It's a well-documented fact that stress can lower your resistance . . . it can lead to physical as well as mental illness. The constant stress in Maggie's life. What *we* did."

"Yeah, and if you keep it up, you're going to psych yourself into something too, real or imagined. So just relax, okay?"

"You didn't see her, Carly. Talking to her on the phone is one thing but *seeing* her . . ."

"Okay, Grace, if it makes you feel any better, they just arrested a guy in . . . someplace, I can't remember where. And he was in his mid-nineties and responsible for hundreds of thousands of deaths in Auschwitz more than seventy fucking years ago. And he was doing just fine, thank you very much. So much for the email. And your loony fears."

I allow the *loony fears* remark to slide.

"Maybe he didn't have remorse. Maybe he didn't feel like he'd done anything wrong. But Maggie did, that's the difference."

Silence.

"I'm slammed here at work, Grace, I really am. I gotta go, but you take care, okay? Do yourself a favor and pull yourself together."

"You're never worried, are you? You never think about your part in everything. How do you manage it?"

I don't really want to know how she manages it. She manages it without a conscience. Again, I try to wind her up but am unsuccessful.

"No, I'm not worried. Same old whack-job with a chip on his shoulder. Or her shoulder. One of these days hopefully they'll drop dead and we'll never hear from them again." The clattering stops, and her voice drops to a husky whisper. "Until that happy day, no one knows anything. No one can prove anything. We technically did nothing wrong. And there's such a thing as statute of limitations, even if we did. Okay? Got it? Oh, and Grace? Are we really going to do this every year? How many years has it been? Twenty?"

Before the call, I'd hoped this would be the time when I'd make her number disappear from my phone and never speak to her again. But now I know it won't be. As long as Carly continues to take my calls, I'll continue to make them. Why do I care so much what Carly thinks? Because she doesn't care at all.

Maggie was the only one who stayed in Indian Springs. She had family there—roots like the daffodils. Roots that went back generations. But eventually, she too was in San Francisco, spending more and more time at the university hospital. She'd been there before, twenty years earlier when her already slender frame was reduced to nothing more than a reminder of who she had been. Anorexia. Then, twenty years later, the relentless cancer that whittled away at her like a carving knife.

When I last visited Maggie, I was struck by the cruel similarity in appearance from two decades earlier. The taut skin over her cheekbones, tight like a mask. The unhealthy pallor. The terrible thought that a too-heavy blanket would crush her fragile bones, leaving only a pile of dust behind.

Was that only two days ago?

I brought a bouquet of daffodils the day I sang for Maggie in her hospital room. Her parents, reunited long ago by her difficulties, slipped out of the room, taking advantage of my presence for a brief mental-health respite. I knew Maggie couldn't see the daffodils, but I told her they were there.

Maybe she heard me, and it brought her some comfort.

Maybe the daffodils were really meant for me.

CHAPTER ONE
Indian Springs: Twenty-Two Years Earlier

I was born to be the perpetual new girl. I don't mean that I was quick to adapt and loved new situations. On the contrary, change was hard for me, and I didn't have the effervescent personality that could smooth my transitions. So I was born to be the new girl because I met everyone's expectations.

My brother, Luke, was the opposite. He was handsome, yes. He was athletic, yes. Not too much bothered him, and he wasn't even required to have a winning personality. But he did. So while Luke was busy deciding how to fairly distribute himself and his many talents as a senior at Indian Springs High, I was busy trying to disappear as a sophomore.

As the children of missionaries, our education had been carried out mostly through homeschooling and mission schools, wherever they were available, but I was far enough ahead in my studies that my parents, with the school's blessing, decided to skip me ahead a grade. Every five years we were required to spend a year back home, although it didn't feel anything like home to me. But when Dad broke his back falling off a ladder in Guatemala, we returned three months early. My only other experiences living in the states had been when I was eight and we spent a year in rural Georgia where my mother grew up. And another year in that same small town when I was only three. This time, because of my father's medical condition, my parents moved us to Indian Springs, which was close to San Francisco, where Dad grew up, and yet far enough away to be affordable. The main reason, though, was the access to good medical care for Dad and, as always, the church community to ease our transition back into the first world.

And what a transition it would prove to be. Nothing prepared me for this country that claimed me on my passport as one of its own. I was accustomed to dusty roads and stray dogs and people whose smiles bore no evidence of orthodontia; market days and clothes my mother sewed on her old Singer from fabrics dyed in brilliant shades of fruit and sunsets and a jungle that creeped up to your window if you allowed it; the Sunday morning serene but blissful faces of worshippers seated on splintered planks in tiny wooden churches; languages I understood spoken side-by-side with languages I didn't; having the ability to interpret a person's meaning by listening to the cadence of their tongue. The movement of their hands. The crinkle at the corner of their eye. This is what I knew.

In Indian Springs, we arrived at night. And when I woke the following morning, I already suspected what a colossal task lay ahead of me. It was almost impossible for me to believe I belonged there with its delineated properties and paved streets that intersected each other at right angles.

The property manager stopped by with the lease and an extra set of keys. A neighbor returned a garden hose he'd borrowed from the last tenants and kept because the house was unoccupied. The mailman pushed his cart along the sidewalk, pausing at our box where he sorted through his bag before selecting a few items to leave behind. Mail addressed to past occupants. Names we didn't know.

I had imagined a life in the states one day, but I didn't think it would be until I was much older. My vision of that life came from old magazines I managed to salvage in the villages where I grew up. The occasional snippets of television I caught during visits to the central medical clinic or the rare family outing to a restaurant which could claim status beyond glorified street vendor. But the magazines didn't prepare me for an entire new set of social cues. A new way of communicating with strangers who spoke precisely and politely but never gave away anything beyond just their words. How to reconcile this world with the one I'd left behind, one I would come to view as a golden time in my life. That I had to figure out on my own, and there was no time to waste.

In preparation for my new life at a new school, I'd gotten the notion that a pixie cut would favorably frame my round face, making me more appealing to others. I'd come up with the idea by myself, inspired by a very outdated teen magazine. Mom would never have thought to impart fashion advice, which was the furthest thing from her mind. Growing up, my hair hung shoulder length and natural as it dried and was shaped by the tropical humidity. Mom would lop it off with a pair of old scissors whenever it got too long. I sensed this wouldn't be enough for first-world respectability, so using the same old scissors, with one eye on the magazine and the other on a mirror in front of me, I recreated the cut as best as I could. Mom helped with the back, claiming she loved not only the modesty of the cut but the look of it too.

What I hadn't foreseen was that the baby fat which made my face round also made my body round. And without the aid of any makeup to hint at my gender (and no breasts to speak of), my pixie cut had the effect of transforming me into a chubby boy—at least, at first glance. While other girls blossomed, I was stuck in prepubescence. Had I not insisted on wearing a skirt my first day at Indian Springs High, I most likely would have been taken for a boy. I was wholly unprepared to be a modern American teen, and yet that's just what I was about to become.

Mom dropped us off across the street on our first day of school. Luke flew out of the car and melded so seamlessly into the crowd, it seemed he'd done it a thousand times before. First day of school for us was February twenty-third, which was going on the 160th day for everyone else.

Still, I felt my chest swell with optimism at the sight of thousands of daffodils lining every conceivable walkway around and leading up to Indian Springs High. Their humble, bowing heads melded into a bright sea of such intense color, I was certain it could shame even the sun. I was Dorothy skipping along the yellow brick road toward the Emerald City and all the adventures awaiting me. Any school of this size was a totally unfamiliar concept to me. Prior to this, the largest school I'd attended numbered thirty students max. Children of missionaries, locals, and the occasional son or daughter of an American diplomat, preferring a religious education.

But somewhere between my mother's car and the intimidating entrance of my new school, my legs grew heavy, my heart sodden with dread. It seemed that pixie cuts were not in style, after all. I didn't see one girl with hair short enough to reveal her ears. Hair was styled, not air-dried like mine which I had lauded for the absolute genius of convenience it would bring to my life. The source of my fashion inspiration had been terribly out of date. I felt deceived by my mother's reassurance.

How had I so badly misjudged this most basic of all teen fashion tenets—the acceptable hairstyle? But it didn't end there because it was soon obvious the pixie cut wasn't my only fashion crime. Blouses tucked into pleated skirts were nowhere to be seen, except on me. The girls wore pants, jeans mostly. Tight-fitting tops revealing developing figures instead of baggy blouses. And if there were skirts, they were unlike any skirt that was part of my wardrobe, which up until that point was a mish-mash of donations of used clothing from strangers, last-minute purchases from Goodwill, and some colorful ethnic fashions picked up on the cheap in countries where we'd lived. I wondered how I was going to convince Mom to let me wear makeup—jeans, I was sure she'd go along with for their modesty. I didn't have a clue as to how to apply makeup and, even if I could convince Mom, she wouldn't be of any help having never touched the stuff herself.

I'd been so proud to learn I would skip a grade in my new school, but now I wondered if that was another huge mistake. It would forever mark me as the girl always at least a year less mature than her peers, and one look around told me that physical maturity mattered here. These kids didn't seem as if they'd be wowed by my intellectual prowess. These kids held themselves as if it was what was on the outside that mattered. That was quite the opposite of what I'd been taught my entire life.

I was just thirteen years old and still playing with dolls.

Somehow, I was either pushed along or managed to push against the throng of students, passing period by passing period. For the most part, I wound up where I was supposed to be, until it came to fourth period English. I'd carefully chosen a seat in the back of each classroom for the strategic purpose of going most unnoticed, but when I heard "take out your books" and saw the images from around the world which adorned our social studies books, I knew I had to make a fast but inconspicuous getaway.

"Miss . . ." the teacher halted his instructions to turn his focus on me before I could make it out the door. That one innocuous word succeeded in turning me into the main attraction for everyone else in the room who hadn't, until that moment, been paying attention to the girl fleeing from the room.

"Grace," I said foolishly. "Templeton." I threw in my last name as though it could somehow diffuse the situation. "I, I think I'm in the wrong class."

"And the right class would be?" He arched a pair of superior eyebrows at me.

"English."

"Then you most assuredly are in the wrong class," he said kindly. "Let me take a look at your schedule."

And while he was doing that and scratching out an excuse for tardiness for my English teacher, I permitted my gaze to stray from the top of my shoes. Most of the students were chuckling softly, but their eyes shifted compassionately when I looked up. What they must have seen in me that day would be a wonder to them—the strange creature who appeared inexplicably in their midst.

But one girl didn't look away, choosing instead to stare directly at me. She wasn't snickering like the others, she observed me as though taking in my entirety and formulating a conclusion which I immediately wanted and didn't want to know. She was lithe, legs covered in faded denim, cuffed at the hem, and sprawled out from underneath her desk. I noticed flip-flops and painted toenails in spite of the somewhat cool February day. Her shoulder-length, strawberry-blonde hair was perfectly coiffed with bangs that dropped to just above eyes I imagined would be green if I could see them. And then she smiled. Not laughed, but smiled. She held my gaze until I was forced to smile back.

I loved her at that very moment.

"Here's your tardy excuse." The teacher's words ripped me from my reverie. "Good luck, Miss Grace Templeton."

And so began anew the muffled giggles and snorts. I didn't dare turn around to see if the girl was part of it. I wanted the image of her cool acceptance—and yes, validation—to carry me through the difficult twists and turns of that first day.

My next hurdle was health class, which was taught, to boys and girls alike, by the football coach. Health, the way it was meant in class, wasn't a subject discussed much around my house. My parents talked a lot about maintaining a healthy body and mind through contemplation, exercise, a balanced diet, and shunning the obvious vices. But when it came to sex . . . well, I knew that somehow my parents had conspired physically to bring me and Luke into the world, but I was short on details and not really keen to get them. I hadn't even begun to menstruate.

Health class in school was about those other things too. Healthy food. Exercise. Staying away from cigarettes, drinking, and drugs. But by February, the teacher had eased into the more personal issue of sex. Girls and boys would be separated for certain classes, Mr. Janke let us know. But there was plenty we could talk about as a group. Premarital sex. Responsibility. How babies can ruin your life when you're not ready for them. Protection if you absolutely must, although abstinence was the preferred method.

My head swam with the details I heard that first day in class. I worried about Luke, who had missed sophomore year in America. How would he ever gain all the knowledge that I would soon possess? I knew my parents wouldn't be much help. From my vantage point in the back of the class, I could see students diffusing the tension with snickers, passing notes, folding paper, spinning pencils, mindlessly thumbing through the textbook, and generally squirming.

But I was fascinated that sex was something which could be discussed so openly and calmly by an adult in front of children. Only my father's calamity had pried me away from my parents' protective cocoon, thrusting me into a world where the words *penis* and *vagina* could be uttered with as much indifference as *peanut butter and jelly sandwich*. From the back of the classroom, I did have the advantage of being protected from the view of most everyone in the class, which allowed me to focus rather than fidget.

As I was furiously taking notes that would have to be hidden deep in my backpack once I got home, I pressed too hard on the pencil in my excitement. The tip splayed helplessly against my paper and no amount of coaxing would anchor it enough to continue to function as a proper pencil. I searched uselessly through my backpack, knowing I'd only grabbed one pencil and no sharpener on my way out the door that morning. To get up and go to the front of the classroom to sharpen my pencil was unthinkable.

"Pssst," a boy sitting next to me hissed.

He reached out to me, a pencil in his hand. When I stared dumbly at him, he jiggled his hand as if to wake me from a deep sleep.

"Thanks," I whispered, taking the pencil and returning to my note-taking, a little less frantically now that I knew I was being observed.

When class was over, I permitted myself a sneak peek at the boy who had offered his pencil. A fuller look than what

I'd previously seen from the corner of my eye. He was tall and gangly, his hair cut short but not stylishly from what I could tell. Luke was broad-shouldered and muscular. This boy was paper-thin; if there was a muscle in his body, I failed to see it. His clothes were rumpled and ill-fitting. The sheen of oil on his forehead highlighted several white-tipped red zits. He wore glasses that looked like they could have been borrowed from my dad. In other words—at least physically—he was my kindred spirit.

"Do you want your pencil back?" I asked his back as he was leaving.

"Nah." He turned around. "You can keep it."

"Thanks," I said. "I'll bring you a new one tomorrow."

And then, a burst of confidence I didn't know existed within me. "My name's Grace Templeton."

"I'm Timothy," he said. "Or Tim. Whatever."

CHAPTER TWO

AFTER DAD'S ACCIDENT, he had surgery in Guatemala to stabilize him before being flown back to the states in an air ambulance. The next two years would mark a long, slow, painful path to recovery, but from my child-centric perspective, I didn't fully understand what that meant for him. I knew that he rarely came out of his bedroom. I knew he slept and read and ate in a special hospital bed, delivered to our home and paid for by insurance. I knew he and Mom lost the ready smiles that had carried me through childhood. I just never considered him as having to adapt in the same way that I was adapting. He was a grown-up, after all.

Although our new house was the nicest one, by objective standards, that I'd ever lived in, I couldn't imagine it ever feeling like a real home. The mail continued to arrive each day, bearing the ghosts of past occupants. Dad's torment was always just yards away, dampening any bright thoughts that might percolate in my brain. Mom was mostly missing, working as a nurse in a hospital thirty miles away where, by necessity, she tended to every patient except the one who needed her most. The neighbors kept to themselves, which was a concept totally unfamiliar to me. On the positive side, we had our first TV, but it was in my parents' room to distract Dad from the pain that was his constant companion.

People travel for miles to visit the daffodils that begin to bloom in Indian Springs each February. The entire town was under orders to display daffodils in every conceivable space. Not exactly official orders, more of a community understanding. If you don't participate, you undermine your community, turn your back on what it stands for—love, acceptance, support during the hard times.

Judgment and ostracism.

Nature's smiles dominate the landscape for a few months, bringing a fleeting fame to an otherwise unremarkable town.

My family was one of the few that didn't live up to our obligation when we first moved to Indian Springs. Couldn't. The bulbs in front of our house were old and hadn't been well-cared for. The plants hadn't been watered properly after blooming season. Mom was too busy taking Dad to his doctors' appointments, and Luke and I were trying to adjust to our new school. Not that we would have known what to do with a daffodil even if we'd had all the time in the world on our hands. Eventually, well-meaning neighbors showed up and replaced bulbs and tended to the ones resilient enough to survive. I'd look out the kitchen window when I was rinsing my breakfast dishes to see an unfamiliar figure, trowel in hand, hunched over the strip of bare earth that edged our front lawn.

I felt keenly the divide between those happy yellow flowers that decorated our new town and the mood that permeated inside my new home.

My first night after school, I lay in bed replaying every minute of my day. I was pleased the work seemed easy enough, and I didn't think I'd have trouble keeping up. I hadn't made any friends, but then I hadn't really expected to. I'd seen Luke during lunch—all the way across the cafeteria from where I'd taken a seat at a table occupied by kids who didn't appear to be a cohesive group. Some were reading. Some were eating. Some were staring at the food in front of them. It seemed like a safe table, where I could take cover during lunch. Luke, on the other hand, was hanging with a group of boys who, to the outside observer, could have been his lifelong friends. I knew he was trying to decide between baseball and swim team. The boys most likely were sent by competing coaches to recruit Luke for their sport.

I thought about Timothy, whom I decided to call by his real name instead of Tim because it was the first one he'd said, so I believed it must be his preferred. I had stocked my backpack with plenty of sharpened pencils and even a few pens for the next day. My homework was done. My clothes were laid out. I'd broached the subject of clothes with Mom who agreed to get me a pair of jeans and maybe a few t-shirts that weekend at the Goodwill.

The walls were so thin between the three bedrooms of our house that I heard every footstep and every squeak of every bedspring. The TV murmured from my parents' room where it had become constant background noise, long after they fell asleep. I waited for Luke to finish up in our shared bathroom so I could brush my teeth and go to sleep on the lumpy used mattress that came with the house.

I thought about the girl who looked directly at me and smiled, refusing to let me go until I smiled back at her. I got up and walked over to my dresser where I stared into the mirror. I pushed my hair flat against my forehead, imagining bangs which grew down to my eyebrows. I knew that my hair grew a half-inch every month. I envisioned myself in one year, with hair that reached my shoulders and was perfectly styled.

I selected a Pixy Stix from my private candy stash hidden from who-knows-who in my dresser drawer. Cherry-flavored. I tore open the top, and poured a small amount onto the tip of my tongue where it mixed quickly with saliva. I pushed the mixture onto my lips, spreading it with my tongue, rubbing my lips together to distribute the red color evenly.

I pictured the girl I wanted to be.

Mr. Janke shuffled our assigned seats once a month, so the next day I was no longer seated next to Timothy, nor was I in the back of the class. But I did manage to catch up with Timothy after class to present him with a brand-new, freshly sharpened pencil.

"Thanks." He dropped the pencil in the front pouch of his backpack and ambled away. Apparently, I'd misjudged our connection. Or his desire to converse with a kindred spirit.

I hadn't seen the girl with the strawberry-blonde hair again, not even at lunch. But then again, there were two lunch periods so she was probably in the second one. I had seen Timothy, though. I originally figured him for a candidate at my adopted table of social isolation but I was wrong again. Timothy hung with a small group of friends, both girls and boys, who seemed to enjoy each other's company. If I had to judge by their appearance, I'd have pegged them for the smart kids.

Timothy never showed any sign of recognition, not even when we stood side by side, waiting in the cafeteria line. I attempted a weak smile and a barely audible "hi," but his gaze by then was already averted, and the sound of my voice was no match for our one-foot height differential. My puny greeting drowned in a cacophony of clattering dishes and clanking forks. Mercifully, the cafeteria server intercepted my smile and smiled back.

"Hi," she said, rescuing me from utter humiliation.

That day at lunch, a girl at my table I'd seen the prior day leaned over mid-chew. She wore glasses which made her somehow less intimidating.

"Are you new?" she asked, and I felt a thrill at the possibility of new friendship.

"Yeah, I just started this week." I turned my upper body to face her, trying to signal my openness to questions.

"Cool. Where are you from?" Her upper lip caught on silver braces when she spoke, producing something akin to a lisp. I'd never seen braces that close before and tried not to stare but couldn't help noticing a tiny sprig of green snagged in the wire of her front tooth.

"Actually, we moved here from Guatemala. A village called Monte Verde."

"Guatemala? Isn't that an island out in the middle of the Pacific? Like near Tahiti?"

I hesitated to start down a path that would lead to all the ways I was different from everyone else, but she seemed genuinely interested and kind.

"Nope. You're probably thinking of Guam. I've been there too."

"Oh, cool," she said, but the way she said it made me think she wasn't impressed one iota. "What grade are you?"

"Sophomore."

"I'm a junior," she said as if to bring our conversation to a close. As if there would be no recovering from the difference in our grades, no going back to two strangers innocently reaching out to each other. The brief flicker of interest in her eyes extinguished. "Well, nice talking to you. Hope you like it here." She flipped open a well-worn paperback novel and was instantly mesmerized. It seemed even a fantasy world was a better bet than a sophomore girl from a country that wasn't close to Tahiti. I wondered if I'd come off as a know-it-all when I threw in the line about Guam. I wondered if I'd humiliated her by pointing out the difference in the two countries. I wasn't sure when another opportunity like this would present itself, and I feared I'd blown my only chance for a friend.

By the third day, I had no illusions about what lay in store for me. The daffodils were nothing more special than yellow bobbleheads. I'd fallen for their promise of new life and fresh starts, but I wouldn't be deceived again. Nobody was interested in forming a friendship with me. Even kids like Timothy and the girl at the lunch table rejected me. I accepted my fate of counting down the days until school was over. Running out the clock. Summer would bring the promise of warmth and sunshine, which I associated with happiness. Maybe Dad would be better by then and we could go back to Guatemala or a different mission somewhere else. Luke could stay behind for college. It wasn't so long to wait. Only a few months.

In health class, Mr. Janke assigned a class project and advised us we were to work in pairs. Glancing down the list of possible topics, I wasn't sure which was more daunting—the subject matter or the act of securing a partner. I glanced nervously to my right and left but everyone was already partnering up, flagging down friends across the room or leaning over to whisper to ones nearby.

"Come up and see me once you've picked your subject and I'll mark you off," Mr. Janke said. Already, more than half the class was lined up at his desk, declaring their partnerships and their preferred topics. A few had to pick second or third choices by then and I still didn't have a partner.

There was a tap on my shoulder, and I swiveled so quickly, I felt a sharp ping followed by a painful twinge in my neck.

"Wanna be partners?" Timothy asked, and a relief so powerful overcame me that tears threatened to spring from my eyes.

"Sure, but . . ."

"I'll get us a topic," he said and walked right past me to the front of the room.

I watched Timothy confer with Mr. Janke, and it was apparent from their knitted brows that there were slim pickings by then. At one point, they glanced over at me, and I forced a smile in return, wondering why I wasn't up there bargaining on my own behalf, but also relieved Timothy was doing it for me. Mr. Janke leaned over his paperwork to note our partnership and whatever subject had been chosen for us.

"Herpes," Timothy said as he walked by my desk.

The rest of class was a blur, a combination of physical illness and unreality. Wasn't it clear to Mr. Janke I was in no way prepared to handle this? Herpes? STDs? What did I know about that world? What would my parents say? And with a boy as my partner? How could I calmly sit and discuss this with Timothy? Where would we work? And when? Would Mr. Janke allow us to work in class, or would we have to meet outside of school? In *his* house or (Heaven forbid) mine? Could I convince him to go to the local library? Was this a sort of date? Was Timothy asking me out on a date? How could I calmly discuss herpes with Timothy when I was already blushing just thinking about it? Would he expect me to kiss him at some point?

I soon had the answers to my questions as I jogged to catch

up with him after class, when it was apparent he wouldn't be waiting for me.

"Umm," I began, betraying my absolute lack of all confidence. "Umm . . . how should we do this?"

I had to walk in double-time, every two steps of mine equaling one of his.

"Do what? The project?"

"Yeah. I mean . . ."

"Don't worry about it. I'll do it myself."

When I looked up at him with what he must have known was alarm, he said, "I'll put your name on it with mine. First, if you want."

"But that would be dishonest, wouldn't it?"

"Why? There's always one person who carries all the weight when it comes to working in groups or with partners. So why not dispense with the pretense? I'll handle it. Make it much easier on the both of us."

Who was I to argue? I knew I had nothing to contribute.

"And anyway," he continued. "Group projects are stupid. They accomplish absolutely nothing, and I prefer working on my own."

So was this why he chose me? Because he knew he could work on his own without interference? Without some meddlesome partner interjecting ideas that he considered stupid?

"Well, what should *I* do? I should at least do something."

"You can give the oral presentation," he said without a glance over at me.

I froze in my tracks, but when I realized he wasn't going to stop, I rushed to catch up with him.

"No, I'm sorry. I can't do that," I said, my voice so small and shaky, I was embarrassed. "I'd rather write the whole thing than do the oral presentation."

Timothy must have heard the panic in my voice because he

looked down at me as though only just then aware someone was at his side.

"Okay, okay. I'll do everything. You can . . . proof the paper."

I seized on that, although by then I was fairly confident Timothy was indeed one of the smart kids and proofing the paper was just a bone he threw to get me off his back.

"Deal!" I said triumphantly.

Physical education was a new horror I'd been able to avoid the first two days. Whoever was in charge of providing me with a uniform either didn't come through or perhaps had forgotten. I was allowed to sit on the bleachers and do homework while the other girls lined up in the gym to perform various aerobic exercises before divvying up into volleyball teams. In Guatemala, physical education meant swinging on a rope under the vivid purple canopy of a flowering guayacan tree or kicking a soccer ball with whoever happened to have one. Usually barefoot.

My luck ran out on day three when Ms. Simms, the PE teacher, presented me with the requisite top and shorts stamped with the name and logo of our school. Since they were several sizes too big, and since I still didn't wear a bra, I changed into my PE uniform by slipping my top over the blouse I wore to school, and rolling the sleeves of my blouse so they wouldn't be visible. I cinched the waist of my shorts by drawing the cord tight and double-knotting it.

Ms. Simms randomly assigned me to a group of girls with whom I was supposed to remain for the rest of the year, and with whom I was expected to bond in the spirit of all that was wonderful about team sports. Introductions were quick and were done by Ms. Simms. Not one girl had a follow-up question for me or anything beyond an obligatory "hi" shadowed by a disappearing smile. On the volleyball court, I mimicked my teammates' actions but failed to serve the ball over the net a single time, missed every ball that came my way, and even succeeded in smacking a teammate in the nose with a wild backward swing. She was immediately excused to go to the nurse's office to tend to the resulting bloody nose. So much for bonding. When all the girls had changed from their PE uniforms back into school clothes, I was still struggling with the double-knot on my shorts. Once again, I arrived five minutes late to English, and this time without a pass.

Another week went by before oral presentations began in health class. They were scheduled so they'd all be done by the end of the week. As I listened to the other kids fumble and flush their way through their reports, I felt immense gratitude that I wouldn't be put in that position. I'd proofed Timothy's report and found it to be professionally written without a single mistake that I could find. But it was filled with embarrassing words and phrases like *genital-to-genital, sores,* and *oozing.* I returned the paper to Timothy without eye contact.

I would be required to go to the front of the class when we were introduced, but after that I could take my seat. Even that was bad enough since I'd developed a cold sore at the corner of my mouth—a sore that always appeared when I was on the verge of coming down with a virus or hadn't been getting enough sleep. It was Monday, and Timothy wasn't there, but I wasn't worried because he'd said we were scheduled for Friday. By then, I hoped my cold sore wouldn't be so noticeable.

I was totally unprepared when Mr. Janke called my name as the next presenter.

"But . . ." I sputtered. "Timothy isn't here today."

"You're scheduled today," Mr. Janke said. "And it wouldn't

be fair to put someone else in your place when they aren't prepared."

"But *I'm* not prepared," I gasped.

Mr. Janke looked down as if to double-check the schedule.

"Why not? Do you have the paper?'

"Yes, but . . ."

"Did you not help write it and go over it?"

"Yes," I lied. But I had read over it.

"Then proceed. This is a joint project so you'll both receive the same grade regardless of Timothy's attendance."

Every eye in the room was turned on me.

I retrieved my copy of the paper from my backpack, all the while cursing myself for not lying and claiming I didn't have it on me. I clutched it with one white-knuckled fist and made my way to the front of the classroom on legs that threatened to buckle.

"I'm Grace Templeton," I muttered to the pages. "And my project—*our* project . . . me and Timothy . . . it's on herpes."

Cue the laughter. It's not that our project was more or less embarrassing than any of the others by nature; it's just that I was such a painfully pathetic and self-conscious orator.

I blearily read the contents of the report that Timothy had written, the words squirming on the page like lethal viruses, waiting to invade my brain and render me a sobbing mess of mush. At one point, I froze, completely incapable of transforming the written word to the spoken one.

"Go on," Mr. Janke said. From the way he said it, I could tell he was already regretting his decision to make me go it alone. He was a kind man. He just didn't want the clowns running the circus. But the gentleness in his voice gave me the courage to continue, and I tried to focus only on that.

When it finally came to the part where I described the visual symptoms of genital herpes, a girl's squeal cut through the funereal pall that had settled over the room.

"Eeew! She has one on her lip."

To which everyone burst out laughing, and I couldn't blame them. I was the perfect target in the perfectly comedic situation for a roomful of high-school students who'd rather be anywhere but there. Even I recognized it as a means to diffuse the tension, and it worked. I instinctively brought my hand up to cover the sore at the corner of my mouth.

But Mr. Janke was furious, calling the girl from her seat and sending her to the office with a harsh rebuke.

When I was done and had received a compassionate pat on my shoulder and a merciful "well done" from Mr. Janke, I took my seat and proceeded to die a thousand deaths.

The next day, Timothy appeared at my desk before class.

"How'd it go? I heard Janke screwed up the schedule and made you give the talk."

For a few seconds, I considered not replying. But my anger got the better of me.

"Where *were* you?"

"Taking the PSAT. Why weren't you there?"

I didn't even know what a PSAT was.

"Nice. I guess you got your way because it's obvious you planned for me to give the talk all along. Hope you're happy. I hope we get an F."

"We didn't. We got an A."

"*That's* a joke. Anyway . . ." I fumed at the memory of my public humiliation.

"I *told* you; Janke screwed it up. We were supposed to present on Friday."

"Oookay. If you say so, I believe you. Wait. No, I don't."

I opened my book and pretended to read.

Timothy shook his head slowly and sighed. "Whatever." He slouched over to his desk.

I squeezed my eyes shut, allowing the tears to wet my eyelashes but not my cheeks.

After that day, we never spoke in class again.

There was a final memorable incident my sophomore year before we were released to the freedom of summer, toward which we all seemed to be racing those final weeks of school. I had a hall pass to go to the library, the purpose of which I no longer remember. The hallways were empty, a preview of their natural state soon to come. I walked slowly, taking advantage of my justified absence from class.

The long hall leading to the library had double doors which opened to the gym. The part of the gym closest to the hall was connected to the boys' locker room by another door. I was only steps away from the double doors when I heard a sudden commotion—voices, yelling, laughter, a slam, and finally pounding. I quickened my pace to witness the source of pandemonium.

When I stared into the gloom of the empty gym, I saw a boy pounding on the door to the boys' locker room. Stark naked, pale and thin, a thatch of dark hair between his legs from which protruded a ridiculous fleshy tube I understood immediately to be a penis. It flopped back and forth as the boy continued to pound on the door, demanding to be let in. His voice was cracked and sounded close to tears.

My immediate thought was one of shock. Boys had hair down there? I thought only girls did. And the penis . . . disgusting. I know I stopped and stared. This was the first naked adult male body I'd seen and I was riveted, yet revolted. How is it we were the same species and so alike in so many ways when our clothes were on?

Because I was focused on what was between his legs, it took me a few seconds to realize it was Timothy. Our eyes met and he turned his back to me, hanging his head, hunching his shoulders, and covering the crack of his butt with one hand. The door opened, and I could hear the teacher (Mr. Janke?) yelling at the tormentors responsible for Timothy's disgrace.

I walked away quickly, burning with shame for the thoughts in my head.

My first thought was that Timothy was a victim, and I never wanted to be a victim. I decided right then to do everything in my power to make sure something like that never happened to me. Thoughts like this hadn't occurred to me in the missionary schools I'd attended, but now I experienced a different reality. One less kind. One that required more strength.

My second thought was that Timothy deserved it.

The last day of school was a half-day basically devoted to standing in line to receive your yearbook and then getting people to sign it once it was in your possession.

There were a few kids I'd met at the loser table where I'd spent every lunch since I first arrived at Indian Springs. The loser table—such a cliché. None of us thought of ourselves as losers, I'm sure. We were just the kids who wanted to blend in and didn't have the means to pull it off. On the last day of school, we sought each other out to avoid the shame of an unsigned yearbook.

After that, I found a quiet corner to sit where I could study the contents of this book. I'd arrived too late for a picture, but I was grateful for that. There would be no visual record of who I'd been my sophomore year. I knew I'd come back as a different girl after the summer. One more in tune with, at least, the fashion requirements necessary to blend in. One who wouldn't wander accidentally into the wrong classroom on her first day. One who wouldn't ever be a victim again.

This book could have served me well if it had been handed to me on my first day of school. I would have known who was who and what was what by carefully perusing its pages. Who was smart. Who was popular. What activities might possibly align with my interests. But I'd known none of that and was still relatively clueless after more than three months of fighting just to stay afloat.

I found Timothy's picture. He stared awkwardly at the camera, his mouth in an imitation of a comfortable smile. I found his name in the index: Chess Club, Honor Society, JV basketball, Debate Club, State Band, and more. I'd suspected, but not known, the extent of his successes.

I ran my finger over row after row of sophomore class portraits until I stopped at the one I'd been looking for all along. There was the girl who had smiled at me on that first day, taking in my entirety as though I was a real person who was visible if you only bothered to look. Her hair and makeup were perfectly done, perhaps in anticipation of picture day. She looked into the camera, unafraid. She smiled but not in an ingratiating way—more in the manner of someone who knows what others don't. I turned to the back to read her list of accomplishments and they were equally as impressive as Timothy's. I flipped back to her picture and stared into her eyes as I had on my first day. But now I knew her name.

Carly Sullivan.

CHAPTER THREE

ONE OF THE first casualties of Dad's accident and our resulting move to California was involvement in our church. Mom took a job as a nurse to support the family while Dad was literally on his back. Luke and I were mainly left to fend for ourselves and help Dad when Mom wasn't around. She continued to attend church service on Sundays, taking me with her, but Luke was often absent due to sports and friends and his summer job as a lifeguard at the community pool. He would be leaving for Sacramento State University at the end of the summer, so my parents let him have his way.

Mom did her best to cement our family to the church community, but there was only so much time in her week, and I was losing interest by the day. This was no longer a church around which my entire existence revolved—social time, work time, the very purpose of our lives, or at least my parents' lives. This was a characterless building twenty minutes away by car instead of the five-minute walk in Monte Verde, Guatemala. Many people attended this church, and I could never know them all. I never felt the personal connection to God my parents led me to believe was a real and tangible thing. He never spoke directly to me. I felt God only through the bond with my parents. He spoke to me only through them.

When I was younger, a voice did speak to me at night. My own voice. It said *I hate God* over and over while I lay in bed trying to sleep. The voice practically drove me mad, and I was sure it was only a matter of time before I was struck by a bolt of lightning for my blasphemy. After weeks of torment, I finally confided in Mom one night when she was tucking me in.

"It's just the Devil talking to you," she said gently. "Tell him to go away and leave you alone."

Which I did.

But he didn't leave me alone. He continued to torment me until, one day, I realized I'd been suffering through this ritual for months with no adverse consequences. I reasoned that if the Devil and God were battling over my soul every night, neither one was winning. Once I reached that conclusion, I felt even more removed from the religion of my parents. The voice in my head went away, and I decided my soul hadn't been worth fighting over, after all.

An immediate benefit of my new church was my first friend, Alice. Alice was a year younger than me, not yet in high school. Summer had turned the hilly countryside the delicious color of butterscotch. Oleander bushes provided splashes of taffy pink. A honeysuckle vine in our backyard oozed a heady scent that teased my newly awakened hormones. Life was out there to be had. The bees proclaimed it in their lazy droning. The scent of cut grass. The clacking of sprinklers. Alice and I were ready to venture out beyond our homes.

Our favorite spot was the drugstore where we perused the cosmetics department. We thumbed through fashion magazines, studying the images we saw and putting them together with the objects on the shelves that somehow achieved the desired results. Eyebrow pencils, lip gloss, mascara, eyeliner, and so on. Neither of us wore makeup so we weren't sure how to apply it, but we continued our due diligence. Occasionally, a store clerk would shoo us away.

"This isn't a library," he'd say. "If you're not going to buy it, don't ruin it for someone who will."

But one day, a representative from a cosmetics company visited the store. We were enraptured while we watched her perform miraculous makeovers on willing participants who would then, hopefully, purchase products from the line she represented. We spent hours as wide-eyed voyeurs. Then, just as she was packing up to go, she seemed to take pity on us, or perhaps she saw a chance to influence the next generation.

"You gals want me to make you pretty? Real quick . . . I've only got a few minutes."

Alice didn't dare, but I flew to the seat she had set up for the occasion. With my eyes closed and my lips pooched out, I barely breathed for fear of interfering in my expected transformation.

"Take a look," she said at last, holding a mirror up in front of me.

"Wow! You look amazing," Alice exclaimed breathlessly.

A stranger looked back at me from the mirror. But she was a stranger I loved. I made careful notes about each product the rep had used and, after wiping my face clean with tissues and makeup remover, Alice and I rushed to my house before returning with my entire savings from my allowance. At home, my stash of makeup remained hidden in the back of my closet inside one of my shoes. I practiced every night when everyone was in bed until I could paint a fairly decent face within a matter of minutes.

As if my hormones suddenly awakened from a deep sleep

by my newly (and still secretly) purchased cosmetics, I finally began to menstruate. Mom had fretted for the past few years because I was already fourteen with no change-of-life in sight, but the doctor did tests and detected no red flags.

"She's just a slowpoke," he said, which I'm sure had the effect of reassuring my mother, but did nothing for my self-esteem.

Even Alice already had her period, and she wouldn't start high school until the fall.

But when it finally did come, I wondered why I'd ever wished for it in the first place. It felt like a hoax perpetrated on all of womankind. Mom's proclamation that I was "finally a woman" didn't seem like a fair tradeoff for what I had to endure. I didn't think I'd ever be one of those girls who flaunted their menstrual cramps in the locker room every month. It seemed so glamorous when I was on the outside looking in. Sophisticated even. The reality, for me, was a disheartening loss of independence.

Another casualty of our move was my own body dysmorphia. I'd been slightly round as a young girl but never perceived myself to be anything beyond healthy and happy. In fact, I never gave much thought to my appearance, and this absence of self-obsession was only reinforced by my parents, who stressed inner beauty and good deeds. After moving to Indian Springs, everything changed overnight. From my first day of school, I never thought I looked good enough. I spied flaws each time I passed a mirror and began to see my own image as a receptacle for everyone else's disgust. It would take me years to get back to the place I'd once been.

During the time I was envisioning a shortcut to supermodel looks through the miracles of makeup, I discovered, quite by accident, my *golden ticket*, as I came to call it. Alice and I were at the drug store, standing in line to make our daily candy purchase so we wouldn't be declared *personae non gratae* at the magazine rack. I was spending an inordinate amount of time thinking up ways to reinvent myself for junior year of high school. Makeup. Check. Longer hair. Check. More acceptable clothes. Check. Slimmer figure. No, that wasn't happening. I looked at the candy in my hand.

"I'll be right back," I told Alice. "Meet you outside."

I replaced my M&Ms on the shelf and looked around for a less fattening alternative. I spotted a bag of sugar-free hard candies that might just satisfy my sweet tooth and had zero calories. I bought it and was on my way.

By the time I got home, my stomach was cramping slightly, but it wasn't time for my period—I had just finished. I sat on the toilet, and a stream of diarrhea flowed painlessly from me. Once it was over, I felt fine. A few more days of experimenting with the hard candies allowed me to put two and two together. When I stopped eating them, the diarrhea went away. But when I weighed myself a few days later, the scales showed a decline I hadn't been able to achieve on my own. Here it was at last. My golden ticket—an easy path to weight loss without giving up food. I would soon be a svelte girl, and Mom would be none the wiser, since I could continue to eat as I always had. Anyway, it wasn't like I was doing anything illegal. Mom would probably approve of my sugar-free choice since she was always harping on the dangers of too much sugar. Instinctively, I suspected it might be wrong—nothing should be that simple. But what if it was, and I was just the first person to stumble upon it? Still, I didn't share my secret with Alice, who knew everything else about me. Sharing secrets that reached into the darkness of my bowels was too shameful. Too personal. And so deep I didn't understand it myself.

"It's gonna be great being at the same school," Alice said

one hot, lazy day. We were lying on my bed, a honeysuckle scent ushered through my open window by a powder-soft breeze. "But will you still be my friend since I'll just be a freshman, and you'll be a big important junior?"

I didn't see why not. I'd always had friends across a spectrum of ages in my past life, and Alice was only a year younger than me. Americans stuck together overseas since we were such a small community of expats. We didn't divide ourselves according to age because there'd be nobody left to socialize with if we did.

"Of course, why wouldn't I be?" I asked naively.

"Just remember you said so," Alice said presciently. She was light years ahead of me in so many ways. "Anyway, what should we do today? I'm bored."

"I dunno. What do you wanna do? Go to the drugstore?" I was thinking that my golden ticket stash was getting low. Also, I needed more Vaseline, which I'd been using to treat my resulting sore bottom.

"I'm tired of the drugstore. Do you think Luke could get us into the pool? We could go swimming."

"I guess so."

I wasn't really big on swimming, and it showed in my lack of technique and skills. Luke was a natural and always looked for a place to swim wherever we lived, whether it was Lake Atitlan in Guatemala or the Pacific Ocean in Guam. In addition, I now had my appearance to consider. Every morning I'd been taking some of Luke's hair gel and mixing it with a bit of water to smooth my hair into submission. What resulted was, in my opinion, a classier version of my longer pixie cut. My bangs now swept to one side, curling over my right eye to just behind the corresponding ear. When my face was made-up, I hoped I looked quite fashionable, so I wasn't anxious to get my hair wet.

"Let's do it. Please."

"Okay, lemme check with Dad and see if he needs anything. I guess I should make some lunch for him before we go."

I rustled through my belongings before coming up with the latest version swimsuit I owned. It wouldn't win any fashion awards but it was functional, if a little small. The elastic in the legs was loose from age, and when I glanced down at the tops of my thighs, a few pubic hairs poked through. I pulled on a pair of shorts over the swimsuit, and resolved to just sit by the side of the pool and watch if Alice wanted to swim.

I chatted briefly with Dad and then fixed him some canned soup and a few microwaved hot dogs. That and a can of soda would hold him until Mom or I came home. Dad was so quiet those days, I hardly knew what to say to him. I couldn't break through the wall of depression I didn't know existed, and he seemed equally baffled by me. We were a family that dematerialized after stepping into the transporter that beamed us to our new world. But once we rematerialized, it was as though elves had sneaked in and deviously shifted our atoms around until we were almost, but not quite, unrecognizable to each other.

The last thing I did before leaving the house was apply my makeup and stuff makeup-remover pads in the pocket of my shorts. That had become my routine.

From Alice's house, we took the city bus which eventually made its way to every corner of Indian Springs. Since most people got around by car, Alice and I often found ourselves nearly alone when we needed to get somewhere. That day we occupied the bus with two older lilac-haired women sharing a lunch or perhaps a weekly appointment at the hair salon. A Latina mother and her two children crowded together in a bench seat meant for two, the little girl peeking at Alice and me over the seat and then ducking whenever we caught her with a smile. The musical lilt of their Spanish words triggered a longing in my heart for the language which felt like home but was already untangling itself from the hard wires of my brain.

Our stop was the city park, a massive stretch of land intended to provide at least one recreational option for every citizen. We walked by the playground where tots played on structures the likes of which I had never seen during my child-hood. A ground covering of tanbark cushioned children from injury and dissuaded the cats, who had turned out in droves for the sandbox my father made for me in Ecuador when I was five. Further on, two men took turns grunting at each other across the net of a tennis court—one of the few in use since many of the courts were empty at that hot, quiet time of day. Further down were barbecue pits and picnic tables, shaded by Valley Oaks. And just beyond those was the community pool. For girls our age, the pool was the only attraction at the city park. We were too young to go to San Francisco by ourselves but too old to find much of interest in our hometown.

Wafting chlorine-scented clouds stung my eyes and nose when we walked through the door to the ticket sales office of the pool.

"Can you tell Luke Templeton his sister needs to see him?" I asked the sunny-haired girl behind the counter. Her nose and cheeks were lightly sprinkled with freckles, and her arms were smooth and tanned. She disappeared to find Luke while her male counterpart in looks stared at me through the glass barrier.

"You're Luke's sister?" he asked as though he could hardly believe it.

Luke appeared minutes later with the girl at his side. She smiled warmly at me.

"Hey, you two!" Luke said. "What's going on? Dad alright?"

"Can you get us in for free?" I got right to the point.

"If you can't, I can pay," Alice offered. She was wide-eyed as she always was in Luke's presence. Everyone loved him. Even I had no complaints, and I was his sister, which I understood to mean that technically I should at least occasionally hate him.

"Sure, come on in," he nodded to the girl who buzzed us in. "What did you do to your face?" he asked me.

"Just a little makeup." I hadn't considered Luke might notice my altered appearance. "Don't tell Mom, please." From the corner of my eye, I saw the girl smile crookedly before looking down at the stack of papers in front of her.

"I think she looks great," Alice piped in. "It really accentuates her eyes, don't you think?"

"You look ridiculous," Luke said. "Don't know why you think you need that stuff. You're pretty enough the way God made you."

Luke wasn't in the habit of interpreting God's Word for anyone's benefit so I took it as a compliment. I also knew its value was questionable since, of course, Luke would say that no matter what.

"So you won't tell Mom?"

"Nah, but I still think it's dumb."

We followed him to his lifeguard chair, a throne where his word was the law when it came to reigning over a pool tangled with squirming, slippery bodies.

"No running!" he bellowed at two boys who shrank under his rebuke. I was proud that my brother had this kind of authority and awed that he could distinguish a drowning kid from a playing one.

Parents were mostly absent except in the kiddie pool. Children who passed the swimming test and were at least ten years old could be at the pool by themselves. Alice and I were technically old enough to skip the test.

"Go on and knock yourself out," he said. "I'm here if you need anything."

I dragged Alice as far away as possible from Luke. With our towels rolled under our arms, cocooned in the scent of sunscreen, we made our way over browning bodies to a small patch of grass that, surprisingly, hadn't yet been claimed.

Alice threw down her towel. "I'm going in," she said. "Come on."

I thought about my embarrassing bathing suit. Even Alice outdid me in that department with a cute but modest two-piece. I thought about my hair, which would be stiff to the touch if anyone actually touched it. I thought about the makeup which would most likely result in raccoon eyes if I were to take a dip. How had I come so quickly to the place, after arriving in the states, where I voluntarily forfeited fun?

"No, I'll watch. You go on ahead."

Alice didn't need persuading. She slipped into the water like a seal and was soon lost in the soup of bathers. I lay back in a pose of relaxation that I hoped made me look like someone accustomed to sunbathing by the side of a pool. The sharp sting of the sun on my face was hard—a dry heat unlike Guatemala or other countries where I'd lived. The multitude of squeals and shrieks and laughter coalesced into a monotonous drone that reached my brain as nonsensical chatter. It was soothing, and I began to feel sleepy. Within minutes, a daydream was well on its way to transforming into a real dream when a shadow fell over me, darkening the inside of my eyelids. I opened my eyes and sat up, temporarily dazed.

"Carly wants to know how you know Luke," said a pretty brown-haired girl.

"Luke?" I squinted into the sun that hovered just behind her.

"The lifeguard. How do you know him?"

The drone of noise disassembled itself into individual voices as I raced from sleep to wakefulness.

"How do *you* know him?" I asked. I wondered if Luke was in trouble for letting Alice and me into the pool without paying and, if he was, what was the appropriate response to her question.

"Everyone knows Luke," she said. "He's like . . . a god or something."

Oh, she's one of those, I thought. I was used to that.

"He's my brother," I said. "So he's not God or even *a* god. He's just a brother."

Having a brother like Luke had its advantages, but it could be tiresome when most of the attention was diverted his way.

"I didn't mean a real god. I just meant . . ." She was tallish and angular. The straight-cut ends of her shiny hair grazed shoulders bronzed from the sun.

"Yeah, I know." Then I remembered the name of the person who had sent her to ask the question. "Who's Carly?" The name was still fresh in my mind. There must be a lot of Carlys, but what if this was *the* Carly?

"That's her over there." The girl pointed across the pool where Carly was sitting on a towel watching us. She lifted a hand and grinned sheepishly.

It was *the* Carly.

"She dared me to ask you. Why don't you come sit with us?" she asked.

I scanned the surface of the pool but still couldn't pick out which watery shape among the masses was Alice's.

"Bring your towel," the girl said.

I shook out my towel and followed her to where Carly was sitting. Later, I realized I should have taken Alice's towel with me. But at that moment, I wasn't thinking of Alice.

"Luke is her brother," the still unidentified girl said to Carly. "Told ya it was something like that."

Carly fixed her practiced irresistible gaze on me. *Her eyes aren't green, after all,* I remember thinking. They were brown.

"She thought you were his girlfriend," the girl said to me.

"She could've been," Carly said, and I felt a thrill unprecedented in my life that this girl thought I—just plain Grace—could have attracted a boy with Luke's obvious qualities. Then Carly giggled, and the thrill receded as I wondered if she was making a joke at my expense.

"What's he like as a brother?" Carly asked. "He seems so sweet."

"He's . . . nice. For a brother. I don't know. To be honest, I don't spend too much time thinking about him, you know?"

"Sit down," Carly said. "Here, we'll scoot over to make space. Do you want an iced tea? We have extras." She pushed a can toward me while I spread out my towel next to hers. I could smell the scent of her sunscreen mixed with the sharp tang of sweat. She pulled sunglasses down from the top of her head, but I could still see her eyes through the smoky gray glass.

"Do you guys come here much?" I asked, absent of anything else to say but not wanting a silent space to betray what I assumed would be my boring personality.

"Nearly every day," the brown-haired girl said. "Or at least whenever we can. We're working on our tans, right Carly? Carly has a pool at her house but—"

"It's more fun to come here," Carly interrupted.

"And watch your brother," the girl said. "He's a senior, right? Did he graduate?"

"Yeah, he's leaving for college in the fall."

"Ahhh . . . too bad," Carly poked the girl lightly in the ribs. She turned to me. "Maggie's heartbroken now."

"There's still the summer," I said brightly without thinking about what I was doing. I was offering Luke as an incentive. If they were at the pool nearly every day, I could be there too.

Dangling the alluring possibility of a Luke encounter could be my ticket to hanging out with them. Acceptance by them.

"Ha ha," Carly said. "Yeah, Maggie, there's still the summer. You never know what might happen."

We all laughed, Carly and Maggie and me. At that very moment, the laugh sealed something between us. It was obvious nothing was going to happen between the girl, who I now knew was Maggie, and Luke. Luke was college-bound and wouldn't be interested in high-school girls anymore. But we already shared a secret, the three of us. Maggie liked Luke, and we were going to make a game of it for the rest of the summer if I had my way.

I didn't know at the time how many more secrets we'd be sharing in the years to come.

I worked hard to maintain my appeal over the next ten minutes. I noticed Luke watching me at one point, and at another point I saw Alice talking to Luke who pointed in my direction. I'd almost forgotten about Alice. As she made her way over, stopping to retrieve her towel on the way, I'm ashamed to say that my only thought was how to explain away her presence.

"This is my friend, Alice," I said when she was standing beside us. "I . . . uh. We go to the same church. Our parents are friends."

"Hi, Alice. Sit down with us. Maggie, scooch your towel over."

Maggie giggled and scooched.

After that I made no further mention of Alice, nor did I try to include her in our conversation. Carly and Maggie were nice enough. Carly even asked probing questions of Alice in her disarming way—flattering, in the absolute focus she maintained whenever she spoke to you. As if no other person existed for her in that moment. As if her interest in you were something to be coveted, won, perhaps even fought over.

But Alice didn't respond the way I did. Perhaps it was her

age and immaturity, I reasoned. Perhaps it was jealousy. What I never considered at the time was that perhaps she saw something in Carly I was incapable of seeing.

"We'd better go," Alice said after another half hour. "I told my mom I'd be back by now."

"She knows where we are," I said. "She knows you're safe with Luke. I don't think she'll care if you stay a little longer."

"We have to go too." Carly stood and gave her towel a shake, freeing it of the trampled browning blades of grass still clinging to it. "See you guys soon, I hope."

Following Carly's lead, the rest of us stood like automatons. What would be the point of staying when Carly was gone? The backs of my calves and palms of my hands were imprinted by the pattern of lawn. My cheeks were burning, and only then did I realize I'd neglected to use sunscreen on my face.

"Yeah, definitely," I said. "We'll be back for sure."

But Alice said nothing.

Then Carly folded her towel carefully and draped it across her forearm before picking up her bag. Her figure was perfect without any evidence of cellulite or an uneven tan. Her bikini didn't sag or pull anywhere. After a day in the sun, even her hair looked shiny and perky in a sleek ponytail.

"I remember you," she said, looking slightly downward. She was taller than me then and, even though I'd surpass her in height over the next year, I would always think of her as being the taller one. "You came into Mr. Dix's Social Studies class by accident on your first day." She looked over at Maggie as if I was no longer around. "She was so adorable, you should've seen her."

I was bursting with excitement and confidence on our walk home. I wished I had someone I could talk to about the brewing feelings inside me, but I don't think I could have articulated it back then, even if I'd had a willing ear. Alice certainly wasn't interested, that much I knew. She'd been sullen ever since she joined us at the pool and I was angry at her for that but not angry enough to ruin my high.

"I don't like that Carly girl," she said. "I don't trust her. I think she's just using you."

"Using me for what?" I asked indignantly. What could a girl like Carly possibly gain from befriending a girl like me?

"I don't know," Alice said. "She just—"

"You're not making any sense," I snapped. "And she probably doesn't like you either since you were so rude and quiet."

We walked the rest of the way home in silence. The sun had already begun its descent, but its heat would linger well into the night. When we got to Alice's house, she peeled off without inviting me in, which would have been our normal routine. I was frankly relieved.

I suppose I fell in love with Carly that day, although not in a sexual way. Or maybe I'd fallen in love with her the first time I laid eyes on her. The term *girl crush* wasn't yet familiar to me, but Carly was more than a crush. And what is love if it isn't basking in the positive feelings a person bestows on you? Wanting to repay those feelings by pleasing that person in any possible way. Holding that person in the part of your heart reserved for the most intimate and precious feelings. And not wishing to imagine life in any other way.

If it wasn't love, I wasn't equipped to name it.

SAN FRANCISCO

THE NIGHT I graduated from Indian Springs High, Mom and Dad broke the news they were moving to Madagascar where I'd be unlikely to see them for a very long time. Dad was physically recovered but saw meaningful work as the only way to break through the thick wall of his depression. We'd have two months together, during which time they'd help me relocate to San Francisco where I'd accepted a full scholarship from the University of San Francisco. For a person of my means, it was as far away as I could get from Indian Springs, both in character and distance, and that was good enough for me. Mom and Dad were pleased I'd chosen a college with a religious affiliation. That made them feel okay about leaving me behind.

Although I'd never opened up to my parents in any significant way, losing them like that left me feeling orphaned. Unmoored. Luke was finishing up at Sacramento State with a degree in criminology and the goal of becoming a cop. That reality caused me so much anxiety, I spent many nights strangling my sobs with a pillow to avoid the concerned faces of my parents in the morning.

And there had been the first letter. A letter back then instead of an email. It arrived at our house when the daffodils were still in bloom, generic block letters spelling out my name on the outside of the envelope. A San Francisco postmark. No return address.

"A letter for you, Grace." Dad was surprised. I normally didn't get letters or any mail at all.

Even as he handed it to me, I felt the evil of its contents. The malevolence of the ominous block lettering. I shoved it nonchalantly in the back pocket of my jeans and went to the kitchen for a drink, all the while trying to pretend its existence bored me.

In the privacy of my bedroom, I pulled the sheet of paper from its sheath, blank but for six words.

"Will anyone cry when you die?"

At first, it made no sense. *It must be a prank*, I thought, *maybe there'd been a mistake, and this letter was meant for someone else.* But then a wave of nausea felled me, and I lay on my bed, waiting for it to subside. My legs trembled uncontrollably. I was cold enough to pull the blankets over me, and yet, somehow, perspiration soaked through my shirt under my arms and down the middle of my back. I checked the note again to make sure I'd read it correctly and then reached for the phone at the side of my bed.

"What?" Carly answered her private line on the first ring.

"It's me. Grace."

"I know."

"How?"

"Because I just finished talking to Maggie."

"I got a—"

"I know. You got a letter . . . Maggie and I did too. '*Will anyone cry when you die?*' Blah, blah, blah."

"What do you think?"

"I think you should rip it up and flush it down the toilet. Some idiot's trying to scare us. Someone who's probably jealous."

By then I didn't have to ask "Jealous about what?" Carly had long ago provided us with a litany of reasons why we would be the envy of everyone in our school. And their natural target as well.

"Are you worried?"

"Of course not, and you shouldn't be either. Mom's calling, gotta go."

And she hung up.
I called Maggie.
"Are you scared?" I asked.
"Yes. Are you?"
"Yeah, me too."
"Do you think it has anything to do with Jane?"

During my first year of college, I lived in a quad in the dorm—two singles and a double. I shared the double with a girl from Walnut Creek named Marybeth who spent most weekends with her boyfriend in Berkeley. The four of us co-existed comfortably as roommates, and I threw myself into general education requirements with an eye on a degree in psychology. I suppose I hoped to find answers or at least a way to explain me to myself.

In my mind, I'd made a bargain with the universe: take my parents if you must, but then you must also take Carly. And Carly was spirited miles away, thousands to be exact, honing her scholastic reputation at Yale. I would have preferred her to be in Madagascar, but Yale seemed an acceptable alternative. I no longer thought of Carly with a heavy heart laden with love. She was the addiction that I couldn't quite shake, but day by day, I managed quite well. We didn't communicate once the entire first semester. I heard news of her only through Maggie.

Then came daffodil season when all the big changes in my life seemed to occur. Almost exactly a year since the first letter, a second arrived, this one finding me in my dorm at USF, where I thought I'd hidden safely from the world.

Of course, I recognized the block letters and the generic, square-shaped envelope postmarked in the city where I lived. I should have ripped it into small pieces and tossed them in the dumpster outside our building on my way to class.

But I didn't. I dutifully awaited my punishment.

"Karma's a bitch. Are you ready for yours?"

There was no point calling Carly, but I did. In her typical fashion, she downplayed the whole thing, again belittling the sender and casting foul aspersions on their motives. There was no point in calling Maggie, but I did that too. She had just returned to the clinic in San Francisco, her father told me, sick again. Her mother was with her, and maybe I could visit if I had the time. It would probably do her a world of good.

Maggie was the one who stayed in Indian Springs after Carly and I left. A semester of junior college before dropping out. And then came the anorexia which her family referred to as the "sickness." It was doubtful she'd gotten the letter. I wondered if her father had opened it, curious about its strange lettering and lack of a return address.

I imagined Maggie looking out her bedroom window at the wide ribbon of bright daffodils snaking across her front lawn. Golden trumpets heralding the arrival of spring, mocking her bleak state of mind.

And then I imagined Maggie taking a stand and refusing to allow a single morsel of food to pass beyond her lips.

That summer I got a job as a barista at a neighborhood coffee shop. It was one of those places with gold lettering on the windows which blocked most of the street view; tables sticky from decades of use, probably already having seen better days in the sixties; and chairs that yelped in protest at the indignity of being dragged across the old, buckling hardwood floor. Behind the stained marble counter, I normally shared a shift with Carlos, a young man of sunny disposition and compassionate eyes. In the beginning, we covertly sized each other up as romantic potential but settled on friendship. When I first tried my Spanish on Carlos, he gave me the look I would come to know as a substitute for less-kind spoken words.

"And should I speak to you in Norwegian?" he asked.

"British," I said. "And French-German-Swiss."

He gave me the look again.

At the same time, I moved out of my dorm and rented a room in a rundown Victorian where cockroaches fell like rain behind the walls at night. The kitchen smelled like stale cat food, and the kitchen sink blossomed with filthy pots and pans. I used my allotted refrigerator space for single-serve food items sealed against contamination until opened. Surviving kept me focused on everything that didn't eat away at my soul. And since I was in survival mode, with only my barista earnings to carry me through the summer, I was irrationally calm.

Normally, San Francisco is cool and foggy in the summer, but on one particular morning the weather was glorious—clichéd blue skies and sunshine, no clouds in sight. I was beginning to recognize the regular customers at the coffee shop, including a slender, sort of scruffy-looking guy with dark, wavy hair, a baby face, and blue saucer eyes. I'd seen those eyes turned on me a few times, but they had quickly looked away. That day, Mr. Blue Eyes glanced up frequently as he stood in line awaiting his turn. He looked like a man with something on his mind. With *me* on his mind. For a moment, my heart beat icicles as thoughts of Carly and Maggie and the anonymous letters flooded my brain. But when we were finally face-to-face, he simply ordered a drip coffee to go. After he'd paid and was preparing to step aside to wait for his order, he turned back as though he'd forgotten something.

"My name is Nathan," he blurted out.

I was silent, unsure if this was a prelude to something or if the name Nathan was expected to evoke a response.

"I was just wondering . . ." His blue eyes turned bluer in contrast to the pinkening skin that surrounded them. "If you'd like to get a cup of coffee sometime."

Then he burst into laughter.

"I mean . . . Of course you wouldn't want to get a cup of coffee. You work in a coffee shop. Sorry, I'm an idiot. Do you have a boyfriend? And if you don't, would you like to go out to dinner sometime?"

"Move it, Romeo," the man behind him snapped. "Some of us gotta get to work, y'know?"

From behind the espresso machine, Carlos gave him the look.

"Yes," I said so quickly that I almost wondered if someone was speaking for me.

"Yes, you have a boyfriend, or yes, you'll have dinner with me?"

"Yes. Dinner." I felt incapable of more than one-word utterances and was well aware I'd have to answer to Carlos's jabs once this encounter was over.

He took the coffee that Carlos prepared and walked backward into a table before setting it right, then backing out the door without once taking his smile off me.

That smile alone kept me going for the next three days.

Three days later, he returned at his usual time.

"Is this a good day for you?" he asked once he reached the front of the line.

I didn't need to ask for what. "Yes," I said. "I'm off at five."

And at five on the nose, he appeared at the door holding a bouquet of six red roses. His jeans were faded and baggy. He wore workmen's beige-colored boots and a t-shirt that had seen so many washings I couldn't decipher its graphic art.

"Where would you like to eat?" he asked.

My initial impression was that Nathan couldn't afford much, and I sure as hell knew I couldn't.

"How about pizza?" Even that was a splurge for me.

So beginning with pizza, followed by hours walking parallel to the Great Highway and Ocean Beach, we spent a rare, beautifully warm evening getting to know each other. We spread out a blanket and sat on the beach, the sand cool from the memory of foggier nights, starlight dusting our shoulders. We talked until the sun rose behind us, and only the prospect of being late for work chased us from that spot and from each other.

Nathan drove me back to the coffee shop in his old Chevy Nova with ripped red leather seats. He walked me to the door, and only then did he ask for a kiss, which I granted. His breath was stale with pizza and talking and lack of sleep. I knew mine was too. But the kiss—our first. When they say something takes your breath away, it really doesn't, but this kiss did. Quite simply, Nathan took my breath away and then breathed it back into me in technicolor.

Carlos was waiting to tease me mercilessly when I took up my position behind the counter.

"Walk of shame," he said. "Couldn't you at least have changed your clothes?"

"It wasn't like that." I bumped him to the side with my hip. "I'm here, aren't I?"

"Yeah, well, maybe you could've at least showered?" He wrinkled his nose playfully then took a lock of my hair in his hands before letting it fall. "Or run a comb through your hair."

Carlos covered for more than one sleep-deprived order error I made that day. Somehow, though, I survived an entire day of work without having had a single minute of sleep.

When I went home that night, my heart was still singing,

and my lips felt swollen from longing to be pressed against Nathan's one more time. My body ached with fatigue and also with desire. It couldn't have been more than a few seconds before I fell into a deep and dreamless sleep, unperturbed by distressing thoughts.

I hadn't felt that kind of peace in two years.

That first date was followed by others, Nathan always arriving with a bouquet of flowers, even if it was just dandelions he'd found growing in the park. And although I was almost a junior in college, I was still only eighteen—the age at which most kids were preparing to leave the womb of family, and most parents were preparing to cut the cord. That had all happened for me mere weeks after turning sixteen.

Nathan was a first-year medical student at UCSF. He was almost four years older than me but often seemed younger. He had an interest in psychiatry, although his father, a cardiac surgeon, was trying to steer him into a more lucrative field. The grungy clothes and beat-up car—that was just Nathan asserting some independence from his parents, who lived in the upscale city of Palo Alto, south of San Francisco.

"I can teach you how to be poor," I joked one day. "If you really want to know."

He took me in his arms and kissed the irony from my lips. "How could I ever be poor as long as I have you?" It was rank B-movie dialogue. I knew that but loved him for saying it.

We spent the gloom of a San Francisco summer mostly hand-in-hand and sometimes in each other's arms. I was still a virgin. Still trapped by an upbringing I had declared myself free of, but it hadn't yet declared itself free of me. And something more. I was still reluctant to give myself permission to lead a joyful life. I knew I wasn't worthy.

Nathan thought differently, but of course he didn't know my heart. He had patience beyond anything I deserved . . . for my moods, for my unwillingness to fully commit. Nathan was fully there. He became my tour guide through a world I'd inhabited for years but never really explored. We visited Alcatraz, the once infamous prison now populated by tourists. We ate our way through Chinatown and Japantown and Little Italy in North Beach. Nathan shared his love of movies, mostly foreign and indies. I saw, for the first time, the films of Akira Kurasawa, Satyajit Rey, Fellini, and Bergman. The original Hollywood goddesses—Garbo, Dietrich, Crawford, and Davis—became my new screen idols. Golden Gate Park, Coit Tower, Lombard Street, Pier 39. We hit them all.

And when we tired of the summer gloom, we ventured out further to Sausalito which was an impossibly magical and equally fantastical world of small shops and fine dining that real people only visited. We explored the Berkeley campus, inhaling its eucalyptus scent and gawking at stately manors. We walked down Telegraph Avenue, purchased knick-knacks from street vendors, and sampled Ethiopian and Venezuelan cuisine, which was more of a stretch for Nathan than me. We pushed further out, through the Caldecott Tunnel to Walnut Creek, where a surprising world of sunshine and summer and triple-digit temperatures thrived thanks to the Oakland Hills that held back the fog.

Then one day we traveled south to Palo Alto. It was finally time for me to meet the parents, at least, according to Nathan. Their home was palatial and, had he not prepared me in advance, I probably would never have gone beyond its driveway, which was lined with magnolia and crepe myrtle trees. Nathan parked his battered Chevy Nova alongside a gleaming white Mercedes sedan. An inner voice hissed a warning, a déjà vu born from the memory of my first steps toward Indian Springs

High.

Nathan's mother greeted us warmly at the door and immediately instructed me to call her Diane. Fine, silver hair feathered around her face and down the back of her neck. A gold and turquoise necklace swung forward as she leaned to kiss her son on the cheek. Wearing jeans and a fitted t-shirt that shimmered lightly under the chandelier, she looked both strong and fragile. Elegant yet ready for fun.

Dr. Steinburg was his wife's male counterpart, tall and stylish but still retaining his dark hair, thick and wavy like Nathan's. He had an aura of authority, and I didn't have to use my imagination to envision him commanding a surgical team. Equally relaxed in dress as his wife, he sported sandals on feet that looked too groomed to belong to a working man. He didn't offer a first name for my benefit like Diane had.

"You must be Grace," he said, extending a hand which I knew could examine a heart as easily as bringing a piece of sushi to his mouth.

Of course, who else would I be? But those words did me the courtesy of not letting my guard down.

Dinner was grilled salmon and steamed asparagus prepared by Diane. A fresh baguette with olive oil for dipping and chocolate mousse made with avocado instead of cream. When the wine glasses had been refilled two and then three times, tongues loosened, at least Dr. Steinburg's did. Diane glowed from the wine and proximity to her son. I declined any alcohol, not wishing to put them in the awkward predicament of serving a minor.

"I'm driving," I said by way of explanation.

While Diane's questions centered around our social lives—how we met, which friends of Nathan's I'd gotten to know, what we liked to do in our free time, not that she expected we had much of that with Nathan's busy school schedule. Dr. Steinburg was more interested in my life. My parents. Their current whereabouts. Any other close relatives I might have in the area. How I had been educated. He didn't try hard to disguise his suspicion, and I thought I knew why. Every parent might be naturally suspicious of their son's girlfriend coming home for the first time. It was human nature—the desire to protect one's tribe from outside invaders, stealth or otherwise. This line of questioning was different, however it wasn't an unknown occurrence in my life.

Whenever someone heard about my background as a child of missionaries, they seemed baffled by the idea that people would choose to give up all creature comforts in order to impose their will upon those in less developed parts of the world. But of course, I didn't see it that way because I knew my parents' hearts and minds. I understood them in a fundamental way, even after I rejected their beliefs. But I didn't have the ability to convey their goodness and selflessness to others. My parents weren't trying to impose their will. They felt they were sharing a gift more precious than life itself. So I grew more and more tightlipped as the night wore on until Nathan deftly steered the conversation to other topics—school, his mother's art projects, his brothers and their goings-on, and mutual friends.

But it was hard to defend my parents' absence from my life, even to myself. As a child, I didn't have to ask to understand where I ranked in my parents' lives. God was first and foremost. He was above all. After that, my mother and father's love and allegiance to each other came next. Luke and I were always third, and I accepted that at a subliminal level which I never questioned or doubted. That was the way of the world, wasn't it? It didn't occur to me that there could be any other way. And yet, in just a few hours, I'd come to understand that Nathan and his brothers were their parents' priority. First and foremost. But

Nathan bristled against this attention. Burned from the heat it brought to his life, like a magnifying glass focusing the sun's energy on him like a weapon. He rebelled through his Chevy Nova. Through his work boots. Through his girlfriend.

When we left the Steinburgs' house that night, I felt Nathan's urgent need. As though being in his parents' house had diminished him, made him a smaller person, even physically. I couldn't understand why their devotion affected him this way, the same way my parents' inattention affected me. But I wanted to make him whole again the way he'd made me whole that first night. That first kiss. I wanted my Nathan to come back from wherever he'd gone.

In bed in his apartment, we snuggled and kissed as we usually did. Eventually, Nathan whispered goodnight and turned his back to me. This was our way, with Nathan never pressuring me or complaining. Normally I waited for his breathing to grow quiet and steady before turning around and, with my back pressed against his, allowing sleep to carry me into the following day.

But that night, I drew close, pressing my breasts against his chest and engaging him in a kiss that neither of us would or could choose to end. I let my hands play lightly down his back and across his hips, until they slipped into the tight space between us and then further still between his legs. It was only then that Nathan, understanding my invitation, pulled my t-shirt over my head and my panties below my knees. I had become his willing partner.

When I woke the next morning, the world felt like a different place, and I was no longer a virgin.

In the fall, Luke married a girl he'd only been dating for a few months. When she realized she was pregnant, there was never any question they wouldn't have the baby, so the handsome rookie cop married the sweet and lovely Linda. Once I got over the shock of becoming an aunt, I prepared myself to become a bridesmaid. Luke invited Nathan to the wedding, which was in Sacramento, since the Templetons were so underrepresented. Our parents would not be flying in from Madagascar and, with our transient upbringing, we had never made permanent friends and barely knew our extended family. Although he didn't say so, I knew Nathan was happy to meet someone (Luke) who could verify that I really was who I said I was, and not a changeling raised by wolves. Sometimes I wondered if he, like his parents, had his own doubts about me.

I was happy Luke would have a second chance at the close family life that I believe he always craved. Linda was born in Sacramento and had a vast network of family and friends all within a few miles' drive. I was envious, maybe even a little jealous, although Linda assured me that we were sisters now, and I was welcome any time. But I instinctively knew that whatever interest I held for her at that exact moment would vanish once the baby came along.

Indian summer in Sacramento could be hotter than regular summer, and this day in October was such a day. We wilted like lilacs under the intense sun at the outdoor reception. Ducking under the cover of a huge cottonwood on the banks of a murmuring river, I smiled frozenly and made polite conversation with strangers whose names I wouldn't remember an hour later. Uncles and aunts and cousins and in-laws blurred into a faceless mass of confusion. Nathan stayed firmly planted by my side, occasionally disappearing before reappearing with a drink or some food, reminding me to eat and drink in that daze of a day.

I stood stiffly in my lilac-colored bridesmaid's dress which hung loosely, a size too large due to the last-minute notice and frenzy of the event. Luke and Nathan stood behind me while I was being regaled by Linda's father who'd apparently decided to take it upon himself to catch me up on their family history. I listened politely with one ear while my other ear was trained to the far more interesting conversation taking place just behind me.

"Take care of her," Luke said to Nathan. "She hasn't had an easy time of it, and I worry about her."

I whipped my head around, the smile on my face melting into disbelief. Luke had been worried about me? Whatever for? I didn't think anyone other than Nathan spent serious time thinking about me. Luke dropped his eyes, and Nathan stepped forward and took my hand firmly in his.

"Doing okay, Babe?" he asked.

"Yeah . . . why wouldn't I be?"

Linda's father chuckled politely before making his escape.

The wedding was so surreal, a week later I could barely remember what happened. I remember clinging tightly to Nathan, surprising him with my sudden, passionate attention. Perhaps he thought a wedding was arousing my own nesting instincts, but the truth was I felt I was about to be abandoned again. This time by Luke.

After a week, Nathan brought up his conversation with Luke.

"What did he mean by you haven't had an easy time of it?" he asked one Saturday after picking me up from work. He pulled into a rare parking space near his apartment then reached behind him for his book bag. School was in session so my scholarships had kicked in and I only had to work weekends.

"Ah, I don't know. Maybe my parents leaving when I was so

young. Not having family around." The tiny hairs on the back of my neck telegraphed a warning.

"You should spend more time with Luke and Linda," he said. There was nothing unkind about those words, but I took it that way. Luke and I had an understanding which didn't require our physical presence. Nobody in the world but Luke understood what my life had been like. Who our parents were. The mishmash we became because of how we'd lived. I didn't need Nathan to push me toward Luke.

"Are you trying to get rid of me?" I asked, trying my best to sound light-hearted.

He leaned over and kissed me. "Of course not. But . . . it's just strange. It seemed like there was something more he was getting at."

He looked blankly at me. An open face inviting any confession I was ready and willing to make. And I was ready. But I wasn't willing.

"I guess Maggie's whole thing really weighs on me," I said instead. "I feel awful every time I see her."

Maggie was back at the eating disorder clinic. I'd been visiting, but it wasn't easy seeing her so physically wasted and obviously bent on self-destruction. In that respect, Luke was right. In so many respects.

"Babe, why don't you let me go with you? I'd like to meet Maggie, and maybe it would make it a little easier on you."

"No. No, I don't want that."

Had I answered too quickly? Too adamantly? It's not like Maggie and I ever talked about anything meaningful or personal when I was with her. Most of the time her mom was there. I just didn't want Nathan mixing with that part of my life.

"Okay. I was just offering," he said, and I could tell he was hurt. "You know my family and friends. But I don't know any of your friends. You must have other friends back in Indian

Springs. Maggie. There must be others."

"No. You wouldn't want to meet them," I said, feeling slightly panicked. "They . . . I don't have any friends there anymore. You wouldn't have liked my friends in high school anyway."

"I'm a likeable guy. I give most people a chance. Why would you say that?"

I was setting a trap for myself. Or maybe, subconsciously, Nathan was setting one for me. But I knew how I'd feel if he kept me from the important people in his life. Whenever we went out on the weekends, it was with his friends, not mine. I knew, if I were in his position, I'd feel hurt and confused just like he was feeling right then. The interior of the car felt uncomfortably close. It felt like a cage.

"High school was shitty," I mumbled. "I was too young. I got involved with the wrong people. Can we get out and go inside or maybe walk somewhere?" I felt the familiar sting of needles of perspiration under my arms. It seemed as though Nathan should be able to see the frantic beat of my heart beneath the thin material of my top. The throbbing pulse in my neck that seemed on the verge of hatching a migraine.

I hung my head, allowing my hair to curtain my thoughts. It hadn't been short since my unfortunate pixie cut. At that moment, I marveled that I'd once been a girl confident enough to expose her fully unadorned face so boldly to the world. Nathan lifted my chin tenderly with the tip of his finger, swiveling my face toward his as he did.

"Sure," he said as kindly as he did everything else.

I was unfathomably angry with Luke.

I should have known, though, that I hadn't closed the subject. Nathan was only giving me time to rebound in the way he had of taking a step back if it would eventually lead to two steps forward. It came up again one night in bed when we were basking in the after-glow of sex. A glass of red wine in one hand, fingers of the other tracing paths through the lush thick waves of his hair, I was opened completely to Nathan.

In the dim light of the room, his blue eyes appeared gray, thoughtful.

"Just so you know," he said. "I've been thinking about what you said. About your high school." It was clever, I remember thinking. He hadn't made it about Luke this time. This time it was about what *I'd* said. It made me complicit, as though, somehow, I owed him an explanation. A clarification. "The people you said you hung out with in high school . . . in what way were they the *wrong* people? Was Maggie one of them?"

"Way to ruin the mood," I said withdrawing my fingers from his hair. I gulped the last of my wine and placed the glass on the bedside table.

"How were they the wrong people?" he repeated. "And why don't you want to tell me? Haven't I earned the right to be curious about your life?"

How much was I obligated to share now that we were practically living together? I knew I owed him some degree of honesty.

"Yeah, Maggie and I were friends in high school. She's fine, but I was young and the four of us, well mainly one of us . . . but we weren't always so nice, and we did some mean things that I'd rather not dwell on. I just want to forget about that part of my life. Put it behind me." The sex and wine mixed in my head to make me not exactly eloquent, but more forthcoming than I would otherwise have been.

"*Forget?* Have you forgotten?"

"No."

"Exactly. So, tell me . . . what kind of mean things are we talking about here?"

With the thin film of fermented grapes wrapped around my tongue and my brain, I wondered if I was actually slurring my words or just imagining it.

"The kind of mean things that kids in high school do to each other. Didn't you ever do anything mean to someone in high school?"

"No, not intentionally. Not anything that anyone ever brought to my attention."

The way Nathan was looking at me, I felt like a cluster of cells he might examine under a microscope in med school. As though he was breaking me down into more manageable portions, easier to decipher. He was studying me dispassionately instead of watching over me with love, and I hated the way it made me feel. I decided to throw Carly under the bus, and fast.

"There was this girl. Carly. And she . . . I guess you could say she bullied us into doing things we wouldn't have done on our own. But maybe not exactly bullied in the physical sense but . . . I don't know. She had this power over us, and I know that sounds ridiculous, but she had power over me at least. I don't know why. I guess I was young and . . ."

"And what?"

I gulped hard. "And I think I may have been in love with her."

Nathan sat up straight and looked at me as though meeting me for the first time. "You're into girls?"

"No, no. You see, that's why I didn't want to start this. I knew you'd take what I was saying out of context."

I felt like crying. What had I just done?

"Out of context? You said it, not me. You said *I think I may have been in love with her*. I'm not upset, I just wish you could be honest with me, that's all."

He sounded upset to me.

"I didn't mean it that way." I realized the conversation had taken a turn. Nathan was no longer interested in the mean things I'd done in school. Now he only wanted to know if I was *into girls*. This was a far preferable alternative, so I went with it. "A girl crush thing. You know. I looked up to her and she was beautiful and smart and . . . who wouldn't be in love with her? But it wasn't a physical thing. It wasn't what I have with you, nothing has ever been like that. It was an emotional thing . . . maybe it's hard for guys to understand."

He stared at me as though trying to get a read on his truth-o-meter.

"Where is this Carly now?" he asked, reducing her to an object through the article in front of her name. Reclaiming for himself whatever power Carly might still have over me. His tone was distinctly disdainful.

"*This* Carly," I said carefully with just enough humor in my voice to diffuse while teasing him away from the initial line of interrogation, "is at Yale studying business."

"Phew!" He shook his head to acknowledge the power of my statement. "She really is smart. Do you have a picture of her?"

I thought that an odd and prurient request, and yet somehow it didn't surprise me.

"Somewhere, maybe. If I find one, I'll show you."

Nathan leaned over and cupped my face with both hands. He kissed me at first tenderly, and then more forcefully as though he wanted to swallow first my tongue and then my soul.

"I just want you to always be honest with me," he said between heavy gulps of passion-laden breath. Even for a dimly lit room, his eyes were blurry. Unfocused.

He rolled on top of me, and I could feel his hardness against my damp inner thighs. I could feel his desire. We made love, grasping for each other in the way a drowning person will reach out for another. Pulling them under. He went deep, deeper than he'd ever been. And when we finished, which happened quickly, Nathan was asleep before I could even kiss him goodnight.

I stared into the darkness, trying to bring myself slowly back to the world where logic and reason prevailed over animal lust and instinct. I had opened the door a crack for Nathan but I didn't let him in. But by leaving the door slightly ajar, I allowed the monsters to come rushing back.

That March, another letter came, this time finding me at the coffee shop where I worked. I had given up the lease on the room I was renting and was living full-time with Nathan. I expected the letter this time. This time I didn't open it. During my break, I went into the back and burned it in the sink.

"What are you doing?" Carlos asked, when he came back to locate the source of the burning odor.

"Getting rid of an old love letter," I said. "I don't want Nathan to find it."

"Aaaah. Don't know how I feel about that," Carlos said. "But I guess it's a good thing as long as the dude's out of the picture for good."

"He is," I said and somehow felt that by burning the letter, I'd put an end to it.

I didn't call Carly. I didn't call Maggie. I was certain that I had not only survived, I had triumphed.

But a week later, when Nathan came home with a bouquet of daffodils, I'm sure he didn't expect the reaction he got. I'm sure he thought their stark, bold beauty would bring cheer to the gray, drizzling day.

Instead, I burst into tears and, claiming a migraine, took to my bed for the rest of the night.

CHAPTER FOUR
Indian Springs

I CONTINUED TO visit the pool, almost daily. I bought a pass for the entire month so as not to be dependent on Luke to let me in. Mom paid for half, reasoning it was a healthy summer activity for a young girl. Not surprisingly, Alice never went back with me; in fact, we'd barely spoken since that day. I missed Alice and tried to catch her eye at church one Sunday, thinking I'd extend an olive branch. But she either pretended not to see me or she really didn't. And I didn't want to run after her, potentially humiliating myself.

Mom also agreed to buy me a new swimsuit after examining the loose elastic around the legs of my old one.

"Oh my," she exclaimed. "This won't do, will it?"

It was still a one-piece, but at least it fit me and could pass for current fashion.

The first week I went to the pool by myself, Carly and Maggie were only there three times. The first time I saw them, but they didn't see me, and I was too nervous to go over and talk to them. The second time, I purposely walked right past them, and when Maggie called my name, I acted surprised to see them. They invited me to sit with them, which I did. The third time, I worked up the nerve to invite myself.

"Can I sit here?" I asked obsequiously, and they scooted over to make room for me.

After that, it just became a thing. Either Maggie or Carly would wave me over when I came out of the girls' changing room. If I got there first, I claimed their spot and waited for them to arrive. On days when they weren't there, I lay poolside just as I'd seen them do, jumped in for a quick dip, and was usually on my way home after less than an hour. I didn't chat with Luke while he was working, but I knew he always had his eye on me—Mom probably told him to do that. I think Luke was trying to make sense out of Alice's sudden disappearance and my two new friends, but he never asked outright.

One day, Carly, Maggie, and I were lying on our towels, placed like three dominoes, side by side facing the sun. I was wearing a pair of cheap sunglasses I'd gotten from the drugstore and a floppy hat pulled over my face, just the way Carly and Maggie did when they were tanning. Carly propped herself up on her elbows to reach for a drink.

"Wow, Grace, you're so lucky. Your stomach is so flat," she said.

Maggie, who was in the middle, removed her sunglasses and turned her head to look at me.

"You really *are* lucky, Grace. Your belly's below your hipbones. Look at me—I practically look like I'm pregnant."

Which she didn't.

I felt a warm glow that wasn't from the sun. To think these two girls envied something about me . . . something physical. Well, they were goddesses in my eyes—Carly especially. I struggled for a way to respond that would make me seem impressively oblivious to my physical attributes without seeming ungrateful to them for their compliment.

"I . . ." I sat up while keeping my stomach sucked in to maintain the appearance of my most precious asset. I either heard, or felt, a whoosh pass through my head from ear to ear. Then I felt an odd sensation as though someone was closing the door to my brain. A flash of unreality, an out-of-body experience. I looked for Luke to reassure myself he was still there. The lifeguard's seat, with Luke sitting in it, lurched to my left. The grass and towels and all the half-naked bodies on either side of him began to spin slowly until I couldn't get a steady fix on anything. I closed my eyes and fell backward, feeling the thump on the back of my head. My world went from bright to a pinpoint of light to darkness. My hearing went from muffled noises to total silence.

Later on, they told me I resurfaced after about three minutes. When I did, it was in reverse. First the muffled noises and pinpoint of light, and then finally the bright lights and confusing noises. Luke was kneeling on the grass, holding my upper body in his arms. I smelled his sweat and sunscreen and became terribly dizzy. I turned my head to one side and threw up. Then Luke was standing with me cradled in his arms, and I don't remember much else between that time and when I was home lying in my bed.

Late that afternoon, the doctor, who attended our church, made a house call.

"Dehydration," the doctor pronounced.

"Dehydration? Grace, aren't you drinking enough? Is it too much time in the sun, Doctor?" my dad asked.

The doctor looked at me meaningfully, as though we shared a secret. "Grace, have you had any sudden weight loss?"

"No, I mean—"

"She's a growing girl," Dad interrupted. "I mean—she just recently went through the change, kind of late, my wife said. So she's been shooting up and slimming down. That's natural, isn't it?"

I was beyond embarrassed to have two grown men discussing my menses in front of me.

"You're eating right though, aren't you, Grace? No funny business," the doctor went on without acknowledging my father.

"If you mean dieting, Grace eats like a horse," Dad said.

I couldn't get a word in edgewise, not that I wanted to.

"Okay, let's just say you take it easy for a few days," the doctor said. "Stay out of the sun. Get lots of rest and drink lots of liquids. And make sure you're making healthy choices in your diet," he said again in that conspiratorial way. "Give me a call if there are any more . . . episodes."

As soon as the doctor left, I threw the candy in the garbage. My golden ticket wasn't worth losing days spent in Carly's company. I drank about a quart of water and then tried to convince Dad that I was well enough to go to the pool the next day, but he wasn't having any of it.

"You'll stay home through the weekend, and then we'll see how you're doing."

All I could think about was how Carly and Maggie would move on from me during that brief period of time. I had to be there in person to constantly reinforce whatever it was about me they found interesting in the first place. If not, I'd be forgotten, or they'd find some new friend to take the spot where I'd become accustomed to laying my towel. Or worse yet, I'd humiliated myself by throwing up on their poolside sanctuary. Would they even want me to sit with them anymore? This was a distinctly possible calamitous outcome of the golden ticket, and I needed to have an immediate answer. But no amount of arguing with Dad would persuade him and, I think for the first time, he wondered what had happened to the sweet and docile daughter who had never exchanged an angry word with her parents. I imagined he was chalking it up to my menses and the strange and unfathomable ways of women.

The next day was Saturday. I was pouting alone in my room, having refused breakfast as a somewhat protest hunger strike. Mom was having nothing to do with this after my "episode," and to entice me she'd left a pitcher of lemonade and cookies on my dresser.

A few minutes later, she was back.

"There's someone here to see you," she said, and I expected Alice. I was almost gleeful, thinking about how word had gotten to her about my fainting spell, and she was arriving with her tail between her legs to beg my forgiveness. But it was Carly.

"So this is where you live?" Carly plopped down on the bed beside me.

To say that I felt uncomfortable was an understatement. Up until then, Carly only knew I had a hot brother and a flat stomach, nothing more. But now she was in my cramped bedroom, surveying my meager wardrobe in the tiny closet, which had unfortunately been left open. An old Barbie I didn't have the heart to get rid of was perched beside the cookies and lemonade on my dresser. Another one sat sideways on my windowsill, her legs primly straightened in front of her, her head cocked to take in the outside view, her hair obviously recently groomed. My plain-spoken and unglamorous mother had greeted Carly at the door and ushered her to my room. It was a worst-case scenario.

To Carly's credit, she didn't look horrified.

"I just wanted to see how you were," she said. "Maggie couldn't come but she says hi. I was worried about you."

I believed her.

"I'm sorry," I said. "For barfing. Hope I didn't get any on you."

"Not on me," Carly said. "But you got it all over Maggie's towel. Don't worry, she's not mad."

"Oh, yuck. Tell her I'm sorry."

"Actually," Carly's mouth turned up in a mischievous smile. "It was hilarious. I mean, Luke acting like the knight in shining armor, sweeping you into his arms—the look on Maggie's face before she started screaming her head off." Carly laughed, an unexpectedly vulgar sound so at odds with the reserved, ladylike persona she displayed to the world. It startled me, as though I'd suddenly become aware that someone else was in the room with us. "Too bad you were passed out and couldn't see it."

"Yeah," I said. "I guess it must have been pretty funny."

I didn't really think it was funny, not even in hindsight with Carly's take on it. But I was glad she saw it that way. Better that than to be repulsed by me.

Mom popped her head in. "Can I get you girls anything?" she asked. She eyed the pitcher of lemonade, still untouched. "Carly, if you can get Grace to drink something and have a few of those cookies, I'd be much obliged."

"Yes, Grace. Have some, please." Carly stood and walked to the dresser where she poured a glass of lemonade and picked up a cookie. "Here. Be a good girl," she said, handing them to me. She winked at Mom who smiled back and then left us alone, closing the door behind her.

"By the way, I think your mom loves me," Carly said. "Parents always do. Eat and drink so she has a good impression of me. Like I'm your miracle worker."

She laughed again. That ugly bark that seemed to come out

of nowhere. I downed the lemonade and gobbled the cookie. Truth was, I was starving and thirsty, and the need for my hunger strike was over.

"Don't make yourself sick," she said as she was leaving. "Just in case you're being a naughty girl."

By Monday, I'd been released by my parents to do as I pleased. By Monday afternoon, I was basking in the warmth of sun and friendship, cemented by Carly's foray into my private life.

CHAPTER FIVE

Even in July I could feel the summer slip away and, along with it, the naïve girl I'd been only six months earlier. Nothing's quite as treacherous as a small town cradled at the bosom of that month, lush with intoxicating earth aromas sent airborne on waves of heat; the sounds of children drunk on slip-and-slides and cherry popsicles; grandfathers hiding under floppy canvas hats, pruning rosebushes and checking on the well-being of dormant daffodils.

Into this heady mix, add roving bands of youth on the cusp of independence, looking for their own version of happiness in a small town. Unsure exactly what happiness is supposed to mean as hormones transform them daily, hourly, springing surprises that constantly catch them off guard. Coping with baffling mood swings that arrive without warning and at unexpected times. Carving out a space for themselves somewhere between the idiocy of childhood and the conformity of adults, while rejecting both adult and child. Looking for a way to amuse themselves while keeping a foot in both worlds.

These kids, like me, were never sure what the rules of the

game were. They knew what their parents said on one hand and what their peers were saying on the other. They mostly faked it each and every day. And if they faked it wrong, they went home and spoke rudely to their parents, slammed the doors to their bedrooms, and cried into their pillows. These were the kids who looked to hitch their wagon to someone giving the appearance of strength. Someone like Carly. Someone who made it look easy.

Once I'd been accepted by Carly and Maggie, my social world expanded beyond just the swimming pool. In reality, what we did was hardly any different from what I'd done with Alice. None of us could drive, although Carly would have her license in October and Maggie the following March. I wouldn't even turn fifteen until weeks before our junior year was over but I took personal pride in the onset of Carly's approaching adulthood. She already had a learner's permit, although that wasn't helpful to us that summer. So we walked to places where we could hang out. The drugstore where we could stock up on cosmetics and test out shades of lip gloss. I'd finally gotten Mom's permission to wear a conservative amount of makeup. She didn't like it, but she didn't stand in my way. Sometimes Maggie's mother dropped us off at the mall and returned to pick us up hours later. Occasionally, we saw other groups of girls from school there. Carly and Maggie would wave or say hi, but we never hung out with them. We kept to ourselves.

I was a quick study so I listened and learned as Carly and Maggie passed judgment on what was or wasn't "cute" when it came to fashion. I didn't have the wherewithal to buy like they did. But I could amend clothes that Mom and I found on the cheap. I could mold myself into someone who could believably be seen with girls like Carly and Maggie.

Once we went to a movie, and Carly pulled out a flask of alcohol she'd stolen from her parents' bar. She tipped it to her open mouth and then passed it to Maggie. When Maggie passed it to me, I shook my head. I wasn't there yet, although I would be soon. Some boys we knew from school walked into the theater and spotted us. They took seats directly behind us and spoke loudly enough to attract our attention. It was stupid-talk, harmless flirtation.

"Share some with us, Carly," one of them said right as the trailers were starting.

Maggie giggled, and I didn't dare look, but Carly turned around to face them directly and unafraid. She was pretty buzzed by then.

"Go find your own, loser," she said and then turned back and shared a rude laugh with us. I was afraid of what would come next. These boys certainly wouldn't let that insult go unanswered, would they? Carly had surely provoked a war and I was afraid to be caught in the middle. But it only elicited a few whiny complaints, and I thought I heard the word *bitch* murmured at least once. It was the first time I'd ever heard a boy say that about a girl.

"Who's that, Carly? Your little sister?" one of them finally blurted out, a pathetic comeback to Carly's insult.

Carly turned around. "Who's that with you? Freddie Krueger?" She laughed again and then turned back and put her arm around my shoulder. Maggie giggled hysterically into her cupped palms.

"Hey, little sister," Carly said, and I blushed furiously.

"Are you gay for her?" the first boy howled.

"She's my *little sister*, idiot!" Carly answered loudly without turning around. It sent Maggie into another fit of laughter and provoked an angry rebuke from an older couple sitting to the right of us.

After that, I became *Little Sister* or *Lil' Sis* to Carly and Maggie. It lasted about a month—long enough for them to quit laughing about it and for me to quit pretending to laugh about it.

One day Carly summoned us to her house. A stray cat that had wandered into her backyard a week prior had given birth under the back-porch steps. Only three kittens survived.

"Will you guys each take one?" she asked. "I'm going to keep the orange one."

I sized up the two remaining kittens. We'd never had a real family pet although we fed plenty of stray cats and dogs in Guatemala. A cat would be fun and would bond me to Carly and Maggie forever. I'd have to ask my parents, of course.

"I'll take one," I volunteered. Better to ask forgiveness than permission. I'd worry about Mom and Dad later.

"Me too," Maggie said. "If my mom lets me. They're so adorable. Are you going to get the mother fixed?"

"As soon as the kittens are weaned, we'll take her to the pound."

"Aww, that's kind of sad. Won't they just kill her?" Maggie's smile dropped.

"We can't keep a fully grown cat. We don't know anything about her. She's pretty much wild," Carly said.

I watched the three kittens pumping their tiny paws against their mother's teats. She didn't seem wild, so content at that moment, her kittens safe under the porch steps of humans who brought her bowls of food and water. What if she knew that in a few short weeks her kittens would be taken from her and she'd be handed off to likely death? Still, it seemed reasonable, what Carly said. How the cat was wild, and they couldn't take in a wild cat. *But why can't they just continue to feed her outside?* I wondered. Then I imagined asking my parents if we could take in a feral full-grown cat, and I knew what their answer would be.

But it was the way Carly said it. Absent of any self-doubt although, in her defense, she'd had time to process everything. To put her emotions within the context of reality. And how was I any better? I didn't even *want* to ask my parents about taking in the mother cat. I was afraid just by asking I'd jeopardize my chance with the kitten. Maggie looked sad but she didn't step up either.

After tiring of watching the kittens, we sat by Carly's pool in her pristine backyard. Our conversation was already turning to school even with another month of vacation left. Luke was gone. He'd left early to scope out housing and begin the part-time job he'd keep during the school year. Our house wasn't the same without Luke and I began to worry about Dad for the first time—how would he get on without his only son?

"We're like the three musketeers," Maggie blurted out of the blue. "We should call ourselves the three musketeers." That seemed to cheer her a bit, putting an end to the sadness she was feeling over the mother cat's dire future.

"The three musketeers is so cliché," Carly said. "Plus, they were guys, and we're girls. We need something better, so let me think about it for a while."

We all understood that Carly would make the decision, and whatever she decided would be fabulous.

Carly's parents took her to Hawaii for a pre-back-to-school family vacation. For the first time, it was just Maggie and me. We continued to get together, though not as frequently as when Carly was there. And when we were together, it was painfully obvious we could never survive as the two musketeers. Our bonds were with Carly, and without her we were only reminders of her absence. When we talked, it was about Carly. What was she doing right then? What time was it in Hawaii? Was she meeting any cute guys on the beach? How many days—hours—before she returned? Remember when we all did this? Won't it be fun when we all do that?

But before Carly came home, I came to realize that Maggie was a genuinely nice person. I'd never seen that in her before, not really. I'd never actually seen her as anything beyond an appendage of Carly.

"Thirty-six hours before she's home," Maggie said one day when we were painting our toenails in my bedroom. The window was cranked open to neutralize the noxious fumes emanating from the tiny jeweled bottles of gleaming colors. A horsefly tentatively made its way across the window screen, testing for any weakness that might allow passage into our house. "What should we do this weekend?"

"I don't know. Something fun," I answered dumbly. I was never the one to make plans for the three of us. That was Carly's role. Sometimes Maggie's. Even when Maggie handed me the opportunity to decide, I declined it. I was along for the ride, wherever it took me.

"I'll bet you miss Luke," she said dreamily. "Must be lonely without him." She carefully ran a Q-tip dipped in polish remover around the circumference of each toenail. I took a minute to admire her steady hand and precision.

"I guess. Kind of. Mom and Dad miss him a lot, especially Dad. We're going to Sacramento to visit him in a week, so they're excited about that. I might not even go, though."

"If you do, tell him I said hi," Maggie said, and when I didn't respond, she pressed. "I *mean* it." I felt sorry for her because Luke didn't know she existed. Or he did know but she existed as background noise—his kid sister's friend.

My new gray kitten raised its tiny head over the edge of the wicker basket where he'd been sleeping. He stared at us with huge amber eyes that always seemed to register surprise. White tufts of fur sprouted from his ears, giving him the appearance of a miniature bobcat. He padded to the litter box in the far corner and scratched uselessly before relieving himself.

"So adorable!" Maggie said. "I think Bob's the cutest of the three."

Secretly, I thought so too.

"How did you and Carly get to be friends?" I asked Maggie. At times, I viewed Maggie as Carly's equal, but other times she seemed as submissive as me.

"We've known each other since we were seven," she said. She pursed her lips and blew, aiming the jet stream at her drying nails. "She's literally always been there for me, the best friend anyone could have. You're seriously lucky, you know that, Grace?"

"Lucky?"

"That Carly's your friend now. She'll always look out for you. You won't ever have to worry about anything." Maggie threw her head over the side of my bed to find Bob who had disappeared under the edge of my duvet. "Here you are! Oh my God, Grace, you have to clean under your bed. Look at poor Bobby." In a graceful arc of her arm, she brought Bob up to the bed and set him down between us. Dust bunnies clung to his dove-gray fur.

"What would I have to worry about?" I had a sense of the things kids did to each other in American high schools after seeing Timothy's shame in the gym. But I wanted Maggie to confirm the blessing bestowed on me by this unlikely alliance.

"You know. People can be shitty. When I was in fourth

grade I had to wear one of those head things for my braces for a month. It was like . . . wow, one of the worst times of my life. I mean, I don't know how my mom ever thought I could survive that, and I wouldn't have without Carly." Maggie stroked Bob with her palms, protecting against the possibility of stray kitten hairs cementing themselves to her glossy nails.

I looked at the row of gleaming white teeth peeking out between Maggie's lips when she smiled. They were perfectly aligned. Braces were a luxury which wasn't even discussed in my family. My two front teeth angled back slightly, the eye teeth parasitically taking advantage of the extra room. My bottom front teeth fought for space, eventually working out a compromise that involved one moving slightly behind the other. Whatever this head thing was that Maggie had been subjected to, it appeared to have worked miracles in her mouth.

"What did Carly do?"

"You know Rich Benson?"

I shook my head. "I don't think so."

"He was one of the guys sitting behind us at the movies."

"Oh yeah." I thought about the merciless way Carly dealt with those boys. Slicing through their dignity with her sharp words and then finishing them off with a crude and dismissive burst of laughter.

"He was the worst when I had to wear the head gear. He followed me around at recess and made stupid, mean jokes in front of everyone. Carly told me she was going to take care of him, so one day she brought a bike wrench to school. When no one was looking, she loosened the chain on his bike, and after school when he got on his bike and pushed down on the pedal, the whole thing came off and he fell on his face and lost his front tooth."

I grimaced at the thought of falling on my face and losing my front tooth. I thought I detected a slight quiver in Maggie's upper lip. Like she was reliving that time.

"Anyway, after that he didn't have anything to say to me anymore. Everyone was there when he fell, and it was probably the best thing that could've happened to him."

"Seems like you guys really don't like him," I said.

"I don't mind him anymore."

It occurred to me we probably never would have had this conversation if Carly was around. I never heard her brag about herself even though I knew she was one of the smartest kids in our class. She was also first chair flute in the advanced band and one of the top writers for the school newspaper.

"I think it was second grade when we really got to be friends though. We shared a double-desk that year. And I think that was the same year my neighbors' Samoyed was terrorizing me whenever I rode my bike or went out on the street to play. My dad talked to the neighbors about not letting Blizzard run loose, but he kept getting out. Then Carly found a can of red spray paint in my dad's work shed, and the next time she was over when Blizzard got out, she did a number on him. He was this humongous, fuzzy white dog, but by the time Carly was done with him he had huge splotches of bright red all over him. He looked ridiculous."

"Wow! Did you guys get in trouble?"

"Nobody knew we did it. *She* did it. And it didn't hurt Blizzard. We wouldn't have done anything to hurt Blizzard, because it wasn't his fault. It was the neighbors' fault because they couldn't control their dog." Maggie lay on her back, legs over the edge of the bed. She gently positioned Bob on her stomach and continued to caress him until he curled up and promptly fell asleep. "Next time we saw Blizzard, he was completely shaved down to his skin. There was a little bit of red stain on his skin but most of it came off with the fur. Anyway, he never got out again because the neighbors put up one of those invisible electric fences after the spray paint thing."

Neither of those stories was a red flag for me at the time. I don't think we ever truly judge a person except in hindsight, and my history with Carly was only just beginning.

"Blizzard died a few months ago," Maggie said. "It was sad because I actually grew to love him. When I got older, the neighbors would hire me to dog-sit sometimes, and I always felt a little bad about the red paint. He was a good dog, just a little scary when I was small and he was so big."

"Poor Blizzard." I hoped I was suitably matching the sadness I read on Maggie's face. I had a sudden rush of feeling for Maggie. We seemed to connect on a slightly deeper level than I'd ever connected with anyone before. When she talked to me, she expected I was capable of understanding beyond what her words were saying. She gave me credit for an emotional intelligence still in the development stage. She never talked down to me and never made me feel like I was a year younger or not her equal.

"When my parents were going through their divorce, Carly was amazing," she said, her voice taking a perceptible drop in enthusiasm from the prior tales.

My neighbors' dog hurled a dozen high-pitched barks in rapid succession into the stillness of that summer day. From the comfort and safety of Maggie's stomach, Bob twitched his tufted ears without opening his eyes. Maybe he was incorporating the barking into a bad dream. A door slammed, and next door, Mrs. Bailey hollered out something, bringing the barking to an abrupt conclusion and restoring the oppressive and artificial calm that enveloped us.

"I practically lived at Carly's house for a month when that was going on," Maggie said. "My parents didn't care because they didn't want me around to hear them fighting and screaming at each other. They were both so into it, I think they forgot I existed. So Carly just took care of me, you know?"

I nodded yes, although I didn't know. Couldn't imagine what it would feel like to be forgotten by your parents, although I would come to feel a little of it when Mom and Dad moved to Madagascar.

"I was all like—I'm not mad at my parents," Maggie continued. "If this makes them happy, it's better that way. I still love them both. But Carly opened my eyes to what an asshole my dad really was. I mean, he cheated on my mom."

This revelation embarrassed me, and yet I was honored to be trusted with such intensely personal information about her life. I shook my head slowly. Incredulously.

Maggie looked right into my eyes, and I thought I saw the shine of tears on the surface of hers.

"I mean, that's something you can never forgive. Right?"

"Right," I said while wondering if it might be possible to forgive since he hadn't cheated on Maggie.

When it came to Carly, there was always that push and pull, but the pull usually won out in the end.

CHAPTER SIX

A few weeks before school started, Maggie asked Carly and me to meet up at her house. She had a surprise for us. Carly swung by my house to give me a ride. She was driving, as she usually was those days, her mom riding shotgun. From the backseat, I marveled at the way she maneuvered through the streets, made graceful turns at intersections, and glided to a smooth stop in front of Maggie's house. She was so grown-up. A few more months and Carly would be driving Maggie and me around by herself. I could hardly wait.

"I wonder what Maggie's big surprise is," she said after I rang the doorbell.

Maggie flung open her front door before the door chimes finished playing.

"You're going to die," she said, the door partially closed behind her as though she was hiding something. *A dog,* I thought. *A big, white, fluffy dog like Blizzard.* Then she stood aside and opened it all the way. "Ta dah!"

A tall, pale girl stood behind Maggie in the doorway. She had shoulder-length white-blonde hair. Long-limbed and lanky with eyes so blue they were almost clear, like sapphires embedded in ice. Eyebrows that melted into the light color of her skin. She came from behind Maggie and stood by her side. Her long neck. The gracefully awkward way she shifted her body. She reminded me of a giraffe.

"Jane," Carly said, her voice lifting in surprise.

"Isn't it amazing?" Maggie hopped joyfully, her hands held out in prayer position. *Not a dog*, I registered. *But who is this Jane who brings so much joy to the normally subdued Maggie?* I experienced a flash of jealousy. *Does Carly love her too?* "Jane, this is Grace, she's new here too. Grace, Jane used to be my next-door neighbor when we were in eighth grade for a year before her dad was transferred to Chicago."

"But she went to Catholic school," Carly interjected. "Not *ours*."

I knew right then that Carly didn't love Jane like Maggie did. Maybe not even at all.

"Hi, Grace." Jane smiled timidly. She had an open expression and warm voice that was pleasing and disarming. I wanted to like her but was waiting for another cue from Carly.

"Why are you here?" Carly asked and, again, I got the impression she wasn't thrilled by Maggie's surprise.

"My dad got transferred back to the home office so . . . hello Indian Springs," Jane said. I felt an instant wave of pity for her. It seemed she was ignorant of Carly's feelings toward her, but maybe *I* was the one who was misinterpreting Carly's body language. Her choice of words. I hoped so, but when I looked at Maggie, I saw the pure joy had disappeared from her eyes. She seemed guarded. Even worried. "We're buying a house out on Durham Road."

"Way out there?" Carly raised her eyebrows.

"My sister wants a horse so that was part of the parental guilt payoff. You know . . . for moving us again."

"Back to St. Mary's?"

"Hell no!" Jane said. "That was *my* guilt payoff. I get to go to Indian Springs with you guys, so no more uniforms. My sister's going to St. Mary's, but she wanted to." Jane rolled her glassy eyes and smirked.

"Exciting, huh?" Maggie said, but she was looking right at Carly, and she didn't sound so excited anymore.

"Exciting," Carly said in a near monotone, and all doubt left my mind.

"So, come in," Maggie said. "Let's figure out what we're doing today."

We sat around the kitchen table, the other girls politely catching each other up on the past few years, with Maggie doing most of the talking, which was beginning to sound too formal and forced. We swiveled the open bag of chips around like spin-the-bottle, licking the salt from our fingertips and sipping cans of coke. My eyes returned to Jane whenever I thought she wasn't looking. Her posture was slightly slumped in the way of too-tall adolescent girls, but the slope of her shoulders was seemingly perfect, as though carved from marble. The careless way she drew the back of her hand across her mouth to wipe away crumbs and then wiping the crumbs from her hand against her bare thigh. The expression of her eyes which was both far away and intensely personal at the same time. I noticed she wore no makeup except a barely visible lip gloss which vanished after the chips and drink. Her laugh was goofy and silver braces sparkled like diamonds when she smiled. She was natural, completely unselfconscious. She wasn't a girl who seemed used to being judged harshly, or even being judged at all. I wondered how that felt.

A different girl in Jane's gangly body might have come off

as ungainly, but Jane's ease and quiet confidence combined with her strikingly unconventional looks transformed her into something more than the sum of her parts. She had that quality—call it charisma—that defies categorization. The ghost orchid of human attributes, it doesn't discriminate between wretch or saint. Loveliness or hideousness. The strong or the sickly. It's the peculiar allure that draws every eye in the room. Inspires both love and hate. Causes others to change the course of their lives.

Of course, I knew none of that then. I only knew that this girl, unknown to me only an hour earlier, possessed something Maggie and I never would. In my limited lifespan, I'd only encountered it twice before. There was Carly, of course. And a minister in Ecuador who had this same effect on me but, thinking back, I wasn't sure if it was his words or his personal aura. Now I found myself sitting in an ordinary kitchen with two people, each of whom projected larger than life. Didn't Maggie see it as well? Didn't Maggie realize that Carly and Jane couldn't possibly co-exist?

I felt a brush against my ankle which sent a chill up my spine. I looked down to see tiny Princess Leia, Maggie's choice of the three kittens. Jane got up and disappeared down the hall, on her way to the bathroom.

"It's great, isn't it?" Maggie said. "I had no idea she was back until she called me last night."

Carly smiled grimly.

"Now we can be the *four* musketeers." Maggie's cheerfulness wasn't fooling me, and I'm sure it wasn't fooling Carly. She was pleading. Pleading for Jane.

"There weren't four musketeers," Carly said. "And anyway, I thought of a name I was just going to tell you guys today."

Maggie stared at the table and then, as if noticing Princess Leia for the first time, scooped the kitten into her lap.

"What is it, Carly?" I asked after an unbearable silence.

"Well, if you even care," she said, looking at Maggie. "The Kitty Committee. Because we each took one of the kittens."

"I love it," I said. "The Kitty Committee." It felt warm and fuzzy and cute like you'd want the name for your circle of friends to sound. Welcoming and playful. I ignored the obvious. There were three kittens and four people.

Carly hadn't taken her eyes off Maggie.

"It's good," Maggie said. "But what about Jane?"

"I thought it was supposed to be just the three of us," Carly said, and, I admit, I still felt a tiny pang of jealousy at the intrusion of this new girl who was so clearly prized by Maggie.

"C'mon, Car," Maggie said. "We can't just abandon her. She's new, and she was my friend. My parents were friends with her parents. What am I supposed to tell her?"

"Why does she even have to know about our group?" Carly said. "Why can't it just be our thing that doesn't have anything to do with anyone else?"

I'd never seen Maggie stand up to Carly before. It was like watching your parents fight.

"What's the point of a secret group if we're going to be hanging out with Jane? Why can't we just include her? I don't get it."

The bathroom door opened at the end of the hallway, and we heard the slapping sound of Jane's flip-flops moving toward us.

"She has two cats," Maggie whispered urgently.

Another unbearable silence that seemed to go on forever but couldn't have lasted for more than a few seconds.

Carly leaned forward and folded her arms on the table. "Okay, but only if she agrees to abide by the rules."

CHAPTER SEVEN

THE KITTY COMMITTEE RULES

1) Members of the Kitty Committee come before anyone else
2) One for all and all for one
3) No drugs are permitted but alcohol is okay
4) No boys should ever come before or between members of the Kitty Committee (see #1)
5) Absolutely no one else will be permitted to join
6) No one member is above the others
7) If you leave the Kitty Committee, you are dead to the others

The following day, Carly, Maggie, and I met at my house in my bedroom to draft the rules for the newly formed Kitty Committee. Maggie had told Jane we had a club, and she was invited to join. Jane just laughed and said it sounded like fun and what did we do, for which Maggie had no answer.

"What *do* we do?" Maggie asked Carly. She'd been pacing nervously around my room ever since they got there. Carly sat calmly on the floor, bent over from the waist, leaning on her elbows and scratching out notes on the pad of paper in front of her. From Dad's bedroom, the TV blared out a History Channel show about ancient Roman battle strategies.

"We're friends," Carly said without looking up. "Friends who put friends ahead of everything else."

Who could argue with that?

"This next year's going to be the toughest year of our lives, our last year before getting ready for college applications and all. We're going to need to be able to count on each other." She straightened up and looked directly at Maggie, who had joined me on my bed.

"I'm just going to junior college," Maggie said. "But obviously, I want to be there for you guys."

"You should set your sights higher," Carly said. "How about you, Grace? Where do you want to go?"

"I dunno," I said and then thought better of it. "Maybe Sacramento State?" It was more of a question that I threw out to see Carly's reaction. Luke was there, after all.

"You need to set your sights higher too, Grace," Carly said. "You can do better than that, you're smart."

And in that instant, Carly succeeded in infantilizing the two of us. Or perhaps stepping in to take the place of our parents. Either way, I knew I needed her to help me plan out my life. I was just a child but could already feel my future snorting like a raging bull breathing down my neck, ready to trample me if I didn't get out ahead of it.

The Kitty Committee would be my lifeline.

The rules were agreed upon without Jane present since Carly said we were the founding members. I mostly sat silent while Carly and Maggie hammered out the details. Carly was responsible for the bulk of the rules with Maggie adding rule two as her homage to the musketeers and rule six perhaps to ensure her equal voice. Carly pointed out that rule two was already covered by rule one but then seemed to think better of it and agreed with Maggie that it was the perfect addition to our "constitution."

"Rule number seven seems a little harsh," I said, feeling I should at least give the appearance of being part of the decision-making process.

Carly and Maggie both looked at me as though just then remembering I was part of the rules committee.

"Why? Do you plan on leaving?" Carly asked.

"Um. *No!*"

"How about you, Maggie? Are you planning on sticking around, or are you not okay with rule number seven, either?"

Even if Maggie thought it was harsh, the wording of Carly's question left no room for doubt.

"Of course I'm okay with it. Nobody's leaving the Kitty Committee," she said. It was understood that although Jane wasn't in attendance, Maggie spoke on her behalf.

"Well, if everyone's planning on staying, I don't see any problem," Carly said. "So we now have our constitution. All in favor say 'aye.'"

We all said "aye," and, for the first time, I experienced a sense of happiness and purpose derived from being a part of a greater whole. It hadn't happened in church, although I wanted it to—waited and prayed for it, questioned my worth before finally abandoning hope that it would ever happen for me like it had happened for my parents.

"We'll all probably join sororities when we get to college," Carly said. "But there's never going to be a sorority as meaningful or important as this one."

I nodded solemnly in agreement, and even Maggie murmured her assent.

"And one last thing," Carly said as if it was the most

inconsequential afterthought. "We need to have some sort of initiation to prove our commitment. So we'll have to come up with something soon. Okay?"

"Okay," I said without hesitation.

"Maggie?" Carly's eyebrows shot up into question marks.

"Sure," Maggie said, less enthusiastically than me.

Later, I came to understand that Maggie probably sensed the initiation was just another way to make it harder for Jane to commit.

"All in favor?"

"Aye," we all agreed.

SAN FRANCISCO

When I heard Carly's voice on the other end of the phone, I had already survived two years of college, one in an increasingly shaky relationship with Nathan, and three anonymous, vaguely threatening messages, spaced exactly one year apart.

"I'm back visiting the fam," Carly said. "And I'm already going bonkers in this cow town. Care to meet up in the city?"

I suggested a time and place, but Carly wanted to meet at the residential eating disorder clinic where Maggie was currently in-patient.

"I checked on visiting hours," she said. "We can make it."

I'd had something of a transformation since the last time I saw Carly. Gone was the makeup and hairstyling. I wore my hair loose and air-dried, naturally curly or frizzy depending on the fog that day. I'd put on a little weight, which Nathan liked, saying it made me seem healthier. Ripped jeans, a Gypsy top, and an oversized sweater completed my look on that day.

"God, what happened to you?" Carly said. She, of course, was sleek and groomed.

"Nice to see you too, Carly."

While I had gone full-out San Francisco hippie mode, Carly had gone full East-coast preppy. Her displeasure duly registered, she pivoted to the next unpleasantness.

"Let's do this," she said.

This was Carly's first visit since anorexia consumed Maggie's life. I'd visited from time to time, never back in Indian

Springs, which I was unable to face, but whenever Maggie was being treated in San Francisco. She was on a downward spiral but not yet the worst I would come to see. To see her like this was beyond distressing.

Carly and I were buzzed through the entrance after announcing ourselves on the intercom. A young man greeted us warmly, then escorted us to the community room where Maggie waited. She looked up sheepishly, as though caught by surprise—the victim of a cruel prank. Other residents huddled with visitors, some painfully thin, others with no exterior signs of their disorder. The room itself was decorated in warm colors, using soft lighting. Private conversation areas were strategically placed. Soft classical music played in the background. I felt the sadness of that place like a well-worn and familiar sweater. I felt comfortable there.

"This place gives me the creeps," Carly said after only a few minutes of conversing. "Let's get the fuck out of here."

"I can't leave," Maggie said. Her expression was doleful. "I have to give twenty-four hours' notice and get permission."

"Or what?" Carly asked.

"Or I can get thrown out."

"There's no way they'll throw you out," Carly said. "And lose the income stream your insurance is paying? C'mon, grow some ovaries, Maggie."

I was horrified, but the smile that lifted the corners of Maggie's mouth made me rethink my initial reaction. I hadn't seen Maggie smile for a long time.

"Maybe," she said, and I watched her face transform to a more youthful expression as we waited for what would come next. "Okay, follow me and I'll act like I'm going to show you my room. There's an exit door near there that leads to an alley in back of the building. It's not locked from the inside."

Carly's glee was instant. "Ahhh, so maybe you've done this

before?" She waggled her eyebrows conspiratorially.

"Nah, I just go out there sometimes to smoke because there's no smoking inside. I leave the door propped open so I can get back in."

In the alley, Carly took the lead, and, just like that, Maggie and I followed her and the rules of her alternate universe. I poked my finger through the tiny tear in the curtain separating the *now* from the *then,* and yanked. For an instant, I felt absolute freedom like I was feeling it for the first time: the intoxicating siren of recklessness after overpowering its jailor—good judgment; the bond that turned me into a superhero, stronger than I could ever be on my own—my life, no longer just a life but a fantastic adventure. The Kitty Committee.

But by the time we got to Carly's car, I knew we were wrong. We were putting in jeopardy Maggie's standing with the people who were her only current hope for recovery. How could that be a good thing, no matter how much it made her smile? Once again, I had conspired with Carly to ruin a life. From my place in the backseat, I allowed myself a closer look at the prominent vertebrae just beneath the thin fabric of Maggie's shirt. Her shoulders were sharp and bony—inhospitable as a place for anyone to cry on or as a place of nurturing—too fragile to carry the weight of the world. The day was cool, and Maggie hadn't brought a jacket. Gooseflesh ran down her arm. Her hair was dull and lank. I felt sick and, as usual, my complicity had been not speaking up. I'd managed to come so far, and yet I hadn't gotten anywhere at all.

"Where should we go, Grace? It's your city." Carly broke into my thoughts.

I directed her to a small neighborhood coffee shop where Nathan and I sometimes went to read or sit outside at one of the sidewalk tables when the weather was fine. Its main draw that day was its proximity to Maggie's clinic and the hope that we could get her back quickly before anyone noticed she was gone.

"Why don't you and Maggie grab a table? What do you want? My treat."

Was it my imagination or did everyone turn to look when we walked in? Was Carly's voice the loudest thing in the room? Louder even than the angry hiss of the espresso machine, the animated discussion at a corner table—politics, Russian literature, the politics of Russian literature.

"I'll have a croissant," I said. "And a hot chocolate."

"Just get me a glass of water please," Maggie said to Carly's bemused expression.

When Carly returned to the table, it was with a tray overloaded with muffins, cookies, croissants, and three hot chocolates.

"Did you get my water?" Maggie asked, and when Carly didn't answer but proceeded to unload the contents of the tray onto our table, I got up to fetch the water myself.

"So, Indian Springs is just as pathetic as always," Carly was saying when I returned. I set the glass of water in front of Maggie, and she smiled gratefully. "I don't know how you stand it, Maggie."

"Well, I'm here now for a while, at least."

She was still beautiful, I thought. With her prominent cheekbones and height, I could imagine a talent agent giving her his business card, not knowing or caring about the sickness that carved out those features. They wouldn't notice the loss of sheen in her hair or eyes. They wouldn't have known the old Maggie. She could still be a living, breathing mannequin one could easily drape with high-fashion clothes. Soon, she would not even be that.

"So let's catch up," Carly said. "What's been going on, girls? No holding back, especially you, Grace. It goes without saying what's going on with Maggie." The disapproval in her tone was impossible to miss, and Maggie visibly winced at the coldness of her judgment. I ripped off a piece of my croissant and stuffed it in my mouth.

"Nothing," I said, although everything was going on. I could have filled an hour with just what was going on in my head at that very minute.

"Ooh, that sounds exciting," Carly said. She broke off a tiny piece of a muffin, hardly bigger than a collection of crumbs, and held it between her thumb and forefinger as though it was something she should dispose of before finally popping it into her mouth. "Where did you get that water?" she asked, ignoring the hot chocolate in front of her.

I raised my hand to motion toward the entrance where a counter held sugar, cream, coffee stirrers, and a pitcher of water. And only then did I see him coming through the door. Of all the coffee shops in all the towns in all the world, he walked into mine, to reference a line from *Casablanca*. But when Nathan walked in, it really wasn't so surprising. I'd chosen this spot because it was one of ours, one of many but still one. I just hadn't foreseen the coincidence of him dropping by at that time.

Carly and Maggie followed my deer-caught-in-the-head-lights stare which led to Nathan standing in the doorway looking at me. He walked over to our table and put his hand on my shoulder. I hoped he couldn't feel me shrinking from under his touch. He did.

"Grace," he said while looking first from Carly to Maggie then back again. "I didn't know you were here."

"Nathan, this is Carly . . . and this is Maggie. Carly's

visiting, but we don't have much time before Maggie has to get back." My voice felt high and tight in my ill-fated attempt to come across as casual.

"Oh, okay. No problem, just thought I'd say hi."

It *was* a problem, I knew that. I knew it was a problem so significant it would keep us up all night arguing about why I hadn't mentioned it to Nathan. Why I'd chosen to exclude him from the part of my life that most frustrated him. Was most unreachable.

"I'll see you soon," I said weakly. "We won't be long."

Carly took it in like a circus show. Maggie ducked her head and sipped self-consciously and nervously from her glass of water. Even if I'd been a stranger, it would be hard to miss my body language, and these girls were anything but strangers.

"Nice to meet you, Nathan." Carly beamed. "I'm sure Grace will fill us in all about you. You've been keeping secrets, you naughty girl," she said to me while looking at Nathan.

"Yeah, nice meeting you." Maggie shifted her gaze to the table and squirmed in the hard chair, which couldn't have felt comfortable under her protruding pelvic bones.

"Sure, okay," Nathan said. "Nice to meet you all. See you, Grace." He gave my shoulder a perfunctory squeeze and left without ordering the coffee he'd come in for.

"Oookay. I think we have something to talk about *now*," Carly said, her eyes flickering with interest.

But I wasn't in the frame of mind to share Nathan with Carly, who was in the box I'd built around her three years earlier. That was where I needed her to stay. Nathan was in a different box and I wasn't prepared to let him out either.

"He's just a guy," I said. "Nothing much to tell."

"He's cute," Maggie said. "Does he go to school with you?"

"No, he goes somewhere else."

"Someone serious?" Maggie asked, her voice lifting on the

last word.

I wanted Maggie to have a respite by focusing the attention on me instead of her. But there was the fact that I knew Carly was getting a read on me, making me even more determined not to reveal anything to her. She was enjoying every minute of it.

"Nobody serious. Just a guy I'm seeing, sorry to disappoint."

I left out the part about living together and silently begged for Nathan's forgiveness.

Carly pinched off another piece of muffin, having forgotten about the water by then. "It's obvious Grace doesn't feel like sharing with us, Maggie. So let's talk about something else. You. When're you getting out of that awful place?"

"Carly!" I shot her a poisonous look, but she didn't even blink.

"It's okay, Grace. I'm a big girl," Maggie said, but she wasn't. She was childlike. Fragile. "I have to stay until I get better, so however long that takes. But you already know that, don't you?" She exhaled a lungful of regret in a sudden heavy sigh. The smile that had transformed her back at the clinic was gone. She needed to return, I could see it in the slump of her normally graceful posture.

"Okay, let's try something else," Carly said. "Unless you guys just want me to talk about myself, which I'll gladly do." She popped another tiny ball of muffin into her open mouth. I remembered that mouth so well—the places it had been. The things it had said.

"Why don't you do that, Carly?" I invited. "We'd love to hear all about you." Sarcasm had become my passive-aggressive weapon, but it was useless against Carly.

"So why the psychology major?" she asked. "Trying to save the world, are we?"

"It seemed like a good idea when I applied," I said. "It's

something I've been interested in for a while."

Because of you, I wanted to say. To shout.

"What are your plans after graduation?" Carly asked.

Maggie's legs were crossed one over the other. Her raised foot jiggled. She drummed the tabletop rhythmically with her fingertips whose nails had been bitten to below where a nail should naturally end. Carly stared right through her, waiting for my answer.

"I haven't thought that far ahead. Do some advanced studies maybe. Maybe do social work or private practice. I haven't learned enough to figure out exactly what I want to focus on, but I'm sure I will by the time I graduate." I glanced nervously at Maggie. She was like a whistling teapot in danger of boiling over.

"That's going to come sooner than you think," said the girl who'd already planned the next twenty years of her life. "Also, I hope you realize there's no money in it."

I went back to twisting the napkin I'd been holding since Nathan left. Just like that, my future seemed bleak and point-less. Money, which had never mattered to me before, suddenly seemed like the pinnacle of happiness.

"I think it's great, Grace. Really." Maggie picked up her glass and took several small sips of water. But her words didn't have the same impact as Carly's. I knew Maggie would cheer me on no matter what, but it was always Carly's judgment that affected me most.

"Guess who I saw at a money manager internship interview last week in New York?" Carly said. She'd gotten the better of me and was now ready to pivot back to idle chatter.

Maggie and I stared blankly.

"Guess," she repeated, a smile inching its way toward her dimpled cheeks.

"I have no idea, Carly. Who did you see?" She had just

unraveled my future in less than ten words. I was angry with her but even angrier at myself.

"Someone you both know. Someone from the old days. Guess! You guys are no fun."

"Rudolph the red-nosed reindeer."

"You're such a great wit, Grace. Truly."

"You said from the old days. Just trying to be fun, like you said."

Maggie laughed, and I was proud I'd brought back the smile to her face, no matter how fleeting.

"Anyway, I saw Tim LeClerc. Remember him?"

Timothy. My stomach clenched. All of it came rushing back. The herpes report. His naked shame. The rest of it.

"Uh, *yeah*," Maggie said. "Is he still at Harvard?"

"Of course, silly girl. Where else would he be?"

"What's he like these days?" Maggie asked. "I hope he's doing okay."

"He's surprisingly not hideous. I guess the East Coast has been a positive influence for him." As if just remembering, Carly picked up her now cool hot chocolate and downed the contents in a series of gulps. She set the empty mug down in front of her. "What's wrong, Grace? Don't you like your hot chocolate?"

I picked up my cup and took a taste. It had grown cold but was rich and creamy. I drank half the cup, leaving a film of melted whipped cream on my upper lip. I wiped my mouth with the twisted napkin. Why did she have to bring up Timothy?

"I meant what's he *like*?" Maggie insisted. "Did you talk to him?"

"Yes, we talked. I told him I was going to see you guys this week, and he said to say hi."

"Are you kidding me?" The irritation that had been

simmering within me was now too much to contain. "Why would Timothy say hi to *us*?" I often thought that ninety percent of what came out of Carly's mouth was nothing but lies, but I was normally reluctant to challenge her. Life was just easier that way.

"You're not going to believe it, but we were both interviewing for the same internship," Carly said, ignoring my question.

"Why wouldn't we believe it? You two were always competing for the same things."

"No way he's getting this one over me." Maggie and I exchanged a look Carly couldn't have missed. "You'll see," she added.

"I should go," Maggie said. "I shouldn't be here."

Carly pushed a blueberry muffin across the table. It loomed large in Maggie's space—a soldier reporting for duty. Maggie shrank back into her seat.

"C'mon, Maggie. Eat it," Carly said.

Maggie extended a skeletal arm and pushed it away.

"Eat it, Maggie. Enough with the game you're playing."

With her head angled down, Maggie lifted her eyes to Carly. "You think this is a game?"

"It's all in your head. You can control it. Do you think you're not getting enough attention or something? Okay, you've got my attention. You've got Grace's attention. Now stop being so stupid and eat."

"Shut up, Carly!" I hissed.

"No, you shut up! You're just enabling her. Do you think you're going to cure Maggie with what you've learned in Psychology 101? Please."

"No, *you* shut up!" I was fourteen again. "Do you have to ruin everything? Everyone? When are you going to be happy and stop? When's it going to be enough?"

I was embarrassed to realize I was crying. How had that happened? I wiped away the tears with the filthy twisted napkin. Maggie and Carly stared at me with open mouths. The geo-political literati in the corner table were no longer waving their hands in emotional gestures worthy of Tolstoy. Their animated discussion was no longer animated. They were looking right at us. Even the hissing espresso machine was still, the barista suspending his work to check out the table where three girls were at loggerheads, eyeing each other across the table with hateful, spiteful, daggerlike gazes. With tear-stained eyes. How loud had I been? I knew I'd never return to this place again.

"Can you just take me back?" Maggie said. "I really don't want to be here anymore."

"Sure." Carly stood, pushing her chair with the back of her thighs so abruptly it tipped into the table behind us. "You have the muffin, Grace. Although you probably don't need it."

We were all silent on the way back. I insisted on walking Maggie through the alley, so Carly came too. The door was locked. We went around to the front, and they buzzed Maggie in. She'd prepared a story about walking down the alley to the street for a smoke. We hoped the open door wasn't discovered too soon after we left. A few hugs, a few promises to talk soon, and then she disappeared through the door, leaving Carly and me snarling at each other like two hyenas fighting over a carcass.

"Best thing we could have done for her," Carly said, making me both complicit and an ally in one stroke.

"Is that why you snuck her out, because you thought you were going to cure her in thirty minutes over a cup of coffee by bullying her into eating?"

"Hey, nobody's bullying anybody. You have your ways, and I have mine. I've just never seen anyone get anything they really wanted by being coddled along the way."

"Coddled? That's what you think it is? Maggie's ill, Carly. This isn't something she woke up and decided to do one day just to annoy you. Just because nothing else was going on in her life."

"Or is it? Isn't this just an avoidance technique so she doesn't have to grow up and face the real world? Has it ever occurred to you that if something was actually going on in her life she wouldn't be where she is? You might think about that yourself. Life's a bitch, and if you're not strong, everyone's going to roll right over you."

"You're right about one thing," I said. "Life *is* a bitch."

And so are you, I thought. I remembered when we were kids in the movie theater, and one of the boys behind us called Carly a bitch. It seemed so wrong at the time. So crude. A pathetic attempt to match Carly's power through the use of a disgusting word.

"C'mon, I'll give you a ride. Where're you headed?" Her voice suddenly softened.

"Nowhere. I'm going to walk, thanks anyway."

We'd stopped by her car. She looked at me with that direct and disarming gaze I remembered from the first time I laid eyes on her. "Hey, I'm sorry about saying that thing with the muffin—that you didn't need it. You look great, really. I swear you do. I was just mad at the way you were undermining me with Maggie."

I looked away. I was a good two inches taller than her by then. I no longer looked up to her, at least in the literal sense.

"No problem. I didn't take it that way. I no longer strive to be unhealthily thin."

But I did take it that way. And it did hurt. Carly knew that.

"So, this is bye-bye? I'm flying back in a few days, and I won't be coming back to the city."

"This is bye-bye, then."

"I don't want any more frantic calls if another letter comes, okay? Suck it up, I'm just saying. Be strong, Grace. I worry about you."

"Aren't you ever curious about who's sending those?" I asked. "You never even wonder?"

"Nope."

"You're crazy." I tried to keep any hint of admiration out of my voice.

"If I'm crazy, how do you know *I* didn't send them?" Her smile was cold.

I don't, I thought. She wouldn't, would she? What could possibly be in it for her?

Carly leaned forward to give me a hug, but I froze in her arms.

"Grace?" she called after me as I was walking away.

I stopped mid-step and turned my head reluctantly. The fog was coming in, and I wanted to get lost in it. Postpone the time until I got home and had to face Nathan. I wanted it to swallow me up and spit me out on my first day at Indian Springs High. I would double-check my class schedule that day. I wouldn't wander into the wrong classroom. I wouldn't become ensnared in the seductive gaze of a green-eyed girl who would turn out to have brown eyes. Alice and I would have discovered poetry or riding bikes or going to the movies. We would never have gone to the community pool that day or any other day. Alice would have remained my friend throughout school, in spite of our gap in age. I would have graduated from high school, then joined Mom and Dad in Madagascar, assisting them in their good works, even if I couldn't bring myself to help them spread the word of God.

"What?" I said.

"What happened to Bob . . . your kitty?"

"I gave him to Luke when I moved to the city," I said. "He's happier there."

The grand argument I was prepared for never happened. Nathan didn't say a word when he crept into our bedroom late that night, the sleeplessness of his work and studies revealing themselves in tiny crinkles around his eyes those days. Normally, he betrayed his presence one way or another when he came home after I'd already gone to bed. A dropped shoe, a soft cough—testing for my response. Most nights it was enough to wake me from sleep. We'd talk for a few minutes about our day, make love, and then drop off to sleep together. But that night, Nathan stole into the room like a cat burglar, silent, stealthy, without adding a single sound to the stillness of the night. That night I was already awake, my back turned against him. I was prepared to face what I suspected was coming. I wanted to get it over with.

"Hi," I said once he was under the covers. I rolled over to face him. "Busy day?"

He didn't reach for me the way he usually did, even when he was too tired to do anything but sling an arm around my shoulder and cuddle.

"Yep," he yawned. "Have fun with your friends?"

"Yeah, oh . . . not really. Hey, sorry I didn't invite you to sit with us. It wasn't a lot of fun. Believe me, you wouldn't have thought so."

"That's fine," he said. "I couldn't have stayed anyway."

But I knew it wasn't fine, although it would take me a while to have that confirmed.

A month later, it was my turn. I came home from work, expecting to have the place to myself since Nathan was normally still at school at that hour. But when I walked through the door, I found him sitting on our sofa, an overly familiar distance away from an overly attractive female.

"Grace, this is Alisa." He smiled as warmly at me as if I was a visiting auntie. "We're taking a break from the library to do a little studying at home. We won't get in your way, will we?"

Get in my way? They were in my way before I even opened the door and knew they were there. I grunted politely and walked to our bedroom, shutting the door behind me. About thirty minutes later, the murmuring between them, muffled by the closed door, ceased, and I heard our front door open and close. A few minutes later, Nathan came in with a mug of coffee in his hand.

"Want some?" he asked. "I just made a fresh batch."

"No thanks." I lay on the bed holding the same book I'd been holding since I came home. My eyes were foolishly scanning the same few sentences that I'd been scanning for the past thirty minutes. "Who's Alisa?"

"Someone from school. I'm sure I told you about her before."

"If you did, I'm sure you neglected to describe her in detail."

"And that's supposed to mean what?"

"You tell me."

I didn't have to look up to know his face was changing in the way it did whenever he was mad at me. The slightly aggressive tilt of his head. His mouth agape. His eyes burning with indignation.

"I don't get what you're driving at, Grace. Are you suggesting I'm cheating on you?"

"I'm not suggesting anything. I just . . ."

I was suggesting.

"You just what?"

"Nothing." I stared at the book. My eyes stung from holding back tears.

"Okay. Nothing. Great." He turned to walk back to the living room, and I closed the book with a loud clap.

I took my first real look at him since coming home. I checked for any telltale clues—a misbuttoned shirt, messy hair, sockless in our cold apartment. I saw nothing like that.

"I just feel it was inappropriate," I called out to his back. "I also feel like maybe you haven't been totally honest with me. Maybe you're holding back something."

Nathan pivoted slowly, the steaming mug held steady in his hand.

"*I'm* holding back, Grace? Isn't that your specialty? Carly. Maggie. I'm not supposed to ever come into contact with them? Did they even know about me before I walked in that day? Do they even really know about me now?" The color that rushed to his face highlighted the furrows between his brows, etching his features into a hostile mask.

"That's not the same," I said. "They're my friends. And Alisa's a—how's that even the same?" My voice trembled in preparation for battle—for the snappy comebacks I was usually better at than Nathan. At that moment, righteousness felt like it was on my side.

"You tell me, Grace." He seemed sad. Resigned. "You've met everyone in my family. All my friends. And I've met Luke."

I didn't have a comeback for that. It's true I could have pointed out that my parents were halfway across the world, but he already knew that. I didn't want him to ask if I talked about him in the letters I sent regularly to Mom and Dad. I wouldn't be able to lie to him and, even if I did, he'd know. I didn't want to open up the subject of Carly again. So I said nothing.

He left the room, and a few minutes later, he left our apartment. When he came back late that night we avoided speaking. I feigned sleep, and he made no sound to announce his arrival. He slept on the sofa.

Over the next few days, we avoided each other as much as possible, and when we couldn't, we were cordial but nothing more. He was sleeping in our bed again, but we slept back-to-back, as far away as possible without falling off the edge. By the end of the week, we were being kind to each other again, although more familial than anything else. It took us two weeks before we resumed our lovemaking, but it didn't feel the same. I wasn't sure whether something had changed in me or in Nathan, but something was different. He wasn't my Nathan anymore, he was just Nathan. We became roommates with benefits.

Was I capable of making anything in my life work out in a healthy way? Carly's words stayed with me, reinforcing the notion that my education was a futile pursuit. School now felt like a selfish endeavor. If I'd been trying to save the world, like she suggested, at least I would have that. But I wasn't, so I didn't. My relationship with Nathan was a poorly written play in which we were nothing more than two actors walking across the stage and reciting our lines from memory. I felt nothing and began to question if I had ever really felt anything or if I had just been looking for a place to hide—a safe space. If I really loved Nathan, why didn't I let him in? Why did I light a match to a long fuse I knew would eventually blow up and then do nothing to prevent it from happening?

I spent weeks lashing out. At myself. At Nathan. At Carly. Of course, all of it was done without a word being spoken. All of it was done when I lay in bed at night staring at the wall. When I sat in the library at school, pen in hand but nothing on the paper. When I settled myself into the molded plastic seat of a streetcar, lurching from stop to stop.

When the letter came in early March, I steeled myself before opening it.

"It is a man's own mind, not his enemy or foe, that lures him to

evil ways."

Carly had punched me from one side, Nathan from the opposite side. The letter delivered the knock-out blow. I finished up the school year and then gave my formal notice that I wouldn't be returning in the fall.

Once I quit school, it was only a matter of time before I quit Nathan. The two were inextricably linked in my mind. Nathan couldn't be with a girl who had no goals, no future, no way to occupy her time beyond working in a coffee shop and waiting for him to come home. Besides, Nathan wasn't the type of guy who would idly stand by and watch his girl-friend self-destruct. I knew all that, so I kept my plans a secret. I didn't think Nathan would fight for me, for our relationship, so it didn't seem duplicitous to squirrel away my pennies until I had a large enough fund to make my move. When it finally did come, I was right. Nathan didn't fight for me.

One night, sprawled on the sofa in front of the TV on a rare break from school or work, I knew it would be a while before I had another opportunity to say what I needed to say without any distractions.

"I'm not going back to school," I said during a commercial break. "I'm finishing up the semester. I let them know already."

Nathan didn't look at me. Maybe he was ready for this. He didn't seem surprised. Maybe he'd been waiting.

"What're you going to do?"

"I'm going away. I'm going to take some time and just travel. Think about my life."

Even I recognized this lie. I did nothing but think about my life already. This trip was a way for me *not* to think about my life.

Nathan looked at me with wounded eyes. "What about us?"

I took a deep breath. "Don't wait for me," I said.

"Well, I can't force you to love me. So I'm obviously not going to stand in your way." It's what I wanted to hear, wasn't it? "But I can tell you one thing," he went on, and I knew that one thing was never really just one thing. "You're making a big fucking mistake."

He had his parting shot.

I'd carry those words around with me for the next five months. And, once again, I was right. Those six words were so much more than just one thing.

In the weeks leading up to my confession to Nathan, I took care of mundane issues that had to be settled before I could move on. Mending the stray corners of my life before carrying out my plan. I needed a big-girl passport since I no longer traveled with my parents. I needed a suitcase. I needed to decide which of my meager possessions would come with me and which I would donate or toss. I needed a few books to read along the way. And I needed to say goodbye to Luke.

The day before I went to see Luke, I got a call from Alice, who had gotten my number from Maggie's mom.

"It's really good to hear your voice," I said and meant it. She sounded self-assured. Almost grown up. This was the night I would break the news to Nathan, and hearing Alice on the other end of the phone gave me a surge of confidence.

"I've wanted to talk to you," she said. "I think about you a lot. How are you liking college?"

"I'm quitting." I lowered my voice as if the apartment itself could hear my words and relay my message to Nathan before I had a chance to tell him.

There was silence on the other end, and I strained to hear her breathing or perhaps a deep sigh of frustration, but all

I heard was a scraping sound as if she was moving a chair in order to sit down.

"I'm sorry to hear that," she said finally. "I got into Wheaton College in Illinois, and I'm pretty excited about it."

It was hard for me to remember being excited about a major life change. Coming to college hadn't been an exciting time for me. Mom and Dad were leaving soon after, and I hadn't felt ready. Like being thrown into a pool before you knew how to swim.

"Illinois . . . that's such a long way from your family. I'll bet they're going to miss you."

"They're happy for me." She hesitated. "Grace, I just wanted to see how your father's doing. I heard he was sick, and I just wanted to say how sorry I am. If there's anything I can do . . ."

It took me a few seconds to slow my thoughts down to a halt and then start them back up again. My dad was sick long ago. But he'd gotten better. I received regular letters from Mom and Dad—once a week, they came like clockwork. Luke got them too. Nothing out of the ordinary. A description of daily life as Luke and I had known it throughout our childhood. I wrote back, although probably only one for every two or three of theirs. I painted an entirely dishonest picture of my life. Yes, I occasionally mentioned Nathan, but only as a friend, and never was there any mention of our living together. Nor did I mention Nathan's Jewish faith. I was working hard. School was fulfilling. Life was wonderful.

"I think my dad's doing pretty well," I said. "Nothing like when you knew him. He's much better."

"Oh," Alice said, clearly caught off guard. Her manner went from mature to childlike in seconds. She began speaking at double speed. "I'm—I'm . . . gosh, I'm really embarrassed. Sorry. But that's not why I called. I just wanted to say hi and see how you're doing because it's been so long."

"It has," I agreed. "What else is new with you? How's everyone in Indian Springs?"

"You know how it is here," she said. Having had a minute to compose herself, she went back to sounding like the new Alice. "Nothing much changes. I'm glad to be done with high school. It's already getting hot here. I think about you every time I drive by your old house. How's Luke?"

"You mean Officer Templeton?" I laughed, trying to inject some levity into the awkward turn our conversation had taken. "His wife is pregnant again, if you can believe it. I'm about to be an aunt for the second time. But they're still in Sacramento, and I don't get over there too often. How's Reverend Palmer these days? Grumpy as ever?" I asked the last question on a hunch.

"He retired," Alice said. "We just got a new pastor, and he's young and really cool. Actually, he just returned from Madagascar. He knows your parents."

I felt a sudden queasiness as though someone had been peeking in my bedroom window. Watching me without my knowledge. Knowing things about me that I didn't even know.

"Do you still go to church, Grace?" she asked when that didn't elicit a response from me.

"Nah, I haven't been too good about that," I said, not mentioning I hadn't been for years. How could I tell her about the last time I went? How my beliefs had evolved, making us creatures who may as well have been from separate worlds? I still knew how to speak her language, but she would never know how to speak mine.

"You should go back. You really should," she said. "Life can be crazy, and it's always a place you can come to for strength. A place that never changes."

I knew she worried about my everlasting soul, but I couldn't even see my way through my limited time on Earth. I couldn't tell her about the moment that I had decided I was done with the church. Or, rather, when it was done with me.

"I wish you wouldn't do this." Luke sighed. "Most people who drop out of college never go back."

"I will," I said. "When I'm ready."

He leaned forward in his chair, arms resting on his thighs. He lowered his gaze for a second and then looked up, instantly connecting our eyes in a disarmingly frank way. I wondered if this was a tactic he learned from being a cop. Lowering the defenses of the interrogee before catching them off guard when the real questions were about to begin. Luke wasn't a chatty person, but when he spoke, he gave the impression of using carefully selected words. Because of this, people always listened to him. They instinctively knew that whatever came out of his mouth was something of value—or at least came from the best part of him.

"Mom and Dad shouldn't have left when you were so young," he said. "You weren't ready to be on your own."

And even though I had thought the same thing myself many times over the past few years, it hurt to hear Luke say it. Luke was the pillar that held up our family. If he said it, it must be true and not just me making everything about me. I didn't want my parents to be devalued in my eyes. They were good, loving, compassionate people. I didn't want to think of them as flawed parents.

"I've managed just fine."

"Have you?" He split his forefinger and thumb to run down the angle of his jaw. "I happen to think they also made a mistake skipping you up a grade at Indian Springs. You're smart, no doubt, but you weren't ready then either."

"Probably not."

"You know, Grace. You can move in with us and have a

new start in life. Go to Sac State. Linda would love it. No rent, maybe just help out around the house a little when the baby's born. *I'd* love it, and I think it'd be good for you. We'll help you get back up on your feet."

Luke was only four years older than me, but he already felt like a father.

"I can't Luke, really. This is something I have to do." Bob lay in my lap, purring noisily. I scratched behind his tufted ears. He'd grown into an enormous animal.

"Nathan seemed like a good guy. Seemed like he really cared for you."

How could I even begin to explain everything that had happened between Nathan and me?

"He *is* really a good guy. Probably deserves better than me."

"Don't say that, Grace." Luke's eyes radiated pain. "You know that hurts me to hear you say that. You deserve every good thing that comes your way and a lot more." He shook his head slowly as though he couldn't believe a person could have such a low opinion of herself. Especially a person related to him, who had probably never experienced a moment of self-doubt in his entire life.

"Thanks."

"Will you at least give me an itinerary? Some way I can reach you if I need to? Will you promise to write and let us know where you are and what you're up to?"

"Already thought of that." I carefully lifted Bob from my lap, straining my biceps to maneuver his dense weight to the space beside me. He looked at me indignantly before dropping to the floor where he landed with a thud. He sauntered over to Luke's chair where he curled up at his master's feet and glowered at me. I rustled through my purse, coming up with a folded sheet of paper. "Here's every place I'm going to visit and, wherever possible, the contact info for the closest youth hostel."

Luke leaned back in his chair and unfolded the paper. His eyes scanned the front of the page, and then he flipped it to look at the back. "Jesus Christ, Grace! Turkey? Have you never seen *Midnight Express*?"

"If Mom and Dad could hear your language," I teased. "Blasphemer."

His eyes crinkled with good humor, but it seemed to catch him off guard. Perhaps he still battled with the remnants of his beliefs in the same way I did. Struggled to make sense of what was out there if we didn't have the doctrine to explain it in a way we could hold onto. But I didn't think so. I think Luke always knew that he could reach deep and find the answers in himself. Not like me.

"Yeah, sorry about that. I haven't—I guess you can say I've strayed."

"Me too. And I was just kidding."

His dad voice returned.

"But Turkey, really? I don't like to think of you over there by yourself."

"It's fine. I'll be fine. And, yes, for your information, I have seen *Midnight Express* and I'm not planning on smuggling any drugs. Not going to happen."

"Or using," Luke said.

"Or using."

Linda walked in the room, still in a nightgown, her hair in a high ponytail, her face fresh and natural. Tired looked good on Linda.

"He's down for his nap," she whispered although the baby's room was upstairs. "And I still haven't gotten out of my pajamas. We must be crazy having another one so soon." She stood by Luke's side, resting a hand on his shoulder before he pulled her onto his lap.

"Take a load off, woman," he mugged. He brought her face

to his and kissed her playfully on the lips. I felt a sweet burst of joyfulness followed by the sour taste of envy. No way I could ever live in a house filled with this much love. "Did you hear that your crazy sister-in-law's going to Turkey?" he said.

"What? No, Grace. You need to watch *Midnight Express*."

Luke always had a natural instinct to protect those around him. I imagined Linda's same instinct had blossomed after giving birth.

"Yeah, Luke and I have just been through all that. My trip's going to be nothing like *Midnight Express*. It will be more like Ten in the Morning Express. Anyway, what your husband failed to mention is that I'm also going to England, France, Spain, Italy, Germany, and Holland."

"You forgot Portugal and Switzerland," Luke said.

It always surprised me, and always warmed me, to realize how closely Luke paid attention when we were together. His interest was genuine. People loved him for that very reason.

"Good one. Portugal and Switzerland, almost forgot."

"How much money do you have?" he asked. "How long can you make it over there?"

"If I calculated right, I have enough to barely get me through six months if I'm frugal."

"And then what?" Linda cocked her head in that charming, inquisitive way she had, like a puppy.

"And then I get a job over there somewhere."

"You have to get a work visa for that," Luke said. "I don't know how easy that'll be."

"I've been reading up on it. They say a lot of small businesses will hire you off the books and pay you under the table."

I knew a barista was one of those universal jobs you could probably find even in China. So I at least had training in something that made real-world sense, although the actual training wasn't all that demanding. I was also old enough to be a bartender in many European countries where the drinking age was eighteen. Another skill I could pick up quickly. I was good at small talk with strangers. In fact, that's what I was best at when it came to talking and sharing. I knew Spanish and English, so I could probably pick up any of the romance languages fairly easily. Or look for work in England or Spain.

"Hmm. I don't like the sound of that," Linda said. Luke ran his hand up and down her bare arm.

"Just make sure you save enough to pay for a return ticket home," he said. "And if you don't have enough for whatever reason, you just get ahold of me or Linda, and we'll wire you the money to come home. Right, Babe?"

"That's right," Linda said. "Anytime. We mean it. So, what do your parents think about this? And what about that cutie, Nathan? Did you guys break up?" She set her lips in a pout.

The Nathan part was still too painful and too complicated so I left it unanswered. "I haven't told our parents yet, but I'm writing them tonight."

"Ouch!" Luke said. "They're not going to be happy."

"They'll get used to it. Hey, Luke? Dad's okay, right?"

His eyebrows reached for each other over narrowing eyes. "Yeah, why?"

"Alice called last night. Remember her? Anyway, she said something about Dad being sick, and I wouldn't have thought anything of it except the new pastor at Indian Springs just left Mom and Dad. He was in Madagascar with them."

He kept the firm set of his jaw, but I thought I detected a boyish fear in his eyes.

"They seem fine in their letters. Never heard any complaints or anything about Dad being sick." He sounded as if he was trying to reassure himself.

"Me neither. I'll ask tonight when I write, okay?"

I hated to bring sad news into this house so unharmed by

negativity—where life was being created instead of stagnating or ending. I hated to leave Luke. Linda. Even Bob seemed to hold my eyes with his own as if begging me to stay.

CHAPTER EIGHT
INDIAN SPRINGS

THE FIRST DAY of my junior year of high school.

I couldn't help but contrast my first day six months earlier. Luke was no longer there, having already begun college. Somehow that diminished Indian Springs High in my mind. Luke leaving home had expanded my world, holding out a destination which lay ahead but which, for the time being, was out of my reach. He was my trailblazer.

Balancing that was my newfound poise. School finally felt like it belonged to me instead of the reverse. I wasn't a visitor anymore, an eccentric from another world. My hair had grown out and was styled, thanks to the assistance of The Kitty Committee. My clothes were no longer embarrassing. My makeup was subtle but noticeable. Even though I didn't need one, I wore a bra. I was taller. Thinner. I had the confidence of making an entrance with the most amazing person I knew, Carly Sullivan. Her mother had stopped to pick me up along the way. Maggie and Jane waited for us in the parking lot.

"Okay, Kitty Committee, are we ready to rock our junior year?" Carly looked extra confident with an emerald-green top and matching drop earrings that shimmered under the still-hot sun of late August.

We linked our right pinky fingers and then threw those hands up in the air. It was something Maggie had thought up, and Jane giggled at the silliness but went along. There was nothing between us except the promise of a year of fun. Why these girls, each one magnificent in her own way, had decided to include me was still a wonder I grappled with every day as though pinching myself upon awakening from a dream. Why Maggie and Carly only had each other before Jane and I came along was something I never stopped to consider. They were girls with high standards, head and shoulders above all others at Indian Springs High.

I believe we actually strutted through the doors that day, although Jane in her natural gainliness appeared to lope. Class schedules were passed out alphabetically in the gym. We'd meet up afterward to compare. Classes were shortened accordingly that first day to make up for the special first period.

Students began to form groups, nervously scanning schedules side by side with best friends or boyfriends, eyes darting back and forth. I was with Carly for PE but nothing else. Still, if I had to choose one class, that's where I wanted to have Carly watching my back. Maggie had two classes with me. Carly and Jane had three in common, all AP classes that Maggie and I weren't eligible for. But when it came to lunch, Maggie, Jane, and I had first lunch and only Carly had second. It was only a small cloud that slightly darkened our high spirits—after all, the odds of us all being in the same lunch were minimal. Overall, everyone seemed satisfied with the cards they'd been dealt.

We continued to meet in the parking lot every morning,

beginning our day with the pinky salute, but lunches took on a different feel. Without Carly, Jane became our de facto leader, although it was more a matter of Maggie and I acceding to her rather than any inclination on Jane's part to lead. After only a few days, two other girls from Jane's PE class joined us at the table that we'd claimed outside under an eave. Meant for eight people, it seemed more comfortable now that we were five. Maggie brought out wet paper towels and cleaned the benches each day before we sat down. That would become her unofficial duty for the rest of the year. Our trays made cleaning the actual table unnecessary.

By the end of the week, a boy sat with us, clearly smitten by Jane. He was sandy-haired and starry-eyed with a slight lisp and an even slighter limp. He was a drama kid, Jane informed us. She was too. Her ethereal quality was beyond physical beauty, which I wasn't convinced she possessed. It was an unnamable thing, irresistible to those who came close enough to its winsome appeal. I watched her speak to the boy, who I soon learned was named Kyle. I watched the way his eyes consumed her, hair so blonde as to be white, eyes so blue as to be clear, skin so pale and milky it made me think of candle wax. I watched Kyle that day and thought what a wonderful thing to be Jane—to be so admired, perhaps even desired by someone, and yet so oblivious to their esteem.

Although she was a modest person, Jane regaled us with tales of her travels. She had done modeling for a major agency when they lived in Chicago but dropped out when it began to interfere too much with reading and family time. She became scuba certified when they lived on the Gulf Coast and spent every weekend exploring those warm waters, once coming face-to-face with a bull shark that inexplicably turned on its tail and fled. Her passion was skiing, which she hoped to pursue extensively come winter at the family cabin at Lake Tahoe, only three hours away. She loved anything by Jane Austen or Emily Brontë, neither of whom I'd read but was overwhelmed with a sudden desire to do so. Her family always spent Thanksgiving in New York City, where the girls would shop with their mother until they couldn't take another step.

Jane took a great interest in my travels as well. She hoped to travel the world one day, and I opened up to her questions, which would have embarrassed me in the past. Before, the exotic nature of my former life only set me apart and added to the insecurity I felt when I moved to Indian Springs. But Jane made me proud of this side of myself, and I realized with regret that I hadn't fully appreciated the experiences at the time they were happening. I'd experienced them in the reflexive way of children—the way that is our life, not to be questioned or examined too closely. I never stood outside of myself to marvel at the worlds I saw, so vastly different in nature from anything I would ever experience after moving back to the states. I decided if I was ever given another chance, I would do it differently. I'd experience the water from under the surface where life was really happening. The way Jane did.

Maggie and I dutifully reported these stories to Carly when we were all together.

"Did you know that Jane used to be a model?"

"Did you know Jane's family owns a place in Tahoe and she's going to invite us all to go up there for Labor Day weekend?"

"Did you know that Jane is scuba certified?"

Carly didn't react with the same breathless enthusiasm, but then again, it probably wasn't the same hearing the story secondhand. Whenever we repeated one of her stories, Jane would only smile wanly and not add anything of her own. She usually found a way to change the subject, asking Carly about a chemistry assignment or a book they were both reading for

English. It was still one for all and all for one, and Jane had no desire to make it about herself.

It didn't take long for the reality of my parents' decision to skip me ahead a grade to make itself known in an unfortunate way: beyond just the physical development, in which I was always lagging; the emotional maturity; and the social milestones, such as receiving my driver's license long after it had ceased to be a source of pride and excitement for the others. I was smart, sure enough—especially in a small expat school of twenty to thirty students. But at Indian Springs, more than a year younger than my classmates, I was decidedly average, especially in math and science. Compared to Carly or even Jane, schoolwork was time-consuming and difficult.

Keeping afloat became my overwhelming obsession, as my greatest fear was to have my parents realize their mistake and request to have me repeat my sophomore year. As a result, when I wasn't with the girls, I spent every spare minute cramming for tests and puzzling out homework with my dad's help. It was doable. It just meant there was no kickback time for watching TV or being alone in my room with nothing but Bob's company and my own lazy thoughts. I didn't share this struggle with the others. I didn't want them to be reminded of my relative youth.

Maggie, a struggling student herself, would have understood, but it was different with Maggie. Nobody expected her to be school smart, although we all knew she was smart in the ways of the world. I was supposed to be a smart kid, although it had to be obvious to Carly that I wasn't.

Two weeks after school began, Carly called us with the good news. She had conferred with Mr. Sutherland, a school counselor who was also her private SAT tutor, and he'd agreed to rejigger her schedule. She was no longer in the same PE class as me, and she was in one less class with Jane, but the exciting news was that she was now in first lunch with the rest of us.

After that, the Kitty Committee closed ranks. The two girls and the starry-eyed boy who had shared our table soon drifted off to other tables with other groups. Jane's orbit was eclipsed by Carly's.

CHAPTER NINE

Labor Day weekend, I learned, was a bittersweet holiday. Marking the end of summer and reinforcing the beginning of the school year, it served two purposes. Piled into the minivan of Jane's family, I was thrilled to be setting out on my very first excursion without my family. We were all in high spirits, still under the fading spell of hot August nights. Heading for Lake Tahoe, which I'd heard about but never seen, this was perhaps the happiest day of my life before or since.

Jane's parents were a study in contrasts, as were Jane and her sister, Leann. Her father, Mr. Swanson, was pale and lanky like Jane. He sported round spectacles and was slim everywhere except the round paunch hanging over his belt. Jane's mom, who insisted we call her Rita, was a short, stocky, dark-haired brunette. Her eyes were small and dark, darting from person to person when she talked, which was often. Whereas Jane's father spoke softly and slowly and usually not much at all, Rita was a whirlwind of conversation, steering the discussion amongst us girls for the entire three-hour drive.

Jane and Leann were different in the same way—as though

each parent had been granted a version of themselves. Leann was short and compact and sturdy like her mom. Quick-witted to Jane's languid. Bossy to Jane's laid-back. Only ten months apart in age, they seemed like great friends.

"They were supposed to be twins, you know?" Rita said over her shoulder from the front passenger seat. "But Leann was late like she always is, so she had to wait until round two."

In the rear-view mirror, I could see the smile spreading across her husband's face. He reached over and squeezed Rita's knee, then ran his hand up to very near the top of her thigh. I'd never seen my dad do anything like that, even though I knew he and Mom were completely devoted to each other. I'd never seen them just being playful with each other.

"No, no, no, you've got it all wrong," Leann said, her booming voice reverberating throughout the closed car. "I actually was in there too, Ma, but I got one look at Jane's knobby knees, and I knew she'd take up all the room so I swam back to your ovary where I could wait until I had the place to myself."

"Oh my God," Maggie brought her open palm up to her mouth, her eyes creased with stifled laughter. "You guys are crazy."

Leann, who was technically the pesky little sister, was actually older than me by a few months. I called upon the most mature version of myself to be worthy of the big girls. To not be lumped in with the little sister. I couldn't imagine joking like this in front of my parents. In front of Luke. Sex wasn't a taboo subject in the Swanson family like it was in ours, and I loved it despite the blush I felt creep into my face.

"You're cute when you're embarrassed," Carly whispered in my ear, the hot breath passing through her lips to tickle tiny, sensitive hairs deep in my canal. I blushed even more and hoped no one else noticed.

I'd been on road trips before with my family. Plunging deep

into an emerald-green forest in a four-wheel drive, closing in on two hundred thousand miles, over trails that didn't even begin to qualify as roads, unnamed and unmarked on any map as they were. Through brittle, hot deserts even, where a mechanical breakdown would be much more than an inconvenience like ants at the picnic. Where it could be a dangerous, and even deadly, occurrence for anyone not equipped to piece together a car's engine with paper clips, if necessary, the way Dad and Luke could. But I'd never been on a road trip that was designated for pure fun like this one. I'd never been in a car for three hours where the chatter and laughter never ended. Whenever one of us grew breathless with giggling or excitement, there was always someone ready to step in and take over. And then when I caught my first glimpse of a lake so spectacularly blue it would put a cloudless sky to shame any day of the week, I was finally speechless for the first time that day.

We traversed a series of paved roads until finally turning onto a gravel path where we slowly bumped and crunched our way to a cabin with a log-face exterior. But to call it a log cabin would be to shortchange it. It was a splendid home on the shore of the lake that, by that midday hour, was vibrating with the sparkle of dappled sunbeams.

We poured out of the minivan, our legs aching to tackle three hours of pent-up energy. I stretched my arms and heard my spine crack. I breathed deeply, feeling the sting in my nose of the high mountain air, dusty and thin, dry and scented with a subtle spice of pine. I was young and strong and what felt like free. I had friends that I never could have imagined only six months earlier.

For a very brief moment, I thought of Mom and Dad alone in our humble house in Indian Springs. Dad mourning the loss of his best friend, his son, who was off to start his own life. Mom sitting at the kitchen table, poring over medical and household bills, wondering how we were going to make ends meet in this new life of ours. The TV, a constant background white noise—the content and spoken words no longer important or even meaningful except for the distraction it provided to my father's wounded body and soul. For a brief moment, I wished Mom and Dad could be there with me to see what I was seeing. Experience what I was feeling. But I'm ashamed to say, it was only a brief moment, and then Carly took me by the hand and tugged me toward the front door.

This must be Heaven, I thought. *I must be in Heaven.*

Our first day at the lake house was a half-day. Everyone was tired and wanted to shower and unpack and settle in for the next two days. Carly and Maggie shared one room. Jane and I shared the other, with Leann sleeping in a cot between us. Rita whipped up sandwiches for lunch, and we all went down to the beach for a picnic. Afterward, we slipped off our shoes and walked as far down the beach as we could before reaching a jetty of steep, sharp boulders. At the jetty, Rita supervised our re-slathering of sunscreen since the air was thin at that altitude and sunburns were more severe and came on quickly. Then we turned and walked in the other direction, all the way to a marina with a pier where a number of small boats were moored.

Carly walked to the end of the pier while the rest of us rested on the sand in an area shaded by trees. From where I was sitting, I watched Carly carefully studying the boats tied up below her, taking her time to inspect each and every one. When she came back and joined us, she sat close to Maggie, whispering and giggling to the exclusion of everyone else. I worried that Rita and Mr. Swanson would find her behavior odd and even rude. It didn't seem appropriate to be so secretive within our larger group. But no one else appeared to notice or be bothered by it except for me, so I chalked it up to my hyper-sensitivity whenever it came to Carly doing something with someone that didn't include me.

After dinner, board games, and watching a movie, everyone was ready for bed. I was exhausted after the drive, the two-hour walk in the sand, and the combination of bright sun and thin air. The night was cool, and I heard an owl calling to its mate right outside our window. I must have fallen asleep within seconds of crawling under the covers because that's the last thing I remember.

CHAPTER TEN

WHEN I WOKE with a soft hand pressed tightly over my mouth, the house was dark and silent, save for the sleeping sighs of Leann in her cot only a few feet away. Carly leaned over me, her loose hair streaked by moonlight diffused through the lace curtains. With her free hand, she brought a finger to her lips as a warning to keep quiet. I sat upright and saw Maggie doing the same with Jane.

Carly gestured us toward the door, creeping catlike on bare feet, holding her sandals in one hand. Carly and Maggie were fully dressed but ushered Jane and I out of the room wearing only our PJs and slippers. Jane reached for a bathrobe hanging from the door.

"What the fuck are you guys doing?" Jane whispered hoarsely once we were downstairs.

"Time for an adventure!" Maggie's eyes gleamed.

"A Kitty Committee adventure," Carly added as though that should explain everything.

"Let me get some clothes on," I insisted. "I look like an idiot, and you guys are dressed."

"It's three in the morning," Carly said. "No one's going to see you except the racoons Maggie and I just saw outside. C'mon, let's go."

My first thought was, *how did Carly convince Maggie to do this?* My second thought was for Jane, who would be breaking her own family's rules.

"What kind of adventure?" Jane asked warily, although she didn't seem entirely opposed to the idea.

Once we got to the beach, the need to keep our voices low was no longer necessary. Carly guided us with a flashlight she'd found in the kitchen, but the three-fourths moon, amplified by its mirror image on the lake, made it easy to find our way without the aid of artificial light.

"Kitty Committee rule number one," Maggie was deliriously happy, and I wondered if she and Carly had been drinking. "Party on!"

"I don't remember that rule," I said.

"What *are* the rules?" Jane asked. "Maggie, you were supposed to tell me but you never did—except the 'no drug' thing."

"Rule number three: no drugs, but alcohol is cool so drink up." Carly pulled a flask from the pocket of her jacket, and I knew my intuition was right. Carly and Maggie had a head start, well on their way to being tipsy.

I knew that Carly and Maggie drank on occasion, but I hadn't joined in. Jane said she'd gotten high once with some kids at her old school in Chicago, but she didn't like it so she was okay with the Kitty Committee rule about no drugs. I was okay with it too because it was the furthest thing from my mind. In some of the countries where I'd grown up, taking or selling drugs was an offense punishable by a long jail sentence or possibly death. I'd never considered it even after moving to the US with its much more relaxed attitude. I didn't think about drinking either because my parents didn't do it, so it was never around our house.

"You brought that in the car with you?" Jane asked. I couldn't tell if she was more horrified or amused, but I decided the latter.

"We brought the flask—" Maggie started.

"But the vodka was courtesy of your folks," Carly finished. She tilted a swig into her mouth and passed it to me. Without taking a sip, I handed it to Jane who pressed it to her lips and swallowed. "C'mon, lil' sis," Carly poked me in the ribs. "It's time for you to lose your cherry."

"Your alcohol cherry," Maggie giggled wildly. "Don't worry, Jane," she stage-whispered behind her cupped hand. "We refilled your dad's vodka bottle with water. We were busy little beavers while your lazy butts were sleeping. And, by the way, are you aware that you snore?"

"Beavers! Maggie, watch your mouth," Carly yelped.

"I do not!" Jane tipped the flask for another dainty swallow. "Leann does—you must've heard her."

"No . . . It. Was. You." Maggie put her finger right onto the tip of Jane's nose, and they both laughed.

"Don't call me that," I said firmly, soberly considering the company. "I hate it."

Jane wrestled Maggie's finger from her nose, then they both collapsed on the sand in a heap of giggles. But Carly heard me. She heard everything, even when she'd been drinking.

"Call you what?" she asked.

"Lil' sis," I said. "It bothers me when you say that."

"Awww. Then prove you're a big girl like us," Carly said. It felt mean-spirited, and it hurt the way that Carly could pivot so quickly from nurturer to tormentor. I reached for the flask she was holding. I gulped. Once. Twice. Realizing too late that a sip would have been better than a gulp, my throat felt as though a fork was scraping down its length. I wanted to spit it out or puke it out or run for a glass of water or just open my mouth and scream. But I held onto my composure as tightly as I'd ever held on before while the fermented juice made a beeline for the command center of my good judgment.

"Happy?" I stared defiantly at Carly.

"Rule number two," she said without losing the smile on her face.

"One for all and all for one." Maggie called out gaily from her position laying on her back, arms stretched over her head and lifting the hem of her shirt to reveal naked flesh. Jane sat beside her, head cocked as though listening for the thrum of the universe. The moonlight washed out any semblance of color from her hair and bathed the lovely planes of her face. She picked up a handful of sand and drizzled it onto Maggie's bare belly.

"Exactly," Carly said, smiling. "And don't ever forget it." And then softer, so only I could hear. "I'm sorry I called you lil' sis. I promise I won't do it again."

By then I was already plenty buzzed. I warmed from the inside out to combat the cool of the night. I was loved. I was accepted. Life could never be the same.

"So, there's the one for all rule, the no drugs rule—what else did I sign up for?" Jane asked no one in particular. "Tell me before it's too late." She had a peculiar but endearing half-snort-half-laugh that made her seem like a big goofy kid.

"The *real* rule number one," I said.

"Members of the Kitty Committee come before anyone else," Maggie and Carly said in unison with me.

"Before *anyone*? Can Leann be in the Kitty Committee too?"

Maggie, who was in current possession of the flask, passed it to Jane who took a sip. And then another one. All of a sudden it struck me how rules number one and two were vastly different in intent. Carly had questioned the necessity of rule number two when Maggie first suggested it. But rule number two was positive, supportive, inclusive. Rule number one was exclusive.

"Oh, sorry." Carly belched loudly, cushioning what was to come next. "Rule number five: absolutely no one else will be permitted to join."

"Awww, that's sad," Jane said. "I love you guys, but I love Leann too. And I don't think anyone should come before my sister, do you?"

"It's okay, Jane," Maggie said. "This is only really for school, and Leann will be at St. Mary's."

"I guess," Jane said. "What else is there?"

"Rule number six: no one member is above the others," I said. It seemed like something Jane couldn't possibly object to.

"C'mon, get up," said Carly, who was the only one still standing. "Let's go check out the boats at the marina."

Maggie was the first to rise. She extended one hand each to both Jane and me and pulled until she fell backward herself. Then another round of giggling while Jane and I got Maggie to her feet.

"I feel ridiculous out here in my bathrobe," Jane said. "Go on, what are the other rules? So far, I *guess* I'm okay with them."

"Rule number five," Carly said as we trudged through the cold sand in the direction of the pier. "No boys should ever come before or between members of the Kitty Committee."

"That's really just the same thing as rule number one," Maggie added quickly.

"Like, come between how? Are we even allowed to date?"

I wondered if Jane had ever dated before. Or Carly and Maggie? I didn't think so because it had never come up the way you'd think it would as a topic worthy of discussion. *Why would Jane care,* I wondered, *if she'd never had a boyfriend or seriously dated?* But then I decided she might be planning for the future, and I wondered if I should be too. I also wondered why Jane was questioning every single rule, and I had only questioned one, the last one. Even then, I hadn't questioned it so much as remarked on it.

"It's just like guys do," Maggie, who seemed to have appointed herself as explainer-in-chief, continued with her mission of making the Kitty Committee palatable to Jane. "Like guys say 'bros before hos.'"

"Yeah, loser guys," Jane snorted.

"Yeah, loser guys," Maggie agreed, too quickly I thought. "But it's like that. We're not going to let any guy stop us from being friends."

I noticed Carly hadn't offered an explanation for any of the questionable aspects of our rules.

"Well, of course not," Jane said. "Why would we?"

"Exactly," I piped in, buoyed by the alcohol. I took the flask from Maggie and drank a much smaller sip than my first two. "We wouldn't. So that's easy."

Carly smiled at me, and I was proud that I'd explained it so well.

"Okay, please tell me that's it," Jane said. "I don't know how many more of these rules I can take."

"Rule number seven," Carly said. "If you leave the Kitty Committee, you're dead to the others."

I felt the air leave my lungs as if, in that moment, everything rested on Jane's acceptance of a rule even I'd had trouble accepting. My feeble protest had been summarily dealt with by Carly, but Jane wasn't me. Jane had confidence in her opinions. I never contemplated the place where rule number seven came from, but would Jane?

"Oh my God!" She pulled the bathrobe tightly around her as if overcome by a sudden chill. "That is so . . . heartless."

"Again," Maggie said, handing the flask to Jane. "You can't take it at face value. It just means that if you're a real friend, you won't turn your back on your friends."

"And if you do," I added. "You weren't really a friend to begin with."

Even to myself, this sounded like an inane explanation. You're a real friend, and then you're not a real friend, and something about not being a friend in the first place. Who was I kidding? It couldn't be any clearer. Carly had spelled it out exactly the way she intended. Rule number seven bound us in no uncertain terms, and it gave Carly permission to emotionally punish anyone who defied her will. Of course, we knew it didn't mean "dead" in the true sense of the word. But it may as well have.

I believe if the liquor hadn't impaired her better judgment, rule number seven might have been a deal breaker for Jane.

But by then, the rules were clear to everyone and, by her refusal to denounce the Kitty Committee, Jane had signed on. We'd arrived at the marina where the boats were docked and, since this was the outer limits of our walk earlier on, Maggie, Jane, and I turned back in the direction of home.

"Wait," Carly said. "Who's up for a boat ride?"

"We don't have a boat, but Dad says we're gonna get one before next summer."

"What's wrong with one of those?" Carly gestured toward the row of boats bobbing on the water like moon ducklings tethered to the dock.

"Um. They're not ours," Jane said.

"Who's going to know if we bring it back and leave it where we found it?"

Maggie and I exchanged uncertain glances. The flask was

almost empty. Maggie handed it to me as if offering the necessary courage to proceed. I tilted my head and opened wide. I made a big show of shaking out the last drops, even though there were only drops left to begin with.

"Wooh! Grace, look at you." Carly said, apparently unaware I was only swallowing fumes. And I was not about to disavow her of the image of the hard-drinking Grace. "So? Shall we?"

"How about that one?" Jane pointed to a metal canoe that had been dragged up on the beach and was only tied down with a rope. Most of the others on the beach had been chained to trees or metal stakes driven into the ground.

"Uh, don't you need oars to make it go?" Maggie asked.

Finally, an area where I had some actual knowledge, having canoed many times down dark and still rivers canopied in veils of green. It was a favorite pastime of my parents, exploring a country from within via its most intimate arteries, its rivers. In the jungle, you had to be careful, knowing you shared the water with creatures who were happy to eat you or, at the very least, bite you should you remove yourself from the protection of your steely cocoon. I knew how to row. How to drag a canoe in and out of the water. How to get in and out without tipping it over. It didn't take a lot of knowledge, and most of it was obvious, but at least I felt comfortable, although my comfort didn't extend to being in the actual water without the benefit of a canoe.

"It's not to make it go, Maggie." I chuckled as kindly as an elder aunt. "It's to steeeer the canoe."

"Okay, well there aren't any oars to steeeer the canoe," Maggie came back at me, and I wilted a bit under her rare sarcasm.

"How about these?" Jane pulled a pair of oars from underneath the seats of a nearby chained canoe. "These'll work."

With Jane figuratively on board, we were given the tacit approval to steal, or as we preferred to phrase it, *borrow* the boat. Maggie and Carly stripped off their jeans and jackets. I was wearing a shortie to begin with, but Jane removed her bathrobe and left it on the beach with the rest of our clothes, shoes, and slippers. We pushed and pulled the canoe, which was much heavier than it looked, until the last shove into the lake where it finally yielded to our will, obedient to the pressure of even a pinky finger. It was only then I was reminded of the bitter iciness of this high mountain lake, fed by melting snow. Earlier in the day, with the sun bearing down on me, the water had seemed refreshing, even invigorating, to my bare legs and feet. Now it telegraphed a warning I did not heed.

Once we climbed aboard, I picked up the oars and maneuvered away from shore. The water was smooth and glossy like a black opal. On the beach, it made a playful lapping sound, but out there a hush descended from above. I sliced the oars into the water to preserve the stillness the lake seemed to demand at that most private hour, and even the other girls felt it, at least for a while. The night sky was mesmerizing—an explosion of gold dust. A universe with no end.

"Don't go out too far," Jane warned. So I turned the canoe toward the shore and kept it no further than fifty yards away. I steered in the direction of the jetty, not feeling entirely myself, but still lucid enough to properly steer the canoe. Maggie was most far gone, already half-lying, half-sitting on the bottom, her chin resting on her chest. Jane was quiet but watchful, keeping her eye on the shoreline. Carly was quietly composed—I would never have guessed she and Maggie had the same head-start on drinking that night, such different worlds were they inhabiting by then.

As we rounded the jetty, my arms shook from effort and perhaps from the cold as well. The muscles below my shoulders ached from exertion. Even the back of my neck felt stiff from the awkward shifts in position that rowing demanded. I recalled the sensation and knew I'd be feeling it plenty the next day. I turned in a wide arc to go back to the marina and nobody objected. Maggie was already snoring.

"I can't row anymore," I said. "My arms feel like they're gonna fall off."

"I'll take over," Carly said, and the last thing I remember thinking was how quickly she offered and how kind she could be. In order to make room for her, I stood higher than I should have on legs that wobbled more than I realized. My bare foot hit a slick patch of wet and over the side I went.

When I was five years old, our family lived in Haiti. As one of the poorest countries in its hemisphere, the people suffered greatly. Food and medicine were scarce and scarcer still for dogs. Most dogs were feral, surviving on their own from whatever small rodents they could hunt and any scraps they could scavenge. One such dog took to hanging around our house, and before long, he became the Templetons' dog.

He was orange in color with a black muzzle and pointed ears. His eyes radiated innate intelligence. But his skin was scabby, and he most likely had mange because there were patches of missing fur on his body the size of my fist. He scratched relentlessly from a combination of his skin ailment and fleas. Mom said she would try to find medicine to help him, but until then I could only pet him with the bottom of my shoe, and I should never touch him with my bare skin. He wasn't allowed inside our house. Luke and I named him Tramp, and most nights we filled our pockets with leftover scraps from dinner and shared them with Tramp when Mom wasn't looking. Like Mary's little lamb, Tramp followed us everywhere, even waiting for Luke and me while we were in school. At night, he slept outside our front door and barked when other dogs came near. He viewed himself as our protector, and his loyalty never wavered even when scraps of food weren't forthcoming.

Then for two days Tramp was missing. I asked Mom, and she said he'd probably found a new home. A new family. But I never believed that was true. We were his family, and he would never abandon us. The next day we drove into town, which was about ten minutes away. On the street by the side of the road was Tramp's lifeless remains. He'd been hit by a car or a truck, probably three days earlier. Somebody most likely had dragged his dead or dying body to the side of the road. Mom said Tramp was in Heaven, and we'd see him again one day.

And although my faith had diminished and nearly disappeared by the time I went overboard that night in Lake Tahoe, I thought of Tramp in that deep, dark, cold, and watery place.

What I learned about that night, I learned later from Carly and Jane. Maggie, who wakened from Jane's cries, didn't have an accurate recollection. But I hit that cold water, probably no warmer than sixty degrees, and experienced what they call the *cold shock response*. The panic of hitting the water caused an involuntary gulp which sent water rushing up my nose, into my mouth, and straight to my lungs. I felt myself slide beneath the surface of the water, unable to control my arms or legs. They say you see your life play out in front of you, and I did. But not like an old movie reel. Like a peaceful passage where I stopped along the way and snagged that memory of Tramp. And then I continued on to my destination, where I was able to imagine the end and peacefully say goodbye to my family. All of this happened in less than two minutes.

The equal and opposite reaction resulting from my plummet into the lake was to send the canoe further away from me, perhaps about ten feet. And then Jane dove, without a thought for her own safety, toward where she'd last seen my head bob to the surface, mouth agape. Calling out to Carly and Maggie to throw the life jackets overboard, life jackets that none of us were wearing, she held onto one and, pulling me up by the hair, got me to lean on the other. Somehow, they pushed and pulled me into the canoe without overturning it. We were only twenty yards from shore so Jane swam, holding on to the side, while Carly rowed us to the beach.

I remember retching terribly and shivering so violently that I thought my teeth would crack. Carly and Maggie pressed me between themselves to warm me. They rubbed my arms and back. Gave me their own dry shirts, one on top of the other. They carried me between them while Jane ran ahead to bring up her own body temperature. When we reached the pile of clothes, Jane was still shivering but warming up in her dry bathrobe and Carly's jacket, which she took off and put over my shoulders. Our night had turned into an adventure, just like Carly promised.

I fell on my hands and knees and vomited another few times before we got up and went home. There were so many hands touching me, caressing me, gently pushing the wet hair from my eyes. I felt loved, unlike the time I'd passed out at the swimming pool. I didn't think Carly would find anything about this to be hilarious in hindsight.

Back at the cabin, Leann was awake, waiting downstairs for us with all kinds of questions. Angry that we didn't include her in our moonlight adventure. We didn't tell her what happened. Only that we'd taken a canoe out for a ride and left it where it didn't belong. Only that we'd had a little to drink and taken a little dip. Leann shook her head, but there was a hint of admiration in her eyes. A hint of disappointment that we hadn't included her in the fun.

"All for one and one for all," Carly whispered as she helped me up the stairs.

The Kitty Committee had come through for me that night, she was letting me know. And they had.

But it was Jane who had acted to save my life.

CHAPTER ELEVEN

AFTER LAKE TAHOE, I had nightmares for months. Nightmares of being powerless, buried alive, wrapped inside a blanket so dark and cold that I couldn't breathe. I developed sleep paralysis that rendered me unable to speak or move while still observing the external waking world around me. But as time went on, it became more and more rare. And life continued, mostly unremarkably.

With Luke gone, I had a bathroom to myself, except when he arrived home for a weekend, always bearing several duffel bags full of dirty laundry. His monthly visits were something I began to look forward to more than anything else. For two days, my parents and I were inoculated against the normal gloom of our household with the dose of sunshine Luke injected into our lives. On those weekends, I stuck around, basking in revived family memories—ghosts that Luke stirred from their graves. The hours of belonging to each other again were worth everything to me. For two days, which sped by far too quickly, we were no longer strangers living under the same roof. We were a family that shared happiness in an entirely believable way.

When Sunday afternoon rolled around, and Luke returned to school, the rest of us scattered like billiard balls. I sought out the familiar comfort of the Kitty Committee and the diversion it brought from home and school. Mom turned her focus back to church, Dad, and work. The TV went on again, its constant background drone a mournful mantra marking the passage of wasted time.

The Kitty Committee wasn't totally about mischief, and it wasn't always about Carly. Carly and Jane had ambitions which demanded extracurricular activities that bit sharply into their free time. Carly also had private tutoring for the upcoming SATs, and Jane attended an SAT prep class every Saturday. This meant Maggie and I had a lot of alone time, which we often spent together. I knew I wanted to go to college. I just didn't know what I had to do to get there beyond keeping my grades up and taking the few SAT practice tests in a booklet Carly had given me, along with an admonishment to use it. My parents never had "the talk" with me—the college talk, that is. They assumed I'd figure it out the same way Luke did. They assumed when a child left home, they should be prepared to survive on their own. And the way to get there wasn't by having parents coddle them, hold their hand, and map out every step along the way. Ironically, Carly also professed to believe that self-reliance was the key to advancement but, as an only child of two working parents, she had plenty of resources at her disposal.

I never doubted that my parents' faith in my ability to get things done on my own without their guidance came from a place of love and respect. They trusted me to instinctively know the right thing to do. They gave me the basics as a child and assumed the rest would take care of itself. But their trust was deeply misplaced and, because it was so matter-of-factly given, I didn't hold it in high esteem.

Halloween weekend. While other kids put on costumes and partied hard, the Kitty Committee celebrated Carly's sixteenth birthday at a very upscale restaurant in a trendy but tiny Napa Valley town an hour away from Indian Springs. Her parents drove—two cars—and the party included an adult couple, friends of Carly's parents.

I'd never spent much time with Mr. and Mrs. Sullivan. The few times I'd been to Carly's home, they were either not there or busy doing something in another part of the house. Their style was to leave us alone, unlike Jane's parents who made a point of popping into the room to chat for a few minutes whenever we were around. Even Maggie's mom, on the rare occasions she was home, plopped down on the sofa with us and tried to hang out like one of the girls until Maggie shooed her away. I liked her and would have let her stay if she was my mom. No topic was off-limits around her, and Maggie could and did swear without fear of punishment.

Sleepovers were almost always at Maggie's but occasionally at Jane's. When we were at Jane's house, Leann inevitably tossed her sleeping bag wherever we made camp for the night—sometimes we fell asleep in the den, watching movies and eating popcorn; sometimes it was Jane's bedroom; when the weather was still nice, we made up beds on the back porch, falling asleep to the yip of coyotes and the low moans of great-horned owls. Wildlife was one of the perks of living where Jane did, out in the country. Leann kept a horse, and she taught me how to feed it carrots by tucking in my thumb. I loved the smooth, rubbery feel of its surprisingly soft nose and the way it pushed air from its lungs through giant nostrils, which made me think of the blowhole of a whale. I liked Leann a lot and, in many ways, felt most comfortable when she and I were alone, never feeling pressure to be anyone other than who I was. But Leann wasn't part of the Kitty Committee, and she had her own set of friends from her own school.

My house, by mutual consent, was avoided by the Kitty Committee. Nobody ever said as much, but it was never suggested as a meeting spot, and nobody showed up at my house except to pick me up or drop me off. My house didn't have a fun, loose vibe like Maggie's.

So the car ride was the first time I actually got to see Carly interact with her parents, or at least her father, who drove us four girls, Carly sitting up front.

"My baby girl's growing up," he said proudly, as though he was somehow responsible for that fact. He reached over and patted her on the knee, but she pushed his hand away and turned to look out at the darkness beyond her window.

The car smelled richly of leather. It hummed quietly along the two-lane road that twisted through tall trees looming ominously like black giants on either side. I didn't see a single car on the road besides the taillights of Mrs. Sullivan's car, occasionally flashing red at the sharp twists and turns in the road.

"I think you gals are going to like this place," he said. "It's a Michelin three-star restaurant." He made eye contact with us via the rearview mirror, but I had no idea what that meant and didn't want to expose my ignorance, so I simply nodded in approval.

"That's the highest ranking a restaurant can get." Carly craned her neck toward the back seat. "So enjoy because you might never get this chance again."

Jane rolled her eyes at no one in particular, but I caught it and hoped Mr. Sullivan wasn't watching in his rearview mirror.

"It's so exciting that you can drive now, Carly," Maggie said.

"What do you girls plan to do with your lives?" Mr. Sullivan asked abruptly. He was not an unattractive man for his age. He had sandy-blond hair like Carly's, but thinning on top. He had clever eyes capped by bold eyebrows, and his face was strong and square-cut. In his suit, he looked like an important person. My father owned one suit that he wore to funerals, and he'd had it for as long as I could remember, possibly my entire life. It wasn't sleek and tailored like Mr. Sullivan's, who I knew owned an accounting firm where his wife was also a partner.

"I have no idea," Maggie said.

Jane looked at me as if giving me a chance to answer first, but when I didn't, she said, "I like theater, drama, writing . . . I'd love to have a career in one of those fields."

"How about you, Grace?"

I instinctively knew he wasn't so much interested in what we had to say as he was in bringing the conversation back around to Carly while trying to be polite.

"I don't know," I answered truthfully. "My mom's a nurse, so maybe that."

"That's a noble field," he said. And then, proving my instincts correct, "Carly here is going to make a boatload of money." He chuckled. "At least that's what she's been telling us since she was four years old. Haven't you, Carly?"

"Yup, I've heard her say that a lot too," Maggie said.

I wished I could see Carly's face, but I could only see the glossy hair falling across her ear, catching the bluish gleam of the car's instrument panel.

"I always tell her, 'Carly, I hope you'll remember your poor old dad.'" He reached out as if to pat her knee again but withdrew his hand when it was halfway there.

"I'm sure you and Mom will do just fine on your own," Carly said dryly.

"Do you know that ever since she was a little girl, she helped me pick stocks for our private portfolio? I'd say, 'What do you think the old man should buy next?' and she usually steered me right. Didn't you, Sweetheart?"

Was she smiling or frowning? I'd have given anything to know.

"Yeah, Carly's always been really good in math," Maggie said when it was clear Carly wasn't going to answer.

The black giants slid behind us, bathed eerily at every bend in the road by the brake lights of Mrs. Sullivan's car.

"Here we are," Mr. Sullivan said at last, slowing to signal his intent to turn into a driveway I never would have seen had it not been for the gap in the trees and Mrs. Sullivan's sudden disappearance at exactly that spot.

It was a dark place where I could barely see the plate in front of me. I had no idea what to order so I just said, "the same," and pointed to Carly when the waiter came around to me. The adults sat at one end of the table, across from each other for easy conversation. The Kitty Committee sat on the other end—two facing two. It was a stiff and formal atmosphere, and I spent most of the night worrying about which fork to use, where to put my napkin, which water glass and bread plate was mine, and whether I had dressed appropriately. It wasn't at all the treat that Carly had promised. I wondered if I was the only one feeling that way. Were Jane and Maggie enjoying themselves? They seemed to be. Not wishing to interrupt the conversation, thereby calling attention to myself, I reached across Maggie for the bread basket. Carly paused mid-sentence, glanced at me, and barely smiled.

"Maggie, could you please hand Grace the bread so she doesn't knock over your drink?" She spoke to Maggie, but her eyes were fixed on me, and her tone was impatient. I wanted to die, but everyone laughed good-naturedly.

We didn't seem like a group of young teens celebrating a sweet sixteen. I wondered what Carly's parents would think if they could see the way my family ate, often with trays on our laps, sometimes with me sitting on the floor of my dad's bedroom so we could be together. My mom, exhausted from trying to hold everything together. My dad silently nodding to acknowledge our remarks, one eye on the TV, his smiles more like grimaces of pain. I wondered what they'd think of our humble meals in Guatemala—beans, rice, chicken. Luke and I licking our fingers in lieu of napkins, stuffing the greasy left-overs into our well-worn pockets to be shared with Tramp as soon as we dared.

"So, who's next?" Mr. Sullivan dialed up his volume to reach our side of the table. "In the birthday department?"

It occurred to me that Carly's mother hardly spoke to us girls, focusing most of her attention that night on the adult friends. I had to remind myself that there were two parents, not one parent and three adult friends.

"Jane and I are in March," Maggie said. "I'm exactly one day older than Jane." They exchanged amused glances and giggled at that delicious coincidence while a frown line appeared between Carly's perfectly formed eyebrows.

"And you, Grace?"

"She's not until May first," Carly answered for me.

"Oh really, May Day?" Carly's mother showed interest in us for the first time. "That's a lovely day to be born, with some religious significance, you know, apart from what most people think about that date."

I nodded my head because I did know.

"That's a long time to wait for your driver's license, Grace. Good thing you have Carly to shuttle you around in the mean-time," Mr. Sullivan said.

I didn't bother telling them it would be another eighteen

months before I was eligible for a driver's license and neither did Carly or the other girls. Perhaps they weren't really paying attention, or maybe they'd grown tired of the adult intrusion into Carly's celebration. I didn't bother telling them that my family owned one car, and it was fully commandeered by my mother, to be used for our family's survival. Carly already had a nice BMW, albeit five years old, which was earmarked only for her.

I didn't know then that by the time I was old enough to drive, I'd be on the way to losing my family and inventing an entirely new identity for myself—independent adult.

"Carly tells us you've had quite the life," Mrs. Sullivan said, as though just becoming aware of my presence and her daughter's party. She turned to the woman seated opposite. "Grace has grown up overseas in all kinds of different exotic countries," she explained.

"Oh really?" The woman arched a sleek black eyebrow in my direction. "How interesting. Were you a military brat?"

"My parents were missionaries," I said and then added, "and my mom's a nurse." A nurse was usually an easier thing for outsiders to accept. I knew that living overseas to help people through medicine always brought murmurs of approval and even admiration from others. Being a missionary only brought quizzical and fearful looks, as though the next move I would make would be to proselytize.

"Oh, that's fascinating," she said, but she didn't seem fascinated at all.

"I'm sure Grace has some very interesting stories she could share with us sometime," Carly's mom said, making it clear this wasn't the time or place to share my interesting stories. I was frankly relieved. "Jane, I love the way you're wearing your hair up tonight, dear. They say the loveliest part of a woman is her neck, and you're so blessed with a long, graceful neck."

The furrow appeared between Carly's eyebrows again. I thought Carly was beautiful, and I never noticed things like graceful necks. But at that moment, I did notice that Carly's neck was not long. Perhaps it was a little shorter than usual, even compared to Maggie's. Maybe even compared to mine. It was the first shortcoming I noticed in Carly, and it came via her mother's tongue.

"Carly, Sweetheart, ready to add up the check for us?" Mr. Sullivan interrupted. "It's a game we've had since she was little," he explained to the table, his eyes darting from person to person. "She adds up the check, and if she finds any mistakes, she gets to keep the difference if it's in our favor. Of course, if it's not in our favor, no reason to get the poor waiter unnecessarily in trouble, is there?" He laughed loudly at that.

Carly picked up the check and scanned it before shaking her head and handing it back to her father.

"She doesn't do it for the money anymore," Mr. Sullivan went on. "Just our little game, isn't it, Sweetheart?" His arm moved in such a way I could almost swear he was reaching for her knee under the table.

Mrs. Sullivan smiled icily.

CHAPTER TWELVE

I can't pinpoint the moment when I realized Maggie was taking rule number three too much to heart. We often smuggled a beer or siphoned off hard liquor from a parent's stash, but we normally did that as a group. We did it during times when the Kitty Committee had a sleepover or crashed a classmate's party (where we never left each other's sides). When we went to the water park or even the movies. Never enough to reveal our state of intoxication to others, but just enough to instill the sense of *bon ami*, high spirits, and a secret that we alone shared. Just enough to make everything seem a little bit funny. A little reckless. A little daring.

But during the times Maggie and I were alone together, more and more often I suspected she'd had something from her mother's liquor cabinet before I arrived. Maggie's mom was divorced and not often home. She worked, and when she didn't work, she dated unapologetically. That was a concept so alien to me that I couldn't help but pity Maggie. On the other hand, it gave us a place to hang out that was almost always unsupervised. A place where we could speak openly about anything and act out in ways we couldn't have gotten away with at my house. Or Jane's. Or even Carly's, whose parents also worked, but whose home, it was understood, we should never disrespect.

I think it was the day Maggie showed up at school with the unfocused gaze and slow manner of speaking that had become so familiar to me. Like someone just waking from a nap, her eyes remained at half-mast, and her tongue coiled lazily around each word. Looking back, it should have been easy for me to hear that silent cry for help, but I didn't. Drinking wasn't a shameful thing, a crutch, a tool to numb painful feelings. It was an act of rebellion against parents and school and social norms. It was fun. And Maggie was still wonderfully lovable and entertaining at the same time.

First period was American History, a class Maggie and I shared. That morning, Maggie was a little worse off than usual and, in fact, seemed to be barely functioning. When Mrs. Gossage announced we'd be watching a Civil War movie so she could finish grading tests, I was relieved—Maggie could use that hour to get herself straight. Mrs. Gossage was an eccentric with long, graying hair; horn-rimmed glasses with lenses so smudged by fingerprints it was hard to see beyond them; the same pair of Birkenstock sandals, regardless of the outfit she wore; and a very large and colorless mole on her lip that was almost impossible to ignore when she was speaking. Her apparent favorite colors were black or dark brown which magnified, by contrast, the flaky field of dandruff that adorned her meaty shoulders.

Despite her odd appearance, she was one of the more popular teachers in school, not because she had the gift of bringing history to life for her students; in fact, it was quite the opposite—her lectures were dry and tedious. But her students loved her because she listened to us as though whatever came out of our mouths was quite possibly the most interesting thing she'd heard that day. She peered at us through those badly smudged glasses as though we were precious examples of the best of humanity. She valued us and our opinions—both the profound and the ridiculous—so we valued her in return.

It was a good movie, so it didn't take me long to get drawn into the story. I became so engrossed that it was almost thirty minutes before I glanced over at Maggie, who sat in the desk one row up and to the right of mine. By then, her head was on the table, cradled in her arm, and I concluded she was asleep. I winced, hoping she wouldn't snore like I'd seen her do in the past. I nearly pretended to drop something so I could lean forward and jiggle her awake but thought better of it. The volume of the movie was loud enough to cover up a bit of soft snoring, and Mrs. Gossage had stepped out of the room. But the rest of the movie was ruined for me as I became obsessed with watching out for Maggie. After a while, I lost track of the storyline.

Seated in front of me was a girl named Kerry. Directly across the aisle from Kerry was Maggie. Kerry was a friendly girl whom Maggie and I often chatted with before class, but that day the sight of Maggie sprawled across her desk, mouth agape, proved to be irresistible. Kerry glanced back and forth from the screen to Maggie several times before turning around to look at me, stifling a giggle with her open palm. I looked over her head at the screen, pretending not to notice, pretending I was completely absorbed in the movie. But when she reached across the aisle and poked Maggie's shoulder with the blunt end of a pencil, I cringed. Maggie retracted her arm, mumbled incoherently, and turned her head to face the other direction. From where I sat, I could see the glisten of spittle on Maggie's chin and the lower part of her cheek.

The flickering screen in the dark room created a cozy fireplace-type atmosphere. By that time of year, mornings were quite cool, and the heated classrooms were stultifying under the best of circumstances. But gather a roomful of teenagers early in the morning, and anyone could have fallen asleep under those conditions. I had no doubt others were napping as well, and, once I'd lost the storyline, even I felt my eyelids drooping. But Maggie looked disheveled, and it wasn't her first time. I knew that once you were pegged with a particular fault, trait, or weakness, it was impossible to shed.

"Are you drunk?" Kerry asked, loudly enough that even I could hear. An intense wave of sympathy for Maggie washed over me, triggering a fiercely protective instinct I didn't know existed. The girl seated in front of Kerry turned around and looked at her, and then craned her neck to get a look at Maggie. The boy on the other side of Kerry peered at Maggie and let loose a rude snort, his head powered forward by its release. I feared others had also taken notice. Part of me wanted to hide and disassociate from Maggie's shame, but most of me wanted to wrap my arms around her, take her home, and tuck her into bed away from the curious stares and laughter of others. I wanted to protect her from becoming the class joke. The class drunk.

Mrs. Gossage came into the classroom just as Maggie flailed her arm to keep Kerry's question at bay. Unfortunately for Maggie, her hand connected with the history book on the corner of her desk, and it hit the ground like a gunshot. Kerry and I both sprang from our seats to pick it up, but Mrs. Gossage silently motioned us down. Maggie jerked her head up and wiped her damp chin with the back of her sleeve. She looked around cautiously to see if anyone was watching as she slowly got her bearings. She swiveled to face me with an embarrassed smile and rolled her eyes. I smiled back, breathing a sigh of relief that nothing worse had happened. Kerry stared at the screen, and I returned to the movie until, a few minutes later, the bell rang.

"Ladies, stay a minute please," Mrs. Gossage motioned to Kerry and Maggie as everyone filed out of the room. I lingered by the door until Mrs. Gossage noticed me and said, "You can go, Grace."

I moved to the hallway just outside the door, my heart thumping wildly with concern. I tried my best but couldn't hear a word of what they were saying, the noise from the hallway overwhelming the soft voices from within. A minute later, Maggie came out alone. She was smiling, which was a relief. I didn't think she smelled of alcohol, but of course she had her ways—vodka only, mixed with orange juice. It never left a scent on her breath, at least not one I could detect.

"What happened?" I asked, breathless with anticipation. We didn't have far to walk to get to Geometry, so Maggie was taking her time—ambling, but at least she looked better than she had an hour earlier.

"She asked what was going on with me and Kerry, and I said Kerry poked me with a pencil, and we were just kidding around and the book fell."

"Where's Kerry?"

"Mrs. Gossage's still talking to her . . . something about being able to trust us if she has to step out of the classroom. Blah, blah, blah. Anyway, she told me I could go."

"I hope Kerry's not in trouble," I said as we walked into our next class.

Five minutes into Geometry, a student messenger arrived just as Mr. Munson was wiping down the board under a cloud of chalk dust. The messenger, a short red-haired boy I recognized from homeroom, said that Maggie was wanted in Mr. Sutherland's office. Mr. Sutherland was one of two counselors at our school, but he also handled discipline cases.

"Oooh, Maggie's in trouble," Franklin blurted out. Franklin, who was seated in the front of every classroom, the better to be supervised, was a frequent target of Mr. Sutherland's summons. That morning he was giddy at the chance to pile on someone else. And a girl? Even better—no one who would take his taunt as fighting words.

"Maggie," Mr. Munson said. "You're excused." He held up a hall pass, and thirty heads swiveled in order for thirty sets of eyes to feast on Maggie's walk of shame.

"Shut up," Maggie hissed at Franklin, bumping his desk with her hip on the way out.

The rest of class was a blur. Geometry was usually a blur for me, but that day I wasn't even pretending to pay attention. I stared at the backpack slung across Maggie's seat and wondered if I should take it with me if she didn't get back before class was over. But then, just as the bell rang, Maggie returned.

"What happened?"

"Sucks," Maggie said. "Somebody reported me for drinking, so Mr. Sutherland wanted me to take a breathalyzer."

"You're kidding!"

Maggie stuffed her notebook and sweater into her backpack before zipping it shut. Kids from the next class were already arriving, and Mr. Munson looked up from his stack of papers to observe Maggie's activity. He raised his eyebrows quizzically, causing me to wonder if teachers were as interested in student gossip as the kids were.

Maggie slung her pack across her shoulder and lowered her voice. "He called my mom at work, and she said she didn't give her permission for me to take the breathalyzer, so Sutherland said if I didn't, they were going to suspend me."

"So?"

"So I didn't do the breathalyzer, and now Mom has to come

pick me up, and I'm suspended for three days. I don't care. I actually *wanna* go home."

"Don't worry, I'll take notes and get your homework while you're gone. I'll come see you after school today, okay?"

"Thanks," Maggie said. She looked like she was about to cry.

"I'll walk with you."

"You'll be late."

"I don't care. One for all—"

But Maggie wasn't interested in hearing the rest of our motto.

"Mr. Sutherland's an idiot," she interrupted, and I knew she was striking out against her own helplessness and frustration. "I don't know how Carly can stand being in the same room with him for her SAT tutoring. He's all like, 'I'm your friend, you can talk to me.' As if."

I didn't have any experience with Mr. Sutherland other than the day he first welcomed Luke and me to Indian Springs High, but I wanted to be supportive.

"He's a huge idiot," I said, branding myself as one with those words.

We walked by the trophy display case near the front of the school. I'd never actually stopped to look at the shiny brass trophies exhibited there. I'd never seen a single student who did. Who was or wasn't being recognized in that case seemed so remote to my life as to be practically nonexistent.

"He's actually kind of pervy, if you ask me," Maggie went on. "He put his arm around me when I was leaving his office . . . moving in for the bra-strap grope. You know, the supposed supportive pat on the back. Dirty old man."

I'd never considered that a supportive pat on the back could be a pervy thing to do. Maybe because no one had ever done that to me, except perhaps my mom, who I knew was being genuinely supportive. Maybe even Dad when he was still Dad.

Back before I wore a bra, not that Dad would know or care about that. But I believed Maggie. She knew things I didn't.

"Gross," I said. "So who do you think told on you?"

"I guess Mrs. Gossage, who else?"

"Yeah. You thought she was letting you off, but she was just getting you out of the way so she could report you."

And then the words I wish I'd never spoken. "Maybe Kerry?"

Why did I say that? I wanted to offer something that Maggie might prize. An us-against-them thing. I wanted her to have proof that I had her back while she was dozing off. I was her watchdog. Her protector.

"Kerry?" She raised her eyebrows and looked at me curiously. "Why would Kerry do that?"

"I dunno. Maybe she was going to get in trouble for poking you with the pencil. Maybe she was trying to turn it around on you?"

Maggie considered this. We arrived at the front door to the school where her mom would be picking her up.

"She asked if you were drunk," I said. "Anyone could've heard her—people did. *I* heard her."

"She did?" Maggie seemed genuinely puzzled. "Well, maybe it *was* Kerry, and I misjudged her. I always thought she was nice. Anyway, I don't care, she did me a favor—three days' vacation."

Maggie's mother's maroon SUV pulled into the traffic circle.

"You'd better go," Maggie said. She leaned over and hugged me with one arm. "See you later, okay? Maybe Carly can give you a ride to my house. Tell Jane to come too, if she can. Mom won't be back until six, so we can hang out."

The SUV came to a stop in front of us, and Maggie's mom lowered the passenger-side window.

"You'd better get in, young lady. This was a very bad time for me to have to leave work."

"Love you, Maggie," I said. "Sorry this happened to you."

"Love you too, girl. Thanks for always sticking up for me."
Even a half-smile from Maggie felt better than a full-blown
smile from someone else, but it always came at a cost. Even
then, I sensed a limited reservoir of happiness within Maggie,
one that emptied drip by drip. Every smile. Every hug. Every
laugh bringing her closer to a dark and empty pit.

The bell rang, but I stood and watched while Maggie
lumbered down the steps, bent from the weight of her backpack
swinging heavily from one narrow shoulder. The day had started
out cloudy and gray. A weak November sun pushed through the
clouds but was quickly swatted away by the gloom. Only when
Maggie's car disappeared did I move from that spot, turning to
walk the empty hallways, unprotected by a hall pass, trying to
remember if it was a lab day in chemistry and, if so, if I would
be able to slip in unnoticed.

Normally I rushed to lunch, but that day I lingered at
my locker and then stopped at the library to return a book.
Maggie's depression had become real to me that morning,
although I didn't yet have a word for it. And even though I
couldn't or wouldn't name it, I recognized it as a thing that had
the potential to thrive within me as well if I wasn't careful. Just
like Dad fell off the ladder, I could fall into this well of despair.

Carly and Jane weren't like us. They were strong and
unafraid. They would save us—Maggie and me.

"Oh my God, finally!" Carly snapped when I showed up for
lunch.

Seeing the two of them, Jane and Carly, sitting at the table together without the buffer of Maggie or me, was a disturbing sight to behold. It was like seeing a lion and a zebra drinking side-by-side at the watering hole.

"Everyone's saying that Maggie got sent home for drinking. What happened?"

I set my tray on the table and slid onto the bench, ducking my legs under the tabletop. Without Maggie there, I knew nobody would have wiped the benches clean for us.

"It's true," I said. "I was going to talk to you about it." I addressed my remarks to Carly, who had the most claim on Maggie. "She's been doing it a lot lately. Only one time at school before today, and it wasn't that bad . . . not like today. But after school—"

"And you never said anything to me?"

I couldn't take Carly's disapproval. She meant so much to me, and her approval always arrived like a gift whenever it was bestowed. I still woke up mornings in disbelief that Carly was actually my friend. *My* friend. I glanced at Jane, whose eyes were soft. She laid a pale hand over my own as I gulped down my anxiety. The dreary sky had wormed its way into my mood, and I was reminded how unforgiving a Northern California winter could be. Those first days in Indian Springs when I thought I'd never be warm or see the sun again.

"I'm . . . worried about her," I said, my quivering voice giving way to tears.

"Hey," Carly scooted across the smoothly coated metal bench, her voice transforming into a gentle coo. "Don't cry, Grace. Maggie's okay. She'll be okay. That's what we're here for. Right, Jane?" She tucked my hair behind my ear and lightly ran her hand up and down my spine, my muscles releasing their tension in the wake of her touch. I thought of Mr. Sutherland groping for Maggie's bra strap. If he'd been acting from a place of kindness and sympathy, Maggie would have known the way

I knew then with Carly. My tears cleared like a sudden and unexpected spring shower surrendering to the sun. "The Kitty Committee, remember?" Carly said. "That's the whole point."

I nodded yes and looked at Jane, whose eyes radiated sympathy but not agreement. Had I been crying for Maggie or for myself?

"I think Kerry might have told on her," I said, doubling down on my disastrous earlier mistake. I stared at my uneaten bowl of ramen, which was rapidly surrendering its steam and nourishing heat to the frigid day. I pulled the cord of my jacket, tightening the noose around my neck.

"Kerry Thompson?" Carly's eyes popped open. She dropped her hand from my back but didn't move from my side. We were pressed against each other, shoulder to shoulder, thigh to thigh, hip to hip. I felt the warm, moist puff of air leave her lips and enter my lungs. I breathed in her resuscitating breath. Her surprise and indignation. I siphoned strength from the heat of her body against mine. "What does she have to do with anything?" Carly asked. "Why would she even do that?"

It was my now or never moment. I still had the chance to back out, albeit at the cost of making myself look foolish. I forged ahead.

"We were watching a movie in history, and Maggie fell asleep."

I'd told this story to Maggie, hoping she'd understand my loyalty and commitment to her happiness. Kerry had made me uneasy with her obvious delight in Maggie's misery. In the way she'd introduced other bystanders to Maggie's shame. In the way she'd prodded Maggie with her pencil, degrading her as though examining a decaying carcass that she didn't want to touch. Maybe I'd even believed in Kerry's complicity myself, I no longer remember. What I do remember is that my conclusion seemed to please Carly. She wanted to hear more.

"Mrs. Gossage wasn't in the room most of the time, so it didn't really matter. Kerry said something about Maggie being drunk, and everyone sitting around her could hear. I could even hear, and her back was to me. Then she poked Maggie with a pencil, Maggie swung her hand around, and her book fell. So Mrs. Gossage made them stay after. I think maybe Kerry was probably trying to get out of trouble by blaming Maggie because Mrs. Gossage made Kerry stay after, and Maggie got to leave."

"What's she like?" Jane asked. "That Kerry girl."

"She's okay," I answered. "I mean, we thought she was nice, but maybe she's not who we thought she was."

My second thoughts were catching up. Gaining in strength over Carly's approval. I plunged my plastic fork into the ramen noodles and twisted them around and around and around until I'd gathered every last one of them. Then I brought them to my open mouth, my bottom lip pushed out like a platter to catch any potential drips or runaway ramen.

"You really going to eat all that at once?" Jane smirked. I returned the ball of noodles to the cup and looked up at Carly, waiting to see what she would say next.

"It makes sense, though," Carly said. "Mrs. Gossage is really cool, and I can't see her wanting to ruin someone's life. She'd be more likely to keep Maggie after class and have a heart-to-heart talk with her. Ask her to smoke a doobie or something. I'm sure you're right. It *was* Kerry."

We'd gone from Carly's initial disbelief, to my hypothesis, to my qualifiers (the words *think* and *maybe* and *probably*), to a final, unambiguous verdict. And we'd traveled there at lightning speed. Case closed.

"Maggie wants us to come see her after school," I added meekly. "If you guys can make it."

"I have debate club, but I can miss it," Carly said. "This is more important. How about you, Jane? I can drive us."

Jane took a deep breath and released it as a hiss between clenched teeth. "I have Thespians, but I guess I can tell them I have a dentist appointment or something. I could do that, I guess."

"You *guess*? You don't have to come if it's too much trouble," Carly said. It was a hope within a dare. I knew Carly didn't want Jane to come. She wanted to be Maggie's savior over and over again, as though she was rebranding Blizzard with a new can of red spray paint or once again loosening Rich Benson's bike chain and rejoicing in his broken bloody tooth.

I respected and admired Jane. She had everything I wanted and thought I needed. But did she have what it took to fight for us—Maggie and me—with more than just her shining example?

"I want to," Jane said. "It's just that I'm co-president."

"So let your co take over," Carly said. "Isn't that the whole point of co-presidenting?"

Jane scooped a spoonful of yogurt from its plastic container, digging deep for the strawberry preserves on the bottom. She brought the spoon up to her mouth where it waited, barred from admission while she turned something over in her head.

"I'll make it work," she said.

"I feel like I'm in prison." Maggie led the way to the kitchen. "I'm not allowed to leave the house, and Mom put a lock on the liquor cabinet. An actual lock. Can you believe it?" Each of us naturally gravitated to our usual seat around the kitchen table. "Anyone want anything?" she asked half-heartedly.

"I'll get it." Jane swung gracefully from her chair and peered into the fridge. "Let's see. Milk or . . . coke. Chocolate cake! Uh oh, your mom left a beer in here." She emerged holding a coke. "Anyone else want one?"

One of the fluorescent bulbs on the ceiling was in the process of dying—flickering and faintly hissing.

"Bring the cake," Maggie said glumly. "And four forks."

"Sorry, Maggie," I said. "About today. But we're all here for you."

To my ears, I sounded mature and supportive. I had no idea what else to offer beyond gathering the others to visit Maggie during her exile. Being there physically, I realized, was worthless without something more, but what that something more entailed, I hadn't a clue. That was Carly's job. Maybe even Jane's. My job was done.

"We all made sacrifices to come see you today, Maggie," Carly said. "Well, maybe not Grace, but Jane and I did. And we didn't do that just to be here for you, as Grace put it. I don't know why Jane came, but I know why I did. You need to hear this from someone, and I'm not afraid to say it. You're fucking up, and you need to stop."

Jane's corn-silk hair swung as she turned from the refrigerator, a large chocolate cake balanced in her hands. *She looks as surprised as I feel, but why should we be?* I wondered. Carly was right. Maggie *was* fucking up, and she needed to be stopped. Carly was blunt, but who was going to save Maggie from herself if not her best friend?

"Uh . . . thanks, Carly. Nice of you to stop by," Maggie said. "A little moral support would be appreciated."

"Moral support for what? So you can drink and come to school drunk again? Get a grip, Maggie. School's serious, and if it's not serious for you, it should be because it's the only way you're going to get out of this shit town. Not only that, but you make the rest of us look bad by association."

"Rule number three," Maggie deadpanned. "Alcohol is okay."

"Yeah, we drink for fun when we're out having fun," Carly said. By default, Jane and I had become passive bystanders. "Do you want to spend the rest of your life in Indian Springs while I'm out in the world achieving? While Jane and Grace are too? You really want to be here doing nothing? Because that's just where you're headed. Do you want to be a loser? Because right now, that's what you are."

"Carly . . ." Jane said, leaving her sentence unfinished.

I was surprised but pleased that Carly had labeled me as a future achiever, lumping me in with her and Jane. An hour earlier, I wouldn't have thought of myself that way, but the mere suggestion from Carly's lips straightened my spine. I nodded seriously, as though it was a known fact that I would be moving on from Indian Springs in pursuit of serious and important goals. But I couldn't stop myself from biting the inside of my cheek at the callousness with which Carly called out Maggie. I sensed the faint metallic taste of blood on the back of my tongue. Carly and Maggie had known each other their whole lives. They could speak to each other this way, I reasoned, although I doubted Maggie would speak like that to Carly. But Carly didn't do stupid things, did she? She was always in control, wasn't she?

"You guys too?" Maggie looked from Jane to me. "You think I'm a loser too?"

"Of course not." Jane looked down at her can of soda.

"I don't think Carly meant you're a loser," I said. "She just doesn't want you to get in trouble."

Carly's eyes glinted hard at me. "Don't interpret what I did or didn't mean. I *said* what I meant. Is that the way you want people to look at you, Maggie? To look at *us*, your friends? It's one for all and all for one, isn't it? That means we'll take care of you, but you also have to take care of us, and I honestly don't want my teachers to be looking at me and wondering if I'm some kind of a drunk loser. You have to be able to set limits between serious time and fun time."

She got up from her chair and stood behind Maggie, resting her hands on Maggie's narrow shoulders. "You know I love you, right? I'd do anything for you, and I'm only saying this because I love you. So cut it out, okay?" Her voice had softened so convincingly that I could almost believe a different person was speaking. "Okay?" she repeated.

"Okay," Maggie said, her eyes glistening with tears. "It's not like I could do it even if I wanted to, with Mom locking down the house the way she has. And I'm grounded for two weeks."

Carly rotated onto Maggie's lap. She took Maggie's face between her hands and pulled to within inches of her, where they could practically share each other's breath. "We're still going to have fun, I promise you," she said. "And I'm sure your mom will let us visit even if you're grounded. I'll convince her. But you gotta try harder for me, okay? I want you to succeed." She brushed Maggie's cheek with a kiss that, to my eyes, seemed almost sensual. I didn't know Carly was capable of such an intimate and emotional gesture—for lack of a better word, a human gesture. It aroused something within me that was close to jealousy, but was also longing for a kiss like that from Carly. I would never be that to Carly, I realized with a sudden sharp pang of regret. I could never take Maggie's place in Carly's heart.

"I know you do," Maggie said, and Carly stood and walked to the refrigerator, surveying its contents before emerging with a ginger ale.

"Grace thinks Kerry ratted you out," Carly said, her sweet, soothing voice transformed to match the ugly accusation. I imagined a gangster in an old black-and-white movie: a machine gun pointed at the hapless victim; its rat-a-tat-tat ending the snitch's life.

"I know, right? And I always thought she was nice," Maggie said. Princess Leia mewed from underneath the table, and Maggie swooped the nearly grown kitten onto her lap.

"I *think* it was her," I said. "I'm pretty sure, but I can't be a hundred percent sure."

Jane reared her head, glancing up from the fingernails which had preoccupied her until that point—pushing down her cuticles, chipping off old polish, anything but looking at Maggie and Carly. She stared at me, her expression unreadable, a clean blank slate like her wide, smooth brow.

Help me, I thought.

"Oh, it was her," Carly said. "Without a doubt. I mean, who else would it be? Mrs. Gossage? Give me a break."

"Yeah, I agree," Maggie said. "I mean, Mrs. Gossage was really nice to me when we were talking. And she let me go, so I'm pretty sure she didn't suspect anything or she would've just sent me to the office right then."

"So, I've been thinking," Carly said. "We talked about proving our loyalty to the Kitty Committee—to each other—by performing an act of allegiance. And then we never did anything about it. I take full responsibility and admit I've allowed myself to get too distracted by school, and maybe I've been neglecting *us*." She threw out both arms to virtually encircle our group. "Anyway, I'm willing to work on that, starting now. The timing's perfect."

The dying fluorescent light sputtered and blinked as rapidly as a strobe.

"What do you mean?" Jane asked. "Like how would we prove our loyalty to each other?"

Maggie didn't have to ask. She knew how Carly proved her loyalty. By then, I knew it too. Princess Leia was curled in Maggie's lap, relishing her warmth, the soft touch of her fingertips.

"Kerry has to suffer something. Something commensurate with the suffering she caused Maggie. It's only fair."

Maybe Jane isn't ready for this, I thought. At least I'd been prepared. What was needed was a degree of lightness—the air was too heavy, too toxic; the dying light was too anxiety-inducing. My heart fluttered as though escaping through my throat. I coughed, and it slunk back into my chest, resuming its normal beat.

"Commensurate," I said. "That was one of the SAT words." Even though my intent was to bring levity, I regretted saying it the second it left my mouth.

No one acknowledged the comment, through word or deed. It was like, at that moment, I ceased to exist. I'd served my purpose—being Kerry's accuser. Now I was expected to shut up and let bolder and brighter minds take over.

"Who wants to be the first person?" Carly asked. "We'll all have our turns eventually."

Jane and I looked at each other from across the table. Her head shook so imperceptibly that I thought I might have imagined it—the flickering light bouncing off her ghostly locks. I wished I knew. Nobody spoke.

"So no one," Carly said after a cringe-inducing moment of silence. I bit the side of my cheek again. Tasted blood again. Carly's disappointment was palpable, and I felt like I was letting her down—betraying her, even. "If no one else is going to volunteer, I guess I will. Not exactly a promising start to the Kitty Committee, is it?"

"I'll do it," Maggie blurted out.

I exhaled the breath I'd been holding in.

"You can't, Maggie, because this one's for you," Carly said as though that should be obvious to any thinking being. Her hands were folded on the table, and I noticed her nails were perfectly manicured and gleaming. She didn't have chipped polish or overgrown cuticles like Jane. Like mine, which were bitten down to the pink.

"I'll do it," I said, trying my best to sound as if it was really my idea. Without thinking, I brought my hand to my mouth, cleaning under the nail with my lower front tooth.

Princess Leia stood and arched her back before dropping silently to the floor.

"You're amazing, Grace," Carly said. She pulled my hand gently away from my mouth, tenderly positioning it on my lap. Even my mother wouldn't attempt such a blatantly humiliating gesture, and yet I took it as a sign of affection. Carly cared for us. She didn't want us to embarrass ourselves. She wanted us to achieve like her. To be beautiful like her. Carly's hand was smooth, slender, soft, and warm. Mine was big, large-knuckled, chapped, and cold. My hand would never be Carly's hand. And yet. "I knew you'd come through for us," she said.

"Yeah, Grace, thanks," Maggie said. "It means a lot that you'd do this for me." She leaned over to pick up Princess Leia, who was cleaning herself at Maggie's feet. She held up the cat, front legs pointing toward me, hind legs dangling. "Thank you, Grace," she said in a high-pitched voice I took to be Princess Leia's human incarnation.

"Amazing, Grace," Jane said, but only I seemed to hear her.

"What do I have to do?" I asked. I was feeling a little more confident after Maggie and Carly showered me with their approval. A little less anxious. I was coming to the place where I believed I'd done the right thing. And how hard could my assignment be? Maybe I'd have to watch Kerry in class, and if I saw her do something wrong, I'd report it after class to Mrs. Gossage. Maybe even anonymously. I would prove my allegiance to the Kitty Committee before anyone else and then sit back and relax when it was the next person's turn.

"I'm going to think of something," Carly said. "I'll let

everyone know in a few days."

I speared a chunk of chocolate cake with my fork, mostly icing, and brought it to my mouth. It was moist and delicious. I helped myself to a second forkful.

"Wait," Jane said so abruptly that I gulped the forkful of cake, making ugly, throat-clearing noises to help push it down. "Isn't there something about every member having an equal voice? I remember that was one of the rules."

"Rule number six." My voice was raspy with cake crumbs, but I was anxious to prove myself as the most serious member; the only one of us who had memorized the rules verbatim; the only one who would soon prove her allegiance. "No one member is above the others." I had studied these rules at home in the days after we created them. I could recite them in my sleep, and sometimes I wondered if I did.

"So what I want to say is," Jane went on, unimpressed with my recitation versus the rule's underlying significance. "How do we really know that Kerry told on Maggie? What proof do we have beyond Grace's theory? I demand that we address this because we're all equal in the Kitty Committee, and I'm not comfortable with what the others have decided."

I was stung by her words. I'd actually wondered the same thing myself, but hearing it come from Jane, with an almost sarcastic inflection, suddenly fed my own growing doubts—not only about my conclusion but about my self-worth. Maggie turned to Carly for the answer.

"Fair enough," Carly said. "That's a valid point, so let's address it."

Jane's shoulders visibly relaxed, elongating her graceful neck. She'd been heard, and that's all she wanted. Carly had disarmed her. Alleviated her concern that we were rushing into something intrinsically wrong. I glanced at Carly, whose body, in contrast to Jane's, seemed to have coiled tighter.

"I trust Grace—" Carly began.

"I do too," Maggie interrupted.

"I *trust* Grace," Carly repeated, shooting Maggie a warning look to hold her tongue. "But anyone can be wrong. So tomorrow I'm going to do a little investigating. Kerry has PE with me, and I know some of her friends. I'll get to the truth before Grace does anything. Before *we* do anything." Her fingernails clicked out a drumroll on the tabletop. It almost seemed like a comical insert to the black-and-white gangster movie I'd envisioned earlier. "Does that make you feel more comfortable, Jane?"

I already wanted to believe in Carly. Always. So I had no trouble accepting whatever she came up with. But even Jane, whose tension with Carly was almost a tangible thing, appeared persuaded. The strain in her ice-blue eyes melted away. Carly could do that if you let her and didn't know better. And if Jane's concerns were assuaged, mine would be as well.

"Yeah, I guess so," Jane said. "You should really replace that light bulb, Maggie. It's giving me a headache."

"I know. I was just going to say that," I laughed, harder and more falsely than was appropriate.

Maggie got up and flipped the light switch, darkening the room but lightening my mood. It was good to have us together again—a family. The Kitty Committee on solid ground. It was like seeing your parents present a united and cheerful front after a terrible argument—something I'd only witnessed once in my life and hoped never to see again. Carly was smart. Smart in more ways than just school-smart. Carly knew things about people. She could get them to talk about things they might not even *want* to talk about. She could get to the truth, whatever it was. And maybe Kerry hadn't told. Maybe it *was* Mrs. Gossage. Maybe I wouldn't have to do anything after all, and we could find a fun way to prove our allegiance to each other. Our oath to the Kitty Committee.

"In the meantime, let's go over everything that happened," Carly said to Maggie. "Tell me every last detail, and whatever you don't remember, Grace can fill in."

The investigation began like a court procedure. Maggie was the witness taking the stand. Carly was the prosecuting attorney. Jane was ready to jump in with an objection if it was necessary. I was the witness waiting in the wings, waiting to be called to the stand when Maggie's memory failed her.

Maggie recounted the story, beginning with the moment we walked into History until the moment she lay her head on the table and fell asleep. I eagerly filled in every detail I could remember after that, even the ones that didn't seem relevant. After a while, Jane seemed to lose interest and got up to visit the bathroom, content to leave the investigation in Carly's capable hands, now that she had extracted a promise that the truth would prevail. When Maggie got to the part about sitting in Mr. Sutherland's office, she didn't hold back, concluding with, "I really don't know how you can stand him, Carly. He's a such a pervy old man."

Carly didn't brush off Maggie's concerns the way I thought she might. Instead, she asked, and Maggie told about the bra-strap grope. Carly claimed she had felt the same sort of squeamishness about Mr. Sutherland but could never put her finger on exactly what it was about him that bothered her so much. Still, he was an amazing SAT tutor, and her practice-test scores had improved dramatically, so she would just have to put up with his creepiness for the time being. He was tutoring Tim LeClerc too, and there was no way Carly was going to drop Sutherland and let that scumbag Tim outscore her on the SAT.

Maggie was quick to state that it was never her intention to suggest Carly should give up her private tutoring sessions with Sutherland. She could definitely appreciate that sometimes people had to put up with bullshit to get what they wanted. We were all walking on eggshells with each other.

The Kitty Committee didn't start the day we drew up its constitution or even the night at Lake Tahoe when we recited its rules for the benefit of Jane. The Kitty Committee began that day in Maggie's kitchen with three of us unwittingly embarking on the path which would lead to the conviction of Kerry for the crime of Maggie's shame. That was the day the Kitty Committee truly came into its own, displaying its sharp claws for the rest of the world to feel.

SAN FRANCISCO

THE LONELIEST PLACE on Earth is an airport when you're traveling alone. You arrive there on your own, and no one says goodbye when you leave or hello when you arrive. Sitting in my chair, waiting to board, I watched hundreds of people purposefully striding to their assigned gates, where airplanes would swallow them whole and deliver them to cities in which someone would be waiting—a wife or husband, a friend or business associate. For the first time in my life, the absolute unknown was my most positive option, but at the same time, I was blue and wallowing in self-pity. Only the idea of summer in other lands held back the onslaught of the gray San Francisco gloom.

To distract myself, I made mental calculations of flight times and layovers on the twenty-plus hour flight I'd booked in the interest of saving money. I added the ten-hour time change and calculated when would be the best time to sleep, if any, on the plane. I weighed the option of arriving exhausted and toughing it out until I adapted naturally by necessity, when I could no longer stay awake.

I chose Turkey for the beginning of my journey. It was as far away as I could get from anything which hinted of familiarity. I was also impressed by its geopolitical significance, straddling two continents, their cultures and traditions bleeding into each other. Even its flag enchanted me—a field of heart-stopping red and a white crescent moon, sharp points poised to snip the tip of an adjacent star. It seemed magical, and I was in need of magic.

Nathan and I had been unable to occupy the same space, even for the few weeks before my trip, so Carlos kindly took me in, allowing me the use of his sofa. Several days before I left, I received a letter from my parents. It went to Nathan's apartment, but since I was no longer living there, Carlos said Nathan marched into the coffee shop and slapped it on the counter, almost triumphantly.

"It's from Grace's parents," he said, somewhat sullenly according to Carlos, who suspected he was being blamed for harboring me.

I imagine Nathan thought it was the letter from my parents that would shake sense into me, tell me what a fool I was being, and create enough self-doubt that I'd abandon my plans. But of course my parents knew nothing of my plans. Coward that I was, I'd only just sent that letter a day earlier, after having extracted a promise from Luke to let me break the news to them myself. By the time they received my letter, I knew I'd be gone.

Instead, their letter was filled with news of their lives, questions about mine, their hopes and love for me. At the end, Mom mentioned that Dad had been having recurring bouts of the malaria he'd picked up many years ago. Or perhaps it was a new strain, she said—one of the suppressant-resistant variety. In any case, they were seeing a doctor, and Dad would be fine. They were both happier than they'd been in years, although they missed us greatly. It was good to be doing something meaningful again. Making a difference in people's lives.

The night before I left, Carlos stayed over with his girlfriend. The next morning, I woke while it was still dark, folded my bedsheets, tidied up the kitchen, and left a note on the table thanking Carlos for the gift of his friendship and all the laughter and understanding he had granted so freely and unconditionally. The building was quiet, but residents of the other apartments were beginning to stir. I heard the telltale sounds of water rushing through the pipes in the walls and the creaking of hardwood floors that were already old long before I was born. I took one last look around to make sure I hadn't forgotten anything. I thought of my first day of work, how Carlos had evolved from co-worker to trusted friend. The first day Nathan walked into the coffee shop, goofy-eyed and awed by the very thought of me. I placed the extra key on the small table beside the front door. I wrapped a scarf around my neck and quietly closed the door behind me.

The trip itself is only a smudge in my memory, but the full-out sensory assault when I arrived in Istanbul is something I'll never forget. Not having a clue how to navigate the public transportation, I decided to splurge and spend some of my meager resources on a taxi. I would have been an easy and obvious target for any unscrupulous driver, but fate was with me that day and my driver was an older man. Kind, with steely-gray hair, he spoke a little English from his brief stay as a young man in New York City. Mehmet fretted about me, a young woman on her own. As I had landed smack in the middle of rush hour, he had a long time to fret, and we had almost an hour to trade personal histories. By the time he pulled up to the youth hostel that my research indicated was the safest and most modestly priced option, we had become friends.

Fortunately, Mehmet waited to make sure I got in safely because once I'd walked through the narrow passageway to the entrance, I was stopped by a metal gate, chained and padlocked. The padlock was rusted as though it hadn't been used for a while. My heart stirred in my chest, but I took a deep breath and stepped quickly to the street where I broke into a wide smile at the sight of Mehmet's idling cab.

"No good?" He raised bushy, questioning eyebrows.

"No good," I said. My spirits sank. There was no Plan B, and

I didn't have the funds to pay Mehmet to drive me around the city looking for lodging.

He stepped out of the car and opened the passenger side. "Come," he said. "Hungry?" I was famished.

Mehmet explained that his workday was almost over, having started well before dawn. He invited me to his home and, being of an age where instincts and stupidity weigh equally on the decision scale, I took him up on his offer. Another story might have had me never being heard from again, but my story that day took me into the home of a lovely couple. Mehmet and his wife—silver-haired and elegant, gracious and beautiful, warm and nurturing—Azra took to me as though I was a long-lost daughter. I ate food, prepared by her hands, that I couldn't identify, but the smell and taste were sublime. Azra couldn't speak English so Mehmet translated for us, and somehow we were able to read each other's eyes.

I must have done something good in my life, I thought, *to have been presented with this gift.*

After dinner, I was exhausted beyond anything in my previous experience. Azra prepared a small, hard cot for me. Piled with soft blankets, it felt like a cloud. It was where their son slept when he visited from Germany, where he lived and worked, they explained. He would be honored to have me use it in his absence. Mehmet and Azra said they were glad to have my company, and they wouldn't hear of me staying anywhere but with them for as long as I was in Istanbul. They knew, in Germany, someone was showing their son the same kindness they were showing me. It was the way of the world.

Mehmet and Azra gave me the confidence and security to explore every corner of the old city and beyond. They launched me into my new life on a new continent. It had been a gentle transition, but it had to come to an end. After more than three weeks, it was time to plan my next step. I sat in a café sipping the coffee I knew I'd soon be missing. Pen in my hand, paper on the table in front of me, I'd been working on the promised weekly letter to Luke. Soon he could breathe the sigh of relief he'd been waiting for, knowing I was beyond the reach of that Hollywood version of the modern medieval dungeon. I didn't want to go to the place of missing Mehmet and Azra, but it was always there, lurking in the back of my mind along with the anxiety of setting off for the unknown. Turkey had become the known. The familiar. How quickly that had happened.

But the urge to move on was stronger than my anxiety and, thanks to my hosts, I was ready to do so. Mehmet and Azra had given me my traveling feet, reminding me what it meant to understand people beyond just the words they spoke; to respect differences instead of being suspicious of them; to think of myself, once again, as a citizen of an entire world, and not just a member of a tiny group in a tiny school in a tiny town. No one knew where I was, and that was liberating. Exploring a new culture and immersing myself seamlessly in it was challenging but redeeming. Each ordinary life experience was a learning experience when I didn't speak the language or know the names of the streets or even know where to find a public restroom to relieve myself. It was like being born again. My mind was fully occupied with just living, which meant little or no time for worrying. For regrets. For reflection.

A young woman pulled a chair up to an adjacent table and, from the clumsy way she ordered and the English language version of *Atlas Shrugged* clutched in her hand, I pegged her as an American. When she grinned at me, my suspicion was confirmed. Not only had her smile enriched some orthodontist by thousands of dollars (a peculiar American obsession), but no one smiles quite so trustingly, so naively, so openly, and so without an obvious purpose as an American.

"Hi," she tested the waters, probably also having pegged me despite having spent my orthodontic years overseas. "Are you American?"

I nodded, surprising myself with the happiness it brought me to be included in this club after nearly a month of being a stranger in a strange land.

"My name's Rachel." She dragged her chair over to my table. "You mind?"

"No, not at all." I folded the letter to Luke in two and stuffed it in my bag. "I was just writing my brother," I explained. "I've been in Istanbul for three weeks. I'll be heading to Rome in a few days."

"Ooh, Rome." Rachel had long, bright red frizzy hair. Pale green eyes and high pink spots in her cheeks. She wore a sun hat with a wide brim. "I've been traveling with two guys from England that I met on the coast. But they're going to Greece, and I'm trying to make my way to Spain eventually, so we're splitting up. Where're you from?"

I had to think for a minute because that was a question without a true answer.

"San Francisco. You?"

"Seattle."

"Why Spain?" I asked. "I'm going there too. Eventually."

The waiter brought Rachel a cold drink that looked like some kind of an iced coffee or a dark soda. She siphoned off half the glass through a straw before stopping to answer.

"Sorry," she said, gulping for a breath of air. The pink spots in her cheeks faded. "I've been walking for the past two hours, and I'm so thirsty." She bent her head to the straw and bled the glass dry, making a few noisy sounds toward the bottom. "Anyway, to answer your question, my boyfriend's in Spain teaching English for a year. I'm taking a year off after graduation, so I've been traveling and eventually I'll meet up with him. And then who knows? Probably back to the real world and jobs. Why Rome?"

"It's just a plan I made before I left," I said almost apologetically. I thought that maybe I should be more spontaneous like Rachel and the English boys she was traveling with. "I bought my ticket before I left, so now I'm kind of committed. But I think it's time."

"Cool." Rachel pondered my response. "I wouldn't mind going to Rome—all over Italy for that matter. You traveling with anyone?"

"Nope."

"You want some company?"

Now it was my turn to ponder. I didn't have a great track record with friends. As a young girl, I never got too attached overseas, knowing my relationships couldn't be permanent. My family were my friends. Tramp. And then there was Alice, whom I hadn't been so nice to. Carly. My stomach pitched. Maggie. Jane. I felt a gray sheet descend over the sun streaming through the window. There was Carlos—he was a true friend, but we didn't spend significant time together.

"I have a plane ticket already," I said. "So unfortunately, I have to leave on that flight."

Rachel pushed the brim of her hat up, leaned back in her chair, and eyed me. "Are you just saying that to be polite because you don't want my company?"

"No," I said, although I knew I was. I was trying to protect myself from Rachel. And to protect her from me. "It's just that I made the reservation a long time ago so it would probably be pretty hard to get on that flight. And, I mean . . . I know it's expensive to fly."

"I've got lots of money," Rachel said cheerfully. "What's your flight info? There's a travel agency right down the street, and I know they speak English because I've used them before. If your flight is booked, I could take another one. It's always more fun to travel with someone, don't you think?"

There was only one way to answer that without coming across as mean-spirited. And I did like Rachel's open and trusting nature. Her sparkle and unselfconscious manner. In that moment, I calculated Rachel might be someone who would show me the way—a *different* way—to approach life.

"Yes," I said, this time without hesitation. "It *is* more fun when you're not traveling alone. Let's go to the travel agent and check on the flight."

With Rachel as my new ally, my step felt a little lighter. I approached the prospect of leaving Mehmet and Azra with a little less melancholy. I remembered this feeling—the confidence and optimism I had felt when I'd been accepted by Carly as one of her own. Maybe I wasn't a person who functioned well, or even at all, on her own. Maybe I was meant to be part of a pack. But that prospect was so depressing that I shook it off and reminded myself that traveling through foreign countries was nothing like the Kitty Committee. Rachel was nothing like Carly or Maggie. I was a wanderer now. An explorer. I was like Marco Polo, Nellie Bly, and Jack Kerouac. Whatever experiences might come, let them come. I wouldn't ever abide by rules again—at least not the self-imposed kind.

But when the time came to say goodbye to Mehmet and Azra, my newly acquired bravado dissolved into a flood of tears. How could I face never seeing these people again? They'd come to mean so much to me in such a short period of time. They had accepted me unconditionally, and I'd battled dark thoughts at night, wondering if I held them dearer than my own parents, who were loving and well-meaning but somehow never reached this deep into my heart.

"God will protect you always," Mehmet translated for Azra, but I could already read it in her eyes, which glistened with tears.

But they didn't know what God knew, if there was a God. They didn't know what I knew.

A final embrace with Rachel standing behind me. I felt invisible hands on my shoulders pulling me away from Azra, from a place I otherwise would never have had the strength to leave behind. The hands felt so real that, for a moment, I thought it was Rachel pulling me away, but it wasn't.

Mehmet took us to the airport in his taxi—free of charge, of course. He insisted even when Rachel pulled a wad of paper money out of her backpack once we'd gotten to the airport.

"Your money no good for me," he shook his head fiercely, blocking the transfer of cash with his raised palm. "Put away." And he waited to make sure she put it away safely under his protective watch. "Careful," he admonished her. "Keep . . . inside," he pointed to her backpack, mildly irritated at the cavalier way she waved money around without regard for who might be watching.

"I . . ." I began, recognizing immediately the emptiness of what I was about to say. What could possibly measure up to the moment that wouldn't cheapen all the things left unsaid?

He flicked his fingers backward toward the airport entrance. "Go now," he interrupted, sparing us both from the futility of my words. "Have fun. Good life," he said emphatically with a firm nod of his head.

As he pulled away from the curb, he took one last look over his shoulder. His cheeks were silvered that morning with a twenty-four-hour growth of beard. Not wanting to take a chance on missing our plane, he'd left the house without shaving, and I knew that was meaningful, being the fastidious man that he was. I caught my final glimpse of his eyes as I stood smiling and waving goodbye. They were dark and soft, the loose skin underneath draping his cheekbones. He'd been quiet during the ride to the airport. He seemed sad. I thought of Dad during the days right after Luke left for college, days when pain was still his most real and most constant companion.

Mehmet must be thinking of his son, I thought. *So far away. Another stranger in a strange land.*

Hours later, we were in Rome, facing a day so hot it sucked the water out of the Tiber and spewed it into the air we breathed. We located our lodgings and stashed our gear. Thanks to Rachel's generosity, it was a step up from what I'd planned for myself while still maintaining the minimal standards necessary for our bohemian credentials. With what daylight remained, we traipsed around the city, hopping on and off buses along the way, marveling at how easily two-thousand-year-old relics of antiquity coexisted with modern thoroughfares and trendy boutiques. Rome was an enigma, and the more Rachel and I explored, peering into its every nook and cranny, the more puzzling it became. To see so many layers of civilization blotted out, smoothed over, and transformed into something new— Rome was a city that had mastered the art of disguise.

At the end of our third day, we decided it was time to head north. That night, at a bus stop, we met three girls from Canada. Rachel, being the genuine extrovert she was, struck up a conversation, and the next thing I knew, we were all sitting at the sidewalk table of a rundown restaurant, sharing heaping plates of pasta. Vespas buzzed past like mosquitos, mingling their scent of exhaust with Rome's pervading cigarette smoke. Two of the new girls were flying home the next day, but Margaret was staying. She had another month before she had to go home, so naturally, Rachel invited her to join us. Who could resist Rachel? We were a threesome by the following day.

Everything about Margaret was perky. With her short, brown cap of hair, large round eyes, and slightly overgrown front teeth, she was what the expression "breath of fresh air" had been invented to describe. She was just familiar enough to remind me of home, and yet just exotic enough, with her occasional odd pronunciations, to be interesting. On her backpack was an image of the Canadian flag, a leaf which stood on its own stem, every bit as perky as Margaret.

We gathered together the following morning at our prearranged meeting place and mapped out the next few weeks. Having been part of a girl-group before, I didn't expect the easy cooperation, equal voice, and attention paid to all. Those words had only been paid lip service by the Kitty Committee, but Rachel and Margaret lived it.

Margaret and I had rail passes good for nearly everywhere in Europe. Rachel was pay-as-you-go, but she didn't seem to have any monetary constraints. We stopped at the American Express office just before leaving Rome to pick up a fresh supply of cash for Rachel. She offered to pay for almost everything, although we didn't usually accept.

"My dad's rich," she explained. "He's happy for me to have traveling companions."

But I wasn't quite ready to be put on the payroll as a traveling companion. I never wanted to forfeit my options, and leaving anytime I wanted was an option that I kept in reserve but hadn't been tempted to use. Margaret, like me, had finished two years of college; unlike me, she was two years older. Rachel was two years older than Margaret so, once again, I was the youngest, although I was never made to feel that way.

We took the bus to Orvieto, where a French couple offered us a ride to Civita di Bagnoregio, a walled city that was ancient the day Christ was born, built on the side of an extinct volcano. A long, steep climb up a walkway to the town that claims less than ten fulltime residents, it had earned the nickname of "the dying city" as the edges of its plateau were slowly crumbling away. As we traipsed through the narrow streets, my nose buried in the pamphlet recounting the town's history, I knew that had I been five years younger, more naïve, and untouched by life, had I been traveling with my parents, I would have complained loudly and energetically if I'd been forced to make that journey. I wondered if I was finally growing up. Finally becoming equal to the stage of life I was passing through.

Pushing further north by train, the ever-shifting landscape rushed by the windows of our train, reminding me of California. But the villages and cities couldn't have been more different. Italy was a modern country that lived side by side with its past. Everywhere were reminders, from the Arena in Verona to the narrow cobblestone alleyways in Venice. People lived in harmony with their history. People adapted to it, and their lives moved on and were better off for it.

Venice was a city to be happily lost in. Again, Rachel paid for a very modest room which was better than anything I could afford. She reasoned that since she would've been paying for the room anyway, there was no reason to collect money from us. And I let it go because my funds weren't inexhaustible, and I had no good reason to end my journey any sooner than was absolutely necessary. I was already pondering how many and what variety of cold-weather clothes it would take to get me through a winter in Europe, and where I could purchase them at a discounted price. Margaret let it go as well.

In Venice, we met two young men from Germany. They had hashish, they said, and would like to share it with us. I'd never tried drugs before—nothing beyond alcohol, which I considered to be in a different category—a remnant from Kitty Committee days. Nathan smoked weed, but never around me out of respect. But Rachel and Margaret were eager, so we joined them at their place, a nice hotel room on the third floor overlooking a canal. We shut the windows tight, lest the odor leak into the walkway below us. One of the Germans jammed a small wedge of hash into a tiny gold pipe and sucked in the flame from a match. The pipe was passed from person to person, a thin blue trail of smoke rising from its bowl, undulating like a cobra. When it got to me, I hesitated long enough to catch up with my doubts. Everything inside me screamed no, but I was on a mission to bust through all the rules of my former life, so I pulled the smoke into my lungs the way I'd observed the others doing before me. My explosion of coughing gave me away, but by the second and third round I'd gotten the hang of it, and by then it had gotten the best of me.

The lightning bolt from Heaven didn't strike as I had half-expected—instead my hash-head led to an evening of circuitous thought and conversation that seemed fascinating at the time, but in retrospect was often ridiculous. It led to boundless energy and appetite, followed by mild dizziness and extreme fatigue. It led to impassioned longing for Nathan and much second-guessing of my sanity. By the end of the night, I'd broken a Kitty Committee commandment and vowed never to do so again. And by the end of the night, something else had happened. We'd picked up a fourth member of our traveling group—one of the young men whose name was Gunther. Gunther decided he was more interested in going wherever we were going than heading back to Germany with his countryman.

"We're the four musketeers now," Rachel claimed once we were tucked in for the night. A familiar and unwelcome chill skittered down the back of my neck.

"There weren't four musketeers," I said.

Everyone should travel blind at least once in her life. And Rachel was right—it's better if you share it with someone. I'd traveled my entire life but always within the confines of family, so it just felt like moving from home to home until I got to Indian Springs. And once I got to Indian Springs, all I wanted was a way to lock myself down in a solid social foundation, to make myself invincible to forces which otherwise had the power to crush me. But facing each day as a surprise-in-waiting was a new experience for me. Every day, every hour, every minute was a chance to reinvent myself. Life, time, identity—each one became a moving target. Aim. Shoot. And then aim again. I wondered if I could work out a way to make it never stop. To always be one step ahead of myself. But no matter how kind and fun and relatable Rachel was, I knew our eventual destination was Mike, her boyfriend in Spain. Rachel and I were on an adventure, not *our* adventure. I was only a piece of the puzzle that would eventually lead her away from me. Although we were less than halfway to that conclusion, I could already feel its hot breath on my neck. Margaret had paired off with Gunther soon after Venice. Everyone had someone except for me, and I only had myself to blame. I missed Nathan. He had wanted me, but I thought I could live more easily without him. Without anyone. I'd been willing to take that risk but I'd begun to suspect I was wrong.

From Venice, we doubled back to the Dolomites—the Italian Alps. We hiked on trails through mountain-top pastures so high that the clanging chorus of cowbells sometimes seemed like a heavenly orchestra concealed in the clouds. From there we slowly made our way to Lake Como, where we traveled by ferry from town to town, each time being greeted by a scrappy terrier that precisely resembled the dog in the town we had just left behind. Gunther and Margaret, in their near constant state of hash-induced euphoria, found this highly entertaining and had no end of conspiracy theories to explain the doggy clones everywhere we went. It was only when I caught sight of a crate near the boarding ramp that we discovered the dog belonged to a crew member and had been traveling with us all along. His name was Dolce, and he was let loose to take care of business well before the passengers were allowed to disembark.

Those were the lighthearted moments I remember. I also remember my blacker moods. A few weeks earlier in Milan, we came across a couple from France who spoke English well enough to hang out with us. They were somewhat older than our group—perhaps in their thirties, maybe even into their forties. We spent an evening visiting clubs and bars until we were all bleary from lack of sleep. Even then the couple, Michel and Veronique, wanted to keep going, proving that age didn't equal stamina. Instead we invited them to our room, where Gunther lit up the hash pipe and invited them to share a bowl. Although I wasn't imbibing, the closed windows and small room gave me a contact high. As the night wore on and my eyes grew heavier, I felt an acute unease about our new "friends" and wondered if the others were feeling the same thing. Veronique had bruises on her upper arm, and another on the back of her neck. To my foggy brain, she seemed damaged—like Maggie. Michel, on the other hand, gave off a whiff of something else that was uncomfortably familiar. Slowly, over the course of a few hours, he had taken control of our loose free-wheeling conversation. There was a distinct shift in the others' behavior—they were beginning to defer to him, maybe because they perceived that since he was older, he must be wiser. He had an opinion on nearly every subject, and his opinions weren't negotiable. Even Rachel, ever-trusting soul that she was, sensed something amiss. By the time she suggested we call it a night, I saw a diabolical glint in Michel's eyes that I couldn't convince myself was the product of my imagination. They left with promises to meet up with us the following day.

"I don't know about you guys," Rachel said once they were gone. "But I don't want to hang out with them tomorrow."

"I agree," I said, relieved I didn't have to be the one to say it.

"I think he's evil," Margaret said. "Did you see the bruises on Veronique? Wonder if he hits her."

"Do you believe that?" Gunther raised his eyebrows. "That a person can be . . . evil?"

"I do," Margaret said without the slightest hesitation. "One hundred percent."

"I don't know," I said.

"You do realize this is probably the most discussed question in all of history." Margaret lifted Gunther's lax arm and snuggled underneath it. "Philosophers and theologians have been debating that question for thousands of years. We actually talked about it in one of my philosophy classes." Her eyes grew alive with interest.

"I don't think so," Rachel said. "I'm not religious, so I don't see it that way. I think everyone's born pure and innocent. There's no such thing as a bad baby."

"Evil baby," Gunther said, and we all laughed. "What if this evil baby picks up a machine gun and shoots a hundred people? Should he go to jail?"

Rachel smiled and shook her head slowly. "I'm serious," she said. "I think it's wrong to say there is such a thing as evil because societies use it as an excuse to go to war or to enslave entire populations . . . like thinking that people are godless and, therefore, inherently evil was justification for colonialism and the crusades."

"You should've been in my class," Margaret said. "You would've been so awesome."

"I think Michel is evil," I said, and they all turned to me. Surprised.

"Why do you say that?" Rachel asked. The hurt in her eyes made me feel as though I had personally wounded her.

"I dunno." I shrugged my shoulders and slouched forward to let my hair cover my face. It was a terrible response. If I was ready to seat Michel in the throne of Beelzebub, I should at least have a thought-out answer. I should at least have kept my mouth shut.

"I mean . . ." Rachel wouldn't let it go, and I believed at that moment it would shake the foundation of her world were she to buy into the notion of evil. *She must have a very lovely family,* I thought. *A lovely childhood. She must have been very lucky in life.*

"I think that what happens to a child after they're born can influence how they'll react to a situation. Bad parenting, for example. Abuse."

It was as though Rachel had slapped me across the face, but of course she knew nothing of my life. My parents weren't bad parents. They certainly weren't abusive. They were loving parents who had taught me right from wrong. So what did that make me?

"What if a person has good parents?" I asked. "And that person was raised with all the right values and morals. Could a good person become evil? Can they grow up to do bad things?"

The scent of hashish hung thick in the room. The light was low, casting my friends in a less than benevolent light. Dark shadows dropped from their brows to leech all compassion out of their eyes. Their faces, darkened by the weak overhead lights, looked gaunt. Hungry. I felt my senses in danger of spinning out of control. I grabbed onto the leg of the chair I was leaning against, feeling my fingernails dig into the palm of my hand.

"I don't believe that a person who was raised the right way would ever behave in an evil manner," Rachel insisted. "I just don't believe it."

Margaret watched us, her head swiveling back and forth as though she was observing a tennis match. Gunther had sunk to the floor, his head resting in her lap. Margaret absentmindedly sifted her fingers through his wavy, blond hair—silver in the dimness of the room.

"Is there an age when a person's value system isn't fully formed?" I asked, desperate for a convincing answer from Rachel, whom I'd grown to respect. Who seemed to have all the answers, as naïve as I knew they were. "Can a person be lost during that time if they have the wrong influences outside of their family? When their morals are still squishy?"

Rachel considered this. "I suppose that's possible," she said. She regarded me as though we were meeting for the first time. *Rachel, this is Grace. Grace, this is Rachel. I'd like to introduce you to my friend, Evil.*

"Wow, I think we may have smoked more than we realized," Margaret said. Her eyes glazed over. Her eyelids were at half-mast. Her plump lips parted slightly, pushed aside by her endearing front teeth. "This is intense."

I loosened my grip on the chair as my breath returned to its easy rhythm. "I agree with Rachel. I don't think we should meet up with them tomorrow." It was no longer important for Rachel to reassure me—I knew she didn't have the answer. "Let's ditch them and check out of here early. I have a bad feeling."

"Okay, Grace," Rachel reached out and covered my hand gently with hers. "I'm glad you agree because I trust your instincts."

"Come, Evil Baby." Gunther rose to his feet and pulled a reluctant Margaret to her feet with a hand under each of her arms. "Let's go to bed."

There were other bleak moments such as the times when my traveling mates shopped for sundries while I lingered near the postcards searching for an image that could somehow convey thoughts that weren't even clear to me—express my forgiveness and regret via airmail straight into Nathan's heart. Sometimes I'd go so far as to buy one, and then in the evening, after dinner when the others were curled up with a book or with each other, I'd formulate an entire speech in my mind as to all the ways I'd wronged Nathan and all the reasons he might consider forgiving me. Then I'd shorten it to the few sentences which could actually fit onto the back of a postcard. Sentences distilled from the thick stew of confusion boiling inside of me into a palatable and easily digested consommé. I'd pick up the pen I always carried with me and squeeze out those few words into the tiny space meted out for the message, equal in size to the card's destination. Then I'd read it once. Twice. Sometimes three times, before tearing it into shreds.

Nathan didn't know my heart, and he didn't know my history. But he'd been the one person in my life who had tried to get to the bottom of both.

I was sorry to say goodbye to Italy after a month of traveling through its cities, towns, and villages. Between Italy and Turkey, I'd been nourished and, in a sense, reborn. Entering Switzerland, witnessing firsthand its harsh, cold beauty, staring into its glacial eyes—breathtaking yet forbidding—I felt a sense of foreboding as though I'd forgotten something. Something in a dream that would come to me at the most inopportune moment. Walking down a street. Sipping a cup of tea. Losing myself in a book. Or when the hour was late; the night was black and scarred with starlight; and I was laying myself down to sleep, eyelids closing against the cares of the world.

I'd promised Luke constant reassurance in the form of regular communication, but I hadn't upheld my part of the bargain beyond the occasional few words jotted on a postcard on the fly. I had prearranged pick-up locations for receiving Luke's letters, and my previously booked hostel in Bern was next on my list, even though we'd be staying elsewhere. We arrived in that capital city and walked around the entire perimeter in an hour, stopping along the way to see the famed city bears and admire its breathtaking views. While the others relaxed over lunch, I visited the hostel where two letters from Luke were being held for me.

The first letter was mainly chatty about the baby, Linda's pregnancy, and even Bob the cat. The second contained the news that I realized I'd been dreading. Dad was feeling poorly, and the doctors couldn't figure out why he was having this recurrence of malaria or why the medication wasn't working. He told me not to worry (impossible), to enjoy myself, and to get home quickly. It cast a further pall over the country, deepening the uneasiness I'd already been feeling. I wanted to get back to warmer, more familiar climes, but we still had the rest of Switzerland and Amsterdam to explore before heading south for our ultimate destination of Spain.

"I was thinking," Rachel said that night after Margaret and Gunther had retired to their private corner where, by mutual agreement, we didn't look, "do you want me to ask Mike if he could get you a position in the English language school? Since you said you don't have other plans, and you'll be needing the money."

This seemed like the opportunity I'd been waiting for. A way to prolong my travels. To avoid having to make serious life decisions. I spoke Spanish fluently, and Spain was a country that felt familiar to me even though I'd never been there. Rachel would be there for at least a little while until I got my bearings. It was perfect.

"Would you mind?" I asked.

We continued our travels through Switzerland: the alpine villages, lakeside hamlets, and the bustling cities of Zurich and Basel, where Gunther looked wistfully across the river toward Germany. We discussed venturing into Germany, but Margaret, Rachel, and I had laid out our plans, and Rachel and I were anxious to move on. By then, I was already wishing we hadn't included Amsterdam as a destination. Rachel, who could feel Spain and Mike calling to her, was with me, and we assumed Margaret felt the same way. Her time was limited, although she'd already extended it once after receiving a wire transfer of funds from home.

I wish I could remember the names of all the people we met along the way. Of all the countries demarcated on a global map, it seemed one crucial country was missing. It was a realm inhabited by global citizens constantly on the move, searching for something new, seeking something better, looking for answers to whatever they'd left behind. Young people mainly, but also middle-aged and even elderly people. It was a country of shifting borders which I imagined looked something like an amoeba—a giant blob, continuously adapting to its restless population. The country of lost and adventurous souls.

Our last day in Basel, we met for breakfast after an evening of exploration that ended with Margaret and Gunther sleeping on the sofa of Gunther's childhood friend, and Rachel and me in a hostel.

"Well, ladies." Margaret sipped from her cappuccino and then placed the steaming cup on the table. It was a cold but brilliantly sunny day, and a halo of sunlight glowed just behind her head. "You two have been amazing, and I've loved traveling with you, but I think this is where we say goodbye."

I hadn't expected this, although I knew that our bonds were temporary at best. Even Rachel seemed to be caught off guard. "What's up, Margaret?"

"Gunther really wants to show me his home."

Gunther smiled and nodded agreement. He wore a knit beanie with exposed tufts of blond hair curling down over his startling blue eyes.

"And he wants me to meet his family. We're so close to Germany, so it seems like a logical time. Who knows? If all goes well, maybe he'll come back with me to Canada and meet my family."

"Canada, I've heard, is beautiful," Gunther said in his thickly accented English. "Like Margaret." He gazed at her with such admiration that I felt physically wounded by my separation from Nathan. I wondered if Rachel was feeling the same.

"Awww," Rachel said. "That's sad, guys, but sweet. We'll miss you, Margaret. You too, Gunther. But I think you're doing the right thing." She reached across the table and put her hand on top of Margaret's, giving it a light squeeze. "I hope it works out for the two of you; I really do."

There was no logical reason I should feel betrayed, but I did. I barely knew Margaret, although I'd come to enjoy her company immensely in a very short period of time. Even after

Gunther arrived on the scene and she began to pull away, I continued to relish the times we spent together. She was such a pleasant addition to our group. So easygoing, full of interesting but useless information and entertaining anecdotes. And yet the words of the Kitty Committee rang out in my head. Rule number four: no boys should ever come before or between members of the Kitty Committee.

But this wasn't the Kitty Committee. Rachel and Margaret and I were just fellow travelers, citizens of the country of Lost and Adventurous Souls. We were only loosely bound, although our mutual respect ran deep. It wasn't Rachel or me who made Margaret squeal and moan with delight late into the evening after they thought we were sleeping. It wasn't Rachel or me who transformed Margaret's impish smile into a full-out grin, her top lip riding up over her beautifully expressive and boldly visible front teeth, banners of happiness. Technically, Gunther was part of our group as well, although he hadn't been involved in planning the itinerary. And Gunther was a boy, a man. There was also that.

I hesitated for only a moment. "I think it's great," I said. "But I'm really going to miss you. Both of you."

And I realized it was true. I didn't hold it against Margaret that she'd thrown her lot in with Gunther instead of us. I would still miss her a great deal.

I had transformed from a reclusive world traveler to one who recognized her dependence on humankind and human kindness.

By the time we arrived in Barcelona, it had been six months since I'd left San Francisco. Five months that Rachel and I had been joined at the hip. During that period of time, Rachel had become the best friend I'd ever had after Maggie, but I didn't tell her things about my past. Rachel was so good and so certain of the goodness in others, how could I shake her belief in me and risk losing her friendship? I couldn't, although Rachel, more than anyone, would have certainly been a sympathetic ear.

We trudged up the steps to the second floor of an ornate apartment building with a pink façade. The official end to our journey—this was where Mike lived. I was sure the straps of my backpack had left permanent grooves on my shoulders after so many months of traveling. The pack and its contents had become old friends, imprinting my identity as efficiently as a self-portrait. My pack was the shell to my turtle, but now I faced the prospect of planting roots and discarding the shell. Saying goodbye to its familiar and constant weight, which had grounded me to the Earth. Exposing myself to a new society where I'd see the same people every day, go to the same coffee shops and markets, learn the names of the people who worked in those places, and make myself vulnerable to their familiarity. Finding a place to live. And, most importantly, relinquishing the constant presence and reassurance of Rachel, although I'd be staying with them until I found a place of my own. This was what Spain, and more specifically Barcelona, represented to me, and why it lost some of its luster as a result.

"You look different than I imagined," Mike said, squinting between me and a well-worn photograph he was holding in his outstretched hand. Rachel had mailed the photograph to him while we were still in Italy. I didn't doubt that I looked different after all that time. I was road-weary, and the waist of my pants told me I was a lot thinner. I'd been wearing my hair in girlish braids the day of the photo and was certain I must look a good five years older than the image. I laughed.

"Hi, I'm Grace," I said, extending my hand to Mike, who

looked much different than the small photo Rachel carried of him. He looked older, his hair neatly combed and short, his build a little on the heavy side, his eyes kind and creased at the corner with laugh lines. He seemed almost dad-like, although he couldn't have been more than twenty-three. He ignored the handshake and, instead, pulled me to his wide chest and wrapped a large arm around me, gracing me with a friendly back-thumping. Then, moving on from the warm welcome he'd given me, he faced Rachel and held out his arms. She jumped into them, and they wrapped themselves in a cocoon of kisses and necking which made me blush and turn away.

"Sorry," Mike said, remembering his manners after a minute. "C'mon, Grace. I fixed lunch for you. I hope you're all hungry."

I slipped past them through the doorway, scouting for an area where I could make myself invisible if it came to another bout of loving, which it did immediately after the door closed behind us. I sat on a chair in the small dining area and propped my elbows on the table as though I had purposely chosen that moment to sit by myself and reflect on the napkin and fork in front of me. Delicious smells wafted from the kitchen, and I cautiously took a look around. The place was small but tidy and felt homey and welcoming. For two, that is. I knew I'd have to move out soon.

"Thanks for taking care of my girl for me," Mike said over our hot lunch. I ate until I finally stopped from embarrassment, realizing I hadn't eaten with such gusto since I left Istanbul. Maybe Mike gave me that same sense of home and welcome, which freed me to let down my guard and replenish myself. Rachel was a lucky girl. But I'd been lucky once too, I realized. Until I threw it away.

"I set up an interview for you on Friday," Mike said. "Ten in the morning. The guy who owns the school. I think you'll like him, and it's a huge bonus you speak Spanish because that's not even a requirement. Just make sure to never speak it in class." He winked at me. "Kind of defeats the purpose."

Mike was talking like I already had the job.

"Do you speak Spanish?" I asked.

"Si. Un poco," he said. "But seriously, my Spanish sucks. And there's that whole castellano thing here, so even the little I do speak sounds bad."

Rachel couldn't stop grinning at him, and as soon as I'd helped clear and rinse the dishes, I made my excuses to go out and explore the city. The truth was I was bone-tired and would have loved nothing more than to lay down on Mike's couch and continue our conversation. Maybe even catch a few winks. But I knew I had to leave. Five months was a long time to be apart when you were in love, and there was a prearranged mail pick-up location in Barcelona where I was sure there'd be mail from Luke or my parents waiting for me.

The news from Luke wasn't good. Dad wasn't getting better, so they'd flown him to Johannesburg where there were better medical facilities. They were doing further testing. His symptoms were flu-like, achiness and fever that never subsided. Chills. Headache. I remembered how Dad struggled with the pain after breaking his back. How bleak life became for him. For us all. And then he'd recovered and returned to what he loved best only to be slain by this new torment. My stomach clutched with pain and tears sprung from my eyes. It wasn't fair. Life wasn't fair. But then I already knew that, didn't I?

I lost myself in the streets and sidewalks and alleys of Barcelona. I walked until my feet felt like useless and foreign appendages. And then I walked some more. By the time I returned to Mike's apartment, Rachel and Mike were draped in smiles. A modicum of peace was restored to my soul. *People can do this for each other*, I thought. *Bring love and happiness.*

Fulfilment. People could do so much more than cause sorrow. I wanted that for myself.

So much of my life seemed to happen in coffee shops, perhaps because I spent an inordinate amount of time in them or perhaps because people are more open to each other in a coffee shop. More willing to take a risk with a stranger, driven by the intimacy of surroundings and the caffeine. In my experience, I've found that people who sit singly in coffee shops are normally there to observe or be observed. One day, I walked into a café for both of those reasons. And it was there I met Karim—like Rachel before him . . . and Nathan before that.

I hadn't actually planned to enter that particular coffee shop on that particular day. I'd just come from an interview with the owner of the English language school where Mike was teaching, and I was on my way back to his apartment, which I knew would be empty that time of day. When I walked past the sidewalk tables, my eye caught a glimpse of the most beautiful man I'd ever seen. More out of curiosity than anything else, I swiveled on my right foot, thereby applying my emergency brake before passing the entrance to the shop. To someone on the street, I might have looked like I just remembered something which could only be found inside. I hoped I wasn't too obvious.

Beauty being the inexplicable quality it is—nothing more than a fortunate conglomeration of features, the size and spacing of which is pleasing to the human eye—I had to take a closer look. Verify its existence to my own satisfaction. I placed my order and then went outside, holding my drink, and took a seat just behind him where I could observe without risk of being observed. He had thick, shiny black hair tapering down the back of his neck, broad shoulders with a lean physique, strong arms that made his t-shirt seem too small, which may have been his intent. But beautiful people probably have a sixth sense that comes from a lifetime of being watched by strangers. He turned around in his chair and looked right at me. When he smiled, his teeth were white and even. His lips full and sensual. This guy was just plain perfect, at least in a physical sense.

"Hi," he said in a smooth-as-silk voice.

"Hi." I blushed ten shades of hot pink, the kind I could feel down to my chest.

"American?" he asked.

I'd come to realize that Americans were an easy bunch to peg—I was good at it myself. And anyway, there was no use denying my citizenship even if I'd wanted to. I considered trying my Spanish on him to see if he'd fall for it, but I knew my Spanish was the South American variety, and he'd never believe I was from Spain.

"Yep." It was embarrassing how a random collection of facial features had turned me into a gelatinous mess.

"Mind if I sit with you?" he asked, pulling a chair up without waiting for my answer. His English was very good, even with an accent I recognized wasn't Spanish.

I smiled stiffly and waved a hand at the formerly empty slot that he was already occupying.

"Are you hot?" he asked solicitously, his eyes so sincere that I almost believed he was puzzled by my reaction.

"Yes," I said, although the day was only just warm. I twisted my hair into a knot which had the dual effect of cooling the back of my neck and giving me something to do with my hands. I'd been caught red-handed by this man. Maybe he was just having a little fun with me and would soon be on his way, allowing me to slink away with my proverbial tail between my legs.

"My name is Karim," he said. "And yours?"

"Grace."

"Grace is a beautiful name." He smiled wistfully, as if just remembering a favorite aunt with the same name. "I don't get much chance to speak English," he said. "And I'm afraid I might lose it one day without practicing."

"I'm afraid of the same thing," I replied in Spanish. Showing off.

"Ahhh." He raised his eyebrows. "You speak very well. And how does this happen?" he asked in fluent Spanish.

"I grew up in Central and South America—other places too—but that's where I learned Spanish. How about you?"

"When I was much younger, my teacher was from England," he pivoted back to English. "He gave lessons for free to the children who wanted to learn. And my parents encouraged me to take advantage of this gift of language."

A couple came outside to sit at the table Karim had just vacated. The man had a coffee in each hand. He leaned over carefully to set the cups on the table without spilling, and I noticed his companion seized the opportunity to steal a furtive glance at Karim. But Karim seemed to be oblivious to her interest, attuned only to me. I felt proud even though I had only just met him.

He sipped the last of his coffee, which he'd started well before I got there. He leaned back in his seat and pulled a pack of cigarettes from his pocket. He tapped the bottom to partially expel a single cigarette and held it in my direction.

"No thanks," I said. "I don't smoke."

He laughed. "This is what they say about Americans. Very healthy except maybe eating too much."

His smile made me glad that I was at my thinnest. And then I thought of Maggie and the last time I'd seen her. I silently begged her forgiveness for harboring that thought. He leaned forward and hunched over a match then reclined back in his chair. He smiled at me. I recoiled at the smell of the smoke, which I'd never been able to tolerate. It diminished Karim in my eyes, but only for a moment.

"Do you come here often, Miss Grace?"

Hearing my name coiled around those vocal chords and expelled from those lips stirred something very primal in me.

"Yes," I lied, immediately regretting it. If he came here frequently, he'd wonder why he never saw me before. The truth was I'd never been there before and probably never would have set foot there if I hadn't seen him that day. "You?"

"No, never," he said. "I'm only stopping for a short break, and then I must go. I like to try different shops around the city. I've been to many but never here. Please correct me if you hear me say a wrong word in the English." He twisted the corner of his mouth to aim the smoke away from me.

"You're perfect," I said. "I mean . . . your English is perfect. But just say English. Not *the* English."

"Ah, yes, thank you." He smiled, and I wondered how someone who drank coffee and smoked cigarettes could have such white teeth.

We chatted a little more. Aimless topics that I felt were chosen by Karim more for a chance to practice his English than any other real purpose. When he reached the end of his cigarette, he leaned forward and ground it into an ashtray emblazoned with the name of the café.

"And now . . ." He rose to his feet. "Regretfully, I must return to work. It has been my pleasure speaking with you, Miss Grace." He slightly inclined his head to me, and I half expected him to take up my hand and brush his lips against the back of it the way handsome and suave men do in the movies. "I hope you enjoy your stay."

He was about to walk out of my life forever. I couldn't even pass this café again in the hopes of running into him because he'd already said he never came here. *Let him go*, I reasoned. *You saw what you came to see—his beauty up close and in person. You wanted to see if the interior would match the exterior, and yes, he was a nice person, but no different from anyone else you might meet on the street. Polite. Friendly. Say goodbye. Let him go.*

"Can I see you again?" I asked, shocking myself so completely that I felt as if an alien had taken over my brain stem and was breathing and speaking on my behalf.

To his credit, Karim looked a little shocked too. He sat down and leaned forward across the table. He looked down at his hands, as if they would provide him with an answer to my preposterous question, and then he looked back up at me.

"I must be honest with you, Miss Grace," he said sorrowfully. "About two things."

"Grace," I said. "You can just call me Grace."

"Alright then, Grace. I must be honest with you."

"About two things," I repeated stupidly.

"First," he said. "I work very hard and very long hours, leaving me little time for . . . social."

"Socializing," I said. He wanted me to correct him, didn't he? "Me too. Well, not now, but I hope to be working very hard . . . and very long. Very soon." Was I begging? Did the alien now have complete control of me?

"Second," he said, and I noticed he said the word *second* much more firmly than *first*. And then a long pause while he consulted his hands again. "I am promised, or committed, as you say it."

But I didn't say it, I thought. "Oh. Sorry." My face flushed warm.

"I am . . . she is . . . in my home. Where I am from. And I'm not innocent, you understand. But you are a nice girl, and you must know this."

The woman at the table near us hadn't stopped stealing

glances of Karim. And who could blame her, although her companion was about to get angry if she didn't become more discreet. *Innocent?* What did he mean by that? I concluded that it meant he played around.

"She's in your home?" I asked. "Here? Right now?"

"Not here," he said. "In Morocco. We will be married when I've made enough money to return."

"Oh, I see." But all I could think of was that I wanted him. Had to have him. Morocco was a long way away, and who knew if he'd ever have enough money to go back? "Thank you for being honest, but it's okay with me."

"You still care to see me?"

"Yes," I nodded.

We made plans to meet later that night for dinner.

"I was going to whip up my famous paella for dinner tonight," Mike said when he got home that night. Rachel had arrived home only minutes earlier, having spent the better part of her day on a Picasso walking tour. No matter the town or city, Rachel went straight for the art exhibits and museums, while I normally trudged through the streets, window-shopping and hitting the coffee shops when I was too tired to walk anymore. In this way, we were complete opposites and yet had somehow managed to meld into perfect traveling companions.

"I have a date tonight," I announced. "So I won't be eating with you guys. Sorry. I'd have given you more notice if I'd known."

"A date?" Rachel yanked off her shoe and massaged the arch of her foot. She looked up at me with something resembling either pain or amazement. "You mean, a real live romantically inclined get-together with a real live human being type of date?"

"Why're you giving her a hard time?" Mike wrapped a beefy

arm around my shoulder and gave me a gentle shake. "My girl Grace here probably has plenty of dates. Men probably trip over each other to ask her out."

"I'm sorry, I don't mean to. It's just that for the past four months, all Grace has talked about is Nathan and how much she misses him. So forgive me for being a little surprised." She yanked off the other shoe and went to work on that foot.

"Nathan?" Mike looked at me. I was mildly irritated at Rachel for bringing up what I'd told her in private. "Who's Nathan?"

"It's an inquisition," I exclaimed. "Mom and Dad, I didn't recognize you. Anyway, he's just my old boyfriend, but we broke up before I left San Francisco, so no big deal."

"Just your old boyfriend?" Rachel cocked her head as though taking a fresh look at me and seeing things she'd never seen before.

There was a knock on the door.

"That's probably him," I said and then hurriedly added, "his name is Karim."

Karim was indeed on the other side of the door, holding a bouquet of red carnations. I'd assumed our date was casual, but Karim had changed into slacks and a button-down dress shirt. His hair was slick, combed back from his face. Although it was almost dark outside, he had sunglasses perched on top of his head. He looked magnificent, and I felt a little sorry for Mike, the only other male in the room, but almost any man would have suffered in comparison.

"So, you're Karim," Mike said extending a hand which Karim shook. "You take care of my girl, okay? Make sure you have Cinderella home by midnight, Prince Charming." He turned to me and winked.

"Yes, Dad," I laughed and Karim joined in once he caught on to the joke.

Mike looked him up and down. "Damn, you're good looking," he said, apparently having no issues with self-esteem. Everyone laughed, and Rachel finally stopped gawking and introduced herself.

Having assured me before we left that the jeans I was wearing were perfect, I soon saw the reason why. Cinderella's pumpkin for the night was a two-seated scooter, and although I had to close my eyes and hold my breath on multiple occasions, it allowed me to wrap my arms tightly around his waist. His body felt much harder than Nathan's. Leaner. He smelled like some sort of masculine fragrance. Nathan eschewed any artificial scent beyond deodorant and soap, and I'd never been a big fan of it myself, but for some reason it further added to Karim's appeal. Zipping through the streets of Barcelona on that unusually warm night was an aphrodisiac like no other. We finally pulled up in front of a clean but bare-bones Moroccan restaurant which Karim said was very good. We talked for hours over a meal that I subconsciously registered as delicious but barely paid attention to. When Karim looked at his watch, I braced for the evening to be over.

"It's late," he said. "Almost midnight. I should get you back to your apartment."

"You know he didn't mean that, don't you?" And when Karim lifted a quizzical eyebrow, I elaborated. "Mike was just kidding when he said I had to be back by midnight."

"Yes, I know. But, sadly, I have to be at work in five hours."

I felt like an idiot. Of course I hadn't considered that someone who made deliveries to local markets would begin their workday well before most other people.

"I'm sorry. Duh, I'm dumb. Why don't I get a taxi so you don't have to go out of your way?"

But he wouldn't hear of it, so we zipped through the streets, retracing our route until we were back in front of Mike's apartment.

"I had a great time," I said. "And I can tell your English is already improving. So, anytime you want to practice . . ."

We looked at each other, and I imagined all kinds of things I could say to him. But I didn't want to talk anymore, so I leaned over impulsively and kissed him on the mouth. Still straddling the scooter, he hooked one hand behind my waist and pulled me close. I had a thirst for Karim at that moment that felt unquenchable. The heady scent of his cologne made me woozy. He moved his hand up my spine, catching the back of my neck and bunching my hair in his hand. Then he pulled me closer until our lips met and our tongues dove for each other. When his hand found my breast, I knew I wouldn't be the one to stop. Seconds later, still astride the scooter, he pulled away and looked up at me.

"I have always thought that sleep is much overrated," he said. "You?"

"Definitely overrated," I said. "Who needs it?"

"Hop on?" he asked more than suggested. And when I did, he paused only long enough for me to refasten my helmet before buzzing away.

That night began a series of nights, each more lustful than the last. From the moment he knocked on my door, I never doubted I'd end up in Karim's bed. He was only the second person I'd been sexually intimate with. Only the third I'd ever kissed. Nathan and I had approached each other slowly and cautiously, dancing around each other before making our move to intimacy, but with Karim it was immediate and absolute. Two weeks later, I'd moved in with him and was working part-time at the English language school.

Karim was never less than completely honest about his ultimate goal of returning to the woman he would marry, and in case I needed reminding, he spoke of it often. It more than stung, it occasionally made me feel physically ill. But I'd gone in naively believing things might change, and I clung to that. Spain was here and was real. Morocco was close, but on a different continent altogether. I was here. I was real.

"Grace," he said to me one night, our bodies naked under a thin sheet that left him exposed from the waist up. The night was warm enough to leave the window open, allowing in street noises and the flashing light of the restaurant across the street. My fingertips traced the muscles of his chest, raising its tiny hairs on end. "It's a Christian name, no?"

"Yes. I guess so, but it doesn't have to be."

"I believe it has religious significance," he said. "Do you know the significance?"

"The way my parents taught me, grace is God's blessing and help, regardless of whether we sin. But some people use it just to mean . . . like graceful. Or the prayer we say before we eat."

"It's a beautiful name." He stroked the side of my cheek with the back of his long elegant hand. He tucked a loose strand of hair behind my ear. "For a beautiful woman. Are you a Christian, Grace?"

We really didn't know a thing about each other beyond the topography of our naked bodies and the light, easy truths that strangers pass back and forth.

"I don't know. No, I guess I'm not. Well, technically I am because I was baptized." I'd had to answer this question for myself my senior year of high school. Once I'd done that, I had no appetite to revisit the path that had taken me to that place.

"So, technically you are Christian? Are you allowed to believe in your Christian God only technically?"

This was a good thing, right? Taking our relationship to the next level beyond just combining our flesh. Karim wanting to find out what made me Grace. Who I was, beginning with the most basic of all tenets. Constructing me in his mind from the inside out.

"I don't believe, okay? Maybe I'm spiritual, but what's out there is unknowable. How can anyone believe when the world is the way it is?"

"I do," Karim said. "Even though there's much I don't know or understand."

"Then I'm happy for you," I said. "But I don't." I rolled over on my back to avoid his eyes. Discussing religion in bed was out of the realm of my limited experience, and it raised all sorts of warning flags instilled in me since birth. But Karim was a fully integrated man who didn't compartmentalize his life the way I did.

"How would your family feel if you brought me to your village?" I decided to turn the tables. It was a relationship-killing question, I knew that. But we didn't really have a relationship according to Karim.

He propped himself up on his elbow to peer into my eyes, our post-coital hide-and-seek. His brows knit with concern.

"They would be very unhappy," he said. "But you already knew this, didn't you?"

Of course I did.

"Why? Because I'm not Muslim?"

"Well naturally, there's Zayna because they love her like their own daughter. But the other too. Your parents would be the same if you brought me home."

"No, they wouldn't," I lied.

It was the first time he'd said the name of his fiancée, and it hurt to think of her as a real person with a beautiful name. A girl that Karim's parents loved like a daughter. I was only the girl who shared his bed. The girl they knew nothing about. The thought of ideas keeping us apart—religious beliefs or lack of them—that much I could handle.

Karim was a man to Nathan's boy, although only one year older. Karim had been on his own since the age of seventeen, when he left home and moved to a foreign country to help support his family. Nathan had dreams of being a doctor, but they came easily, financed by his parents. He accepted their money while pretending to be poor. Success or failure for Karim depended on his own initiative and ingenuity. Save up his money to buy his own delivery truck. Eventually hire someone to drive for him so he could move back to Morocco and marry Zayna. Start a family. Save up to buy another truck and hire another driver. Karim's dreams were achievable only if he didn't falter. And he had only himself to fall back on.

I had manipulated Nathan, ignored him, punished him for my own insecurities—and yet he refused to leave me. He refused to withdraw his love and, for that, I hadn't respected him. I was the one to leave, long after it was apparent our relationship was doomed. Karim wouldn't have stood for that, even if I had tried, which I didn't. He was strong and resolute. He was gentle and understanding. But his patience had limits because he was a man who had to survive.

I pondered the meaning of grace—the one I had just shared with Karim. God could be sinned against, under-appreciated, and yet my parents told me His love was steadfast. He would never abandon one of His creations or withhold His blessings. But I didn't believe that. I believed it was up to me to find the good in my life, if there was any to be found—the way I had found Karim. The way I had once found and accepted Nathan into my life.

Luke continued to send letters updating me on Linda and my parents. I, in turn, regaled him with the humorous adventures of teaching English in a foreign country, leaving out the part about Karim. Then, one day, Mike received a call from Luke at his home. Mike covered by telling him I was still at work and arranged a time later that night when Luke could call back. Karim drove me to Mike's apartment where I anxiously waited for the phone to ring.

When it did come, the connection wasn't too bad, but hearing his voice for the first time in nearly six months, Luke sounded like an impersonation of himself. Of course, I always imagined him talking to me, and my parents' words too—I could hear their voices in my head. But those voices were my creation, saying the things that I imagined. Now here was Luke, calling from Sacramento, California. And he had something on his mind that was more than gossip. I prayed for it to be news of his newborn child.

"Gracie," he said without beating around the bush. "Dad's really bad off. They're medevacing him back to the States."

"What's wrong?" I asked, and I must have gone ghostly pale. Karim moved to my side and took my hand. Rachel and Mike, who were sitting on the sofa, looked meaningfully in my direction.

"He's very sick. It happened kind of suddenly even though . . . you know, he hasn't been doing great for a while. But this time it must be really bad. They're flying to Miami. Can you meet them there? I can't leave Linda—the baby's coming any day . . . any hour."

"Why Miami?" I stupidly asked.

"No idea," Luke said. I could hear Matty in the background, loudly demanding something in toddler-talk. "Shhh. Go see Mommy," Luke shifted to the tone adults use with little kids, and then back to me, "It's something to do with the air ambulance company—where they can fly into. Anyway, can you go? I have the flight info and the name and directions to the hospital. I've already wired money for your ticket to the American Express office in Barcelona. I need you to do this, Grace, okay?"

"Of course," I said. "I'll get the first flight out."

"Be strong," he warned.

There was no getting out until the next day and even that required super human effort on my part, with Karim, Mike, and Rachel pitching in. That night, I lay in bed with Karim. Our lovemaking was tender, tinged with regret. The lustful hunger I'd felt since the moment I laid eyes on him was already waning. We talked about how long I'd stay in Miami. When I'd come back, although that wasn't immediately knowable. Karim told me how much he'd miss me and how he'd come to depend on seeing me at the end of each day. Looked forward to it hour by hour.

I already knew I would never come back.

That same night I told Karim everything. Everything I'd never told another soul. Even Carly and Maggie's knowledge of my life stopped after high school, which was where Nathan's picked up. And Rachel knew only what happened after Nathan left off. Everyone knew a little piece of me, but nobody knew the whole. Now, finally someone did.

He didn't say anything once I was done. I believed he was shocked to finally know the girl he'd been sleeping with, but his eyes didn't betray a thing.

"I guess I'm lost," I said, breaking the ice. I thought about the country of Lost and Adventurous Souls.

"No, Grace," he said, allowing the softness of his eyes to fall upon me. "You're just not yet found."

By the time I cleared customs at the Miami Airport, I was a wretched and anxious mess. With only the possessions I'd been carrying on my back for the past six months, I stood in line for a cab, trying to come to terms with being back in the States and all the memories that entailed. Miami was a blast of hot, wet heat, even though I'd emerged into the moonlit night. The airport was crowded, noisy, smelled like exhaust.

Once I got a cab, I settled into the backseat and gave the address for the motel Luke had reserved for me—chosen because it was within walking distance to the hospital. I planned to check in, shower, and then hurry over to see Mom and Dad, whom I hadn't seen in nearly three years. I wondered if they'd notice the change in me. I wondered if I'd notice the change in them. Although Dad was faring poorly, I'd seen him that way before. I knew that variant of Dad and didn't relish meeting him again. I wasn't sure if the rumbling in my stomach was for dinner, breakfast, or just plain nerves. I did my best to ignore it.

When I arrived at the motel, the check-in clerk gave me my room key and a message from Luke instructing me to call the minute I got to my room. The room was spartan with a shabby dresser and a squeaky bed with an orange duvet, which I assumed was meant to match the tropical fruit colors of the painting on the wall. The unit air-conditioner belched out a stream of too-cold air. Every corner of the room that wasn't directly in the path of the air was much too warm. The smell was old and musty. The shower grew black patches of mildew in the grout of its old-fashioned tiles—tropical pink. I decided to call Luke before showering.

A woman's voice picked up on the second ring, identifying herself as Nurse Lincoln in obstetrics.

"I was given this number by my brother, Luke Templeton," I explained. "My name is Grace Templeton."

"Oh yes, Grace," she said. Did I detect pity in her tone? Had Luke told her about Dad's scary situation? "Let me see if he can come to the phone. Your sister-in-law is in labor, but I think we still have a little time."

In labor. Things were coming at me so fast. After about five minutes, Luke picked up. This time the reception was perfect; he sounded as if he could have been in the room. My thumping heart stilled at the reassurance his voice brought.

"Grace," he said. "I'm so sorry."

"Why? Don't be sorry. I'm sorry to bother you when Linda's in labor. I just wanted to let you know I was here, and there was a message to—"

"Dad's gone," Luke interrupted.

And still I didn't hear or perhaps comprehend what he'd just said.

"Wh—what? Where'd he go?"

Had I come to Miami for nothing? Had he been transported somewhere else at the last minute?

"He's dead, Grace. He passed. I'm so sorry that you have to face this on your own." His voice cracked into a sob, but he quickly composed himself. "The baby's almost here."

"Where's Mom?" I knew my time to get the answers I needed was short. The baby wouldn't wait. Not even for my terrible news. Maybe Mom was in the same motel as me. Maybe she was still at the hospital. "What happened?" I was too stunned to even begin to feel sadness.

"They never made it out of Johannesburg," he said. "I couldn't reach you because you were already in the air. I don't know what happened, but they think it was lymphoma. Or some type of bone marrow cancer. I don't know. I think Mom will ask for an autopsy. I don't know what she'll do. I don't know if she's coming back yet. I'm sorry—I just don't know anything." His voice started to crack again, and still I was feeling nothing.

"What should I do, Luke?"

"I'm sorry, Grace. I just don't know what to say. I can help pay for a ticket back to Spain. You can come here and stay with us to see what Mom does next. I . . . I just don't know what to say."

"I love you," I said. "Go be with Linda, and tell her I love her. I'll figure it out and let you know."

"I love you too, Gracie." And this time he could barely get my name out. "Bye."

I sat on the edge of my bed, overwhelmed with the desire to cry. But the tears never came. A siren blared outside the thin walls of my room. I was nauseated by the smell and closeness of the room with its thick, tropical air, and the emptiness in my heart and stomach.

Twenty-four hours earlier I'd shared my body with a man who held me like a precious gem. Who'd brought delight in the form of physical pleasure. Who'd listened to the entirety of my life—the story of the real Grace Templeton—and hadn't judged me to be any less. Now I was truly lost. Sitting in a motel room in a strange city. Alone. No plan for my future. No hand to reach out to me. And still I couldn't make myself cry. I tried to think of the last time I cried, but I couldn't even remember. Was it my junior year of high school? Did I cry then? I just couldn't remember.

I left the room, locking my door behind me. I walked through the parking lot littered with empty beer bottles and cigarette butts. A half-empty red slushee was perched on the curb. A discarded disposable diaper wrapped and taped tightly beside it. I tried to imagine the confluence of events that had led these two random objects to share the same space.

The moon was full and huge, and I imagined that somewhere in that city it was bringing beauty into someone's life. Somewhere in that city, a couple sat on the darkened sand, perhaps with palm fronds whispering above them. They looked out at a sea dimpled with city lights and starlight. They held each other tightly and made promises of eternal love while gazing at the moon. The same cruel moon that looked harshly down upon me with its cold, unforgiving eye.

I walked through the streets until I came to the hospital where my father would have been taken. Perhaps he'd still be alive if he'd gotten there in time. I walked further into neighborhoods where dogs barked when I passed, throwing themselves against chain link fences to warn me away. Where cars slowed to see if I was someone worth talking to. Someone worth messing with. But when the people in the cars got a better look at me, they could see I was neither. They sped off—fearful of what they saw, I imagined. Bathing my silhouette in the blood-red of their taillights. A lost soul.

I walked all night, and by the time the sun began to rise, I could no longer feel my legs, numb from exhaustion. I needed to sleep for days. Weeks. I needed to cry. I needed to call Luke and ask after the baby. I walked through the parking lot, passing the same discarded bottles. The same slushee nestled against the same used diaper. Before I even got there, I saw a lone figure seated on the ground, knees drawn up, back settled against the door of my room. My heart froze as I made a sudden turn to the office to avoid confronting the stranger. But then he stood and something in the way he moved triggered a subliminal response.

"Grace?" came Nathan's voice from the shadowy light of breaking dawn.

I walked, almost lurched, toward his open arms.

"I came when I heard," he murmured to my bowed head, my forehead pressed tightly against his chest. He stroked the back of my hair and curled his other arm around my shoulder. "I'm so sorry," he said. "Luke called me. I'm so sorry."

Something clicked in me, a lever releasing all my stored tears. Months of tears poured from my eyes. Years of tears. Sobbing is a pale expression—I was purging years of repressed emotion. Nathan unlocked the door and helped me to the bed where I continued to cry for hours until my tears were completely spent.

Afterward, I slept for two days. If Nathan came and went for food and supplies, I didn't hear him. I slept an unconscious sleep—the sleep of the innocent and the dead. When I finally woke, Nathan helped me pack. I was going home. Back to Nathan. Back to San Francisco. He handed me a small stack of mail that had accumulated since I'd been gone. A very old letter from my parents, which just missed me after I'd already left for Europe. A few rare handwritten lines at the end of the letter from Dad, since Mom was normally the one who wrote and signed both their names. Some paperwork from University of San Francisco—a final tuition statement. A bill from my dentist showing no balance due. And an envelope. The envelope I'd come to expect and dread. While Nathan was in the bathroom, I ripped it open and pulled out the single sheet of folded paper with a single type-written line.

"You can run, but you can't hide."

CHAPTER THIRTEEN
INDIAN SPRINGS

"IT'S SETTLED," CARLY told me over the phone. "I've been asking a lot of questions and there's no doubt in my mind that you were right; it was Kerry who reported Maggie for drinking. Call Maggie and tell her to call Jane. Tell them we need to meet up." *Click.*

I dutifully picked up the phone and called Maggie. "Where? When?" she asked.

I was embarrassed. "I don't know. I forgot to ask."

"It's okay. Tomorrow's Friday, so let's just meet at my place at five. We can grab pizza afterward. Why don't you call Carly back and tell her? I'll let Jane know."

In retrospect, it's odd that none of us questioned Carly about her "investigation," but maybe it isn't so odd because we normally deferred to Carly. She mentioned talking to Kerry's friends. She mentioned talking to Kerry. But she never mentioned exactly what facts or statements pointed to Kerry's guilt. That was just understood.

"So, what do we do?" Jane folded her slice of pizza to trap a tongue of oozing cheese. "And by the way, Maggie, that really sucks. Sorry."

Maggie's mother could never stay mad at her for long, so she relented before the two weeks were up and allowed Maggie to meet us at the pizza parlor, which was packed that time of night on Friday. Families, mostly, but even some kids from our school. We sat in a booth, Maggie and Jane facing Carly and me. It was how we usually paired up in a booth. Carly set the speaking volume to barely above a whisper, which we understood was to protect our closely guarded secrets. We leaned forward to better hear each other amidst the din of crying babies and pinball machines.

"I have some ideas," Carly said. "But it's Grace's decision since she volunteered. What do you think, Grace?"

I didn't exactly feel like a volunteer. I felt more like a chess piece that had been maneuvered into position. A soldier ready to receive instructions for a dangerous but top-secret mission. I only wished someone would give me the instructions.

"I mean . . . I don't really know." I had no idea what was expected of me. "Like, what are we trying to accomplish?" That seemed like a logical question, and one which could buy me time and hopefully provide me with direction. Thankfully, nobody took it for a stupid question—I knew that by the way Maggie's and Jane's eyes shifted from me and landed expectantly on Carly.

"We want her to have an idea of the damage she's done," Carly said. "How it's hurt Maggie. And how she should think twice about doing anything like that again because Maggie has friends who care about her."

"That sounds reasonable," Jane said. And it did. Shouldn't I have known that without asking? But even knowing that did little to illuminate my path forward.

"Definitely. I mean . . ." Carly stared at me while I tried to think of a way to rise to the occasion. "Maybe I should talk to her or something?"

"That's a fantastic idea, Grace," Carly said, leaving me somewhere between elated and relieved. Apparently, I had guessed right. "And Maggie, Grace is putting herself out there for you, so don't let her down. Don't let the rest of us down. Make sure this never has to happen again."

"I will." Maggie hung her head. "I already told you that," she mumbled. Jane reached over and patted the back of Maggie's hand.

"So, it's up to you now, Grace," Carly said. "If you need any help or moral support, just let us know. I kind of have Kerry's schedule figured out if you need to know that."

But it wasn't up to me, and Carly probably never doubted she'd receive a call from me begging for help. I couldn't call Maggie—after all, it was Maggie whom I was avenging. And I wouldn't call Jane who was borderline against it. At least she had been, until she was convinced that Carly had done a thorough investigation. And even then, she didn't show much enthusiasm. No, it was Carly whom I would turn to, as I had ever since I'd met her. Carly knew that all along.

"This is where she works." We stood in front of a store in the mall—a small but popular destination for the girls at our school—one that sold beads, costume jewelry, and t-shirts emblazoned with Japanese anime characters and witty sayings. It was a place we'd always visit during our frequent trips to the mall.

"You're kidding. I didn't know Kerry worked here."

"She said she just started two weeks ago. She works week-ends."

"So you think I should just go up to her and—"

"And just ask when she has a break. Say you want to talk to her. Be nice, okay? No reason to be a bitch about it but be firm, and if you need me, I'll be wandering around the store. You'll be fine, okay?" She grabbed my hand and squeezed. "Let's go."

We walked through the door.

Carly peeled off the minute we set foot in the store, making it seem as if I was there on my own. *She's testing me,* I thought. *She wants to make sure I'm strong. Not like Maggie. I can't let her down.* But Kerry was busy with a customer so I pretended to be perusing the merchandise, being careful to keep my distance from Carly, who had made it clear I was on my own. Kerry spotted me, smiled and waved, and was making her way toward me when another customer intercepted her. They spoke for a minute and then walked together to the register. With Carly off in a far corner of the store, her back turned to us, I don't think Kerry even realized she was there.

Each second that ticked by put my nerves more and more on edge. *Who am I to lecture Kerry?* I wondered. She would probably just laugh in my face. Although I had matured since I first set foot in Indian Springs High and gained confidence, I was still just little Grace Templeton. A girl to these almost-women. And here I was ready to deliver a Mafia-esque warning. *Don't mess with the Kitty Committee*—although I would never publicly expose our secret name. My bowels felt loose, and the fluorescent lights of the store distorted my vision, bringing a surreal aspect to my surroundings. The porcelain cat, waving its front paw up and down and up and down, was delivering an ominous message—*Get out! Leave the store immediately!* But I took a few calming breaths, all the while watching Kerry ring up the customer. After all, I was just going to ask to meet up with her on her break. I could explain it much more gently than the others might imagine. No one would be the wiser because Carly had made it clear that I was on my own. And once I did this, I was done. This was my initiation, and then it would be someone else's turn. I could sit back and give them the benefit of my experience with calm under pressure.

Just at that moment, I felt a hand on the back of my elbow. It was Carly.

"Let's go," she said. "This doesn't feel right."

I'd never been so relieved. This was a reprieve, wasn't it? I hoped it was permanent and not just putting off the inevitable until another time. I'd been ready to do my duty but was more than happy to walk away.

With her shoulder pressed against mine, Carly leaned in even further and flipped open the flap that covered the opening to my purse. "Take this," she hissed, dropping her hand into my bag. I didn't even have time to see what she was giving me. Kerry smiled in our direction, finally free to come over and say hi.

"Bye, Kerry!" Carly called out cheerfully. "We gotta go; catch you next time."

I waved, and we walked out of the store.

"Don't stop," Carly instructed once we were out. "I'll explain. Let's go somewhere where we can sit and get something to eat. Actually, let's go to the car."

I'd never seen Carly like that. Nervous.

"What is it?" I asked. "What did you put in my purse, and why are we running away?"

"I told you, don't stop. And don't look back. We're not

running, and I'll explain everything in the car."

She walked briskly enough that I had to perform an occasional two-step to keep up. Carly had a purse. Why did she use mine? She didn't say another word, and I sensed she didn't want to answer any more questions. Until we got to the car.

I slipped my hand inside my purse while Carly was jostling through hers, searching for the keys. I felt small hard ovals. A necklace. After we got in the car and Carly had locked the doors, I pulled my hand out of my purse, the necklace along with it. It was beautiful. Multiple strands of silver leading to a string of three crystals. I was horrified.

"We can't take this," I said. "We could never wear it. What if someone saw it and recognized it from the store or asked us where we got it?"

"Don't worry, we're not keeping it. We're not thieves," she said, although, technically, I was a thief since I had just smuggled it out of the store without payment. "We're going to send it back . . . with a note."

"What kind of note?"

"A note that you're going to write—anonymously, of course—saying that you heard Kerry bragging about how she stole it, and you couldn't stand by and let that happen, so you took it when she wasn't looking, and you're returning it."

"You're kidding, right?" I slipped the necklace back into my bag lest some passerby glance through the window of the car and immediately know I was handling stolen property. "We can't do that—frame Kerry for something she didn't do."

"And what did she do to Maggie?" Carly asked.

"Yeah, she reported Maggie for drinking, but that's different. Maggie *was* drinking."

"So you think that's okay? What she did."

"No, I didn't say that." Carly was a spider, spinning a web around my defenses with her words. I couldn't think or act quickly enough to keep up with her.

"So, I'm asking you again." She spoke very slowly, as if to a child. "Do you think what Kerry did to Maggie was okay?"

"No, but . . ." I could feel my resistance slipping away. I could feel my friendships with Maggie and Carly slipping away.

"No, but what?"

"You write the note, then," I said. "I'll mail it."

"No, Grace, *you* write the note. This is *your* thing, remember? I'll have my own challenge, and I won't expect you to do it for me."

"Okay, I'll do it," I said grudgingly. "But I'm not doing anything like this ever again."

"Good girl," Carly said. She checked her rearview mirror, put the car in reverse, and slowly backed out of the space. "Remember, not everything's black and white in life. Sometimes you have to do something hard, which might not seem right, to achieve a greater good. I know your parents are super religious, and you probably recite the Ten Commandments before every meal, but what about war? Thou shalt not kill, right? But in war, soldiers have to kill to protect innocent people. Just think of it like that."

"For your information, we don't recite the Ten Commandments before our meals, but *thou shalt not steal* is one of them."

"And I already explained: we're not stealing. Stealing would mean keeping it for our own use. And anyway, the government collects taxes, right? Do we ask to pay taxes?"

"No, but—"

"Exactly. And my dad says that's like the government stealing from us, but it's perfectly legal." She reached over with her right hand and patted me on the back of my arm. I shifted away from her and leaned against the door. I was angry. But I still needed her.

"Mission accomplished," Carly announced brightly that night. It was Saturday night, and we were planning a sleepover at Maggie's. Maybe rent a movie. Order a pizza. Pop some microwave popcorn. A usual weekend night for us. If Maggie's mom was out for the evening, we'd probably share the flask that Carly brought with her. Drown out the taste with Diet Coke. "Grace is the first true member of the Kitty Committee because she's the first to prove her loyalty."

"What happened?" Maggie's eyes opened wide. "What did you say to her? What did she say? Was she mad?"

"Grace, you don't have to share if you don't want to," Carly said quickly. "You'll have the same choice when it's your turn, Maggie."

"I *don't* want to," I mumbled. The package was in the mail. I'd written it just the way Carly suggested. I was still mad. "Everything's fine, though. Where's Jane?"

"Tonight's the opening night of her play, so I was thinking maybe we should all go next weekend to show our support."

"Fine with me," Carly said. "How about you, Grace?"

I had Carly just where I wanted her—extreme solicitude. She was asking for my opinion on nearly everything from the movie we selected to the amount of butter on the popcorn. I could have almost believed I was the center of her universe. Later that night, settled on Maggie's comfortable old sofa, we cracked open the sodas and poured a healthy shot of vodka from Carly's flask into each of our glasses.

"This is to celebrate," Carly said. "To Grace!"

"To Grace!" Maggie leaned over and clinked glasses with me. "Thanks for having my back; you don't know how much that means to me."

"To the Kitty Committee," I said, sending the first swallow rushing down my throat. I'd come a long way in the short time since my first experience with alcohol. I had come to anticipate with pleasure the moment when my overthinking, overanxious brain would be hit by the initial sense of euphoria, followed by supreme confidence and good humor, eventually culminating in a deep and dreamless sleep. It's what I was after that night. And I'd figured out when enough became too much, robbing me of all that I sought from that magic elixir.

I hated what I'd done to Kerry, but I pushed it into a dark recess where actions had no consequences. It was a thing I'd done, but the necklace would soon be back in proper hands, and the actual letter was something nobody could possibly take seriously. The movie for the night was a romance slightly more adult than we usually went for, which initially prompted a lot of talk. We were rarely quiet when we watched a movie together— someone was always interjecting an opinion, laughing at the stupidity of a character, or guessing at the ending. But after watching one scene where the woman was shown topless and a sex scene unfolded beneath the sheets, Maggie and Carly were uncharacteristically quiet. Nobody reached for the popcorn bowl or uttered a word. The fact that the Kitty Committee focused on friendship rather than boys had always been a huge relief to me—I was far from being ready for boys. But for a group of hormonally appropriate teenage-girls, we talked a lot less about sex than one might expect, surprising even me and leaving me to wonder why the subject was off limits or not at least a priority.

"Have you ever kissed a boy?" I blurted out, breaking the awkward silence.

"Umm, yeah!" Maggie snorted out a laugh, to which Carly responded in kind.

"What's so funny?" I didn't know much about Maggie and Carly's past. I knew that Maggie liked someone and kind of had a boyfriend in the eighth grade, the year she lived next door to Jane. I knew Maggie liked someone else her freshman year of high school, but he turned out to be a jerk who dumped her. But I'd never heard too much about Carly's experiences with boys.

"Carly's gone all the way." Maggie's impish smile turned into a leering smirk.

"What?" I'd have been less shocked to learn Carly had robbed a bank. Who was this boy who must have played a somewhat major role in Carly's life and yet was never discussed?

"I fucked Rich Benson," Carly said, still unable to control her giggles.

"I thought you hated him."

"I do. I did. I just wanted to see what he'd be like. And I was tired of being a virgin."

"It was at a party," Maggie said. "Freshman year."

"What was . . . he like?" I wasn't sure how a person could be judged other than maybe if he had bad breath or was cute.

"Little dick," Carly said. "And he didn't even know what to do with the little he had."

Would I know what to do with what I had? And what exactly did I have? How did Carly know? Was she just born knowing? And how had she escaped pregnancy and venereal disease? There were so many things I wanted to know but was too embarrassed to ask. Sex was a frontier I hadn't even considered exploring.

"How about you, Grace? Have you ever kissed a boy?" Maggie asked. By then, the movie had been forgotten and only served as background noise.

"Yeah, Grace. Enquiring minds want to know." Carly sidled up beside me and started to tickle me, with Maggie quickly joining in. Soon, I was robbed of my breath by heaving gulps of laughter so intense they were one step away from tears.

"Stop!" I pleaded half-heartedly. It was torture and pleasure, as tickling often is.

"We'll stop if you tell us everything." Maggie's face was pink with hilarity, and her smile, always contagious, pushed her cheeks apart.

"Everything!" Carly repeated, her fingertips still digging into my ribs.

"Okay, I promise," I gasped. "No, I haven't," I said after catching my breath and wiping the tears from my cheeks. My face hurt from laughing.

"We knew that," Maggie laughed. "We're not idiots, but I'll bet Luke has kissed plenty of girls. Have you ever walked in on him naked?" She waggled her eyebrows.

"Has he ever fucked a girl?" Carly asked. "I mean, you guys being all religious the way you are."

"Shut up!" I threw a pillow at her head, but her reflexes, even under the influence, were too fast. "No . . . I don't know. How should I know?"

"Are you going to be ready when someone wants to kiss you, Grace?" Carly asked, suddenly sober.

"You'd better be," Maggie said. "Otherwise they'll think you're inexperienced and take advantage."

"Boys can tell," Carly said. "Like a sixth sense. Do you want me to teach you how to kiss?"

Maggie unspooled on her back on the floor. Princess Leia, who had been warily observing us from a distance, moved quickly toward her, curling up under her arm. "Carly's a good teacher," Maggie said. "She taught me, and I haven't had any complaints."

It didn't occur to me to ask how Carly could be such a good teacher if she'd only had one sexual experience, albeit *all the way*. It seemed important that I should know how to kiss so no boy would judge me as inexperienced and use that fact for his devious purposes. But the truth is, at that moment, I wanted nothing more than to kiss Carly. If I was completely honest with myself, hadn't I been thinking about it since the day I had first laid eyes on her?

"I guess," I said, and with those words all my anger toward Carly simply vanished.

She didn't hesitate, nor did she seem at all embarrassed. We were already sitting next to each other on the sofa, so she turned to face me.

"First thing he'll do is hold you like this," she said, slipping one arm around my ribcage, centering her hand between my shoulder blades. Her eyes latched onto mine so completely that I was incapable of looking away or laughing to ease the awkwardness. "Then, maybe he'll mess around with your hair a little—guys like to do that." With her free hand, she ran her fingers lightly through the hair above my temple, smoothing it behind my ear. My entire body shivered with delight. She was close enough that I could feel her breath, warm and moist, smelling sweetly of Pepsi and vodka. "Then he'll move in for the kiss." She brought her lips to mine so tenderly it was hard to imagine a boy could be that gentle. That sensitive. Her full lips were insistent, playing against mine, leading me as if in a dance until my lips softened and parted. Her tongue darted in, playing lightly and teasingly with mine while she pushed forward, lowering me until I was lying on my back and she was on top of me. A spark lit between my legs. "Then, if you're not careful," she said, "he'll go for the feel like this." Her hand slipped under my sweater where it lingered on my bare breast for just a moment too long. She gently grasped my already erect nipple between her thumb and forefinger, releasing a gush of slippery wet into my panties. "Oh my God!" she cried out, pulling abruptly away. She sat upright, leaving me floundering for a foothold back to reality. "Grace isn't wearing a bra. I just accidentally touched her boob."

"Gross, Grace," Maggie laughed. "You should've warned Carly."

I was ashamed of the way my body had betrayed me. The

pleasure. The tingling. The release of fluid I initially took for an early start to my period. I knew nothing about the continuum of sexuality. The spectrum across which people could slide back and forth. I knew only that my parents had taught me that homosexuality was a sin, one that another person could lead you into. If this subject had been taught in health, it must have been before I arrived in Indian Springs. Even though I was losing my religion, I feared I would be damned. But if I was damned anyway, then I wanted to do it again and again.

A week later, the Kitty Committee was having lunch at our usual table at school.

"Guess who got fired?" Carly said. "Kerry."

"What happened?" I looked meaningfully at Carly, hoping for a sign it had nothing to do with me.

"She was a new employee and on probation, so they didn't have to have cause. They just told her they were laying her off, but one of her co-workers told her someone reported her for stealing."

"Serves her right," said Maggie.

CHAPTER FOURTEEN

Two EVENTS CAST a pall over what should have been a joyful time of year—the days leading up to Thanksgiving and Christmas vacation. The first happened in November when the SAT results came out. I'd taken multiple practice tests under Carly's tutelage with the insight she'd gained from her own tutoring sessions with Mr. Sutherland. I was thrilled with my results, which were above what I had expected, although nowhere near Carly's league. Maggie skipped the SAT, and Jane had scored reasonably well—better than me, lower than Carly. Everyone was happy except Carly.

"That fucking asshole Tim got a 1580," she said a few days after most students had received their results. "It's no wonder because Sutherland has a hard-on for him."

"I think he's got one for you too," Maggie said. "And every other girl in school."

"I don't mean it that way," Carly snapped. "I mean it's obvious that he gives Tim the special treatment. Spends way more time with him. My session is right after Tim's, and Sutherland's usually running fifteen minutes late by the time I go in. And then he always lets me out early. I'm telling my dad he should prorate what he pays for tutoring because I've been keeping track of the exact number of minutes he spends with me."

"So why would he care so much?" I asked. "About Tim?"

"Duh, he's a guy. Guys are always looking out for each other. The system is so rigged against women."

I'd never spoken to Tim since the incident in health class, but he did strike me as slightly arrogant. Entitled even, as though he occupied a different hemisphere of intellect than the rest of us mere mortals. Tim seemed to me the kind of guy who felt that women weren't his equal. Just like Mr. Sutherland, the way Carly explained him.

"Tim really screwed me over last year," I said. "In health class."

Carly's angry face unscrewed into curious wonder. "In what way?" she asked.

I obliged her and the other two girls with all the facts, which I was still able to recall in visceral detail. I left out the only humanizing anecdote—the one where Tim turned his back to me, ignobly concealing his shame. Tim's shame had been my shame that day. It had been the day I had unwittingly and unconsciously cast my lot with the girl I had yet to meet.

"Oh, Grace," Jane said when I finished telling the story. "I'm sorry for you, that must have been so embarrassing. Tim's locker is right next to mine, and he's a little annoying, but he's never been mean. In fact, he's usually super nice."

"But everyone's nice to you," Carly said, and I thought I detected a sour undertone in her delivery. "Because you're so nice."

I had to admit I would never put the name *Tim* in a sentence with the word *nice*.

"Carly, I don't get it," Jane said, ignoring Carly's sarcasm, if indeed that's what it was. "You should be thrilled. If I got your score I'd be doing a happy dance right now. 1500 is awesome. You'll get in everywhere, for sure."

A week later, Mr. Sutherland announced the winner of our school's National Student Essay Contest. The winning essay would be sent to state finals where it would be judged against other local winners. The winner's name was announced over the school's intercom system right before the bell rang at the end of first period: Timothy LeClerc.

Maggie and I exchanged nervous glances—once again Tim had triumphed over Carly. I think we both knew there would be hell to pay, and one of us would have to pay it. I had already fulfilled my obligation to the Kitty Committee, but Maggie and Jane hadn't, nor had Carly. We had two new enemies. Mr. Sutherland, who was instrumental in selecting the winner of the essay contest, along with a handful of the junior and senior class teachers. Mr. Sutherland, whom Carly was sure had demonstrated favoritism, costing her at least eighty points on her SAT. And Tim LeClerc.

Of course, we all knew that Jane's locker was next to Tim's. I avoided Jane's locker because Tim made me acutely uncomfortable ever since the health class fiasco. I never believed his explanation. Sometimes I had felt his eyes on my back and imagined his delight at having pulled one over on the new girl. I noticed other students also avoided him in health class. He had his own tight-knit group which I saw at lunch, but to most people he was off-putting. Arrogant. That's why he had selected me.

Carly avoided Jane's locker because she instinctively disliked Tim for the competition he presented. Without Tim at Indian

Springs High, Carly would have cleaned up. She would have been the brightest, most successful student in our class without a doubt—the shining star. But Tim was always a dark cloud hanging over her. And as clouds are wont to do, particularly the dark variety, Tim was stealing Carly's thunder.

But Maggie had neither of our issues, and Maggie loved Jane. So Maggie spent as much of her free time as possible in the company of Jane. Maggie cared for me too, but she didn't respect me the way she respected Jane or Carly—one out of admiration, the other out of need and years of habit. Maggie and I were close, and I never doubted she'd do anything for me. I think she believed I'd acted selflessly to defend her honor against Kerry, although she never knew or asked exactly what I'd done. She was never anything but lovely toward me—nurturing as well. But I was the kid sister, at least in my own mind.

I suspected that Carly-free zones (like Jane's locker) were especially enticing for Maggie, who must have grown tired of Carly's occasional wrath and fierce judgments, although they went hand-in-hand with her unshakeable devotion. Maggie had been *the one* for nearly her entire life, and it must have been a heavy burden for her to shoulder alone before the Kitty Committee came along. I sensed Maggie reveled in her newfound freedom. She could still count on Carly's strength and vision as well as what passed for her love. But now she could share that with Jane and me. It must have been a tremendous relief.

"Everyone has to have some skin in the game," Carly said one night. "Not just Grace. There has to be some risk to yourself, and we have to stick together. If we don't, who will? These people shouldn't be allowed to get away with what they do to any one of us."

It was like a pep talk before the big game. Maggie had been wronged, and I'd taken care of it. Now it was established that Tim had wronged me. And Mr. Sutherland had wronged Carly. Maggie listened intently, probably already aware she'd be the next to be called upon. Jane was skeptical.

"How about you? What are you going to do?" Jane asked, but Carly was unruffled.

"I haven't decided yet, but it's going to be something big. Bigger than any of you."

"Yeah? Well, let us know when you decide," Jane said, and I was shocked by her boldness.

A few days later, Rita invited us all over to Jane's for a barbecue. The weather was changing—we'd already had the first rain of the season, and the nights were too cold to go without a jacket. Mr. Swanson braved the cool temperature to tend to the barbecue, eventually delivering a plate heaped with chicken, lamb, and sausages to the kitchen table. After we ate, Leann turned to me.

"Wanna help me feed Frosty?" she asked, knowing I was the only one who shared her interest in the horse.

Frosty had a stable that protected us from the wind, and Leann went to work, cleaning and refreshing Frosty's supply of hay and oats, while I mainly just stroked Frosty's neck. "Do you wanna ride?" she asked once she was done.

Riding for me meant sitting bareback and clutching Frosty's mane while Leann led me around the corral. I loved it.

"Something's going on between Jane and Carly," she said during our third circle around the corral. "Jane won't admit it, but I can tell."

The wind was picking up, driving dust and small bits of hay

up my nose. I sneezed three times in a row. "I don't know," I said, sniffling. "Nothing that I can tell."

But I *had* noticed. Things were tense. It was clear to me there was no love lost between Carly and Jane. They seemed to be play-acting for the benefit of Maggie and me. Mostly Maggie, if I were to be completely honest. Maggie's soul was the prize. If Leann had noticed it too, things must be worse than I realized.

After that, things moved quickly. Carly announced she'd be fulfilling her pledge to the rest of us by getting back at Mr. Sutherland. She'd be striking a blow for every girl he'd ever groped (including Maggie), and every girl whose aspirations he'd crushed in order to give the advantage to some boy. She wasn't squeamish about sharing the details of her plan with us the way I had been. Her plan was twofold. First, she informed her father that she'd been cheated out of tutoring time and given him a detailed accounting, adding up the number of minutes she'd been shortchanged. Carly's dad promised to look into it and have a talk with Mr. Sutherland after the holidays. But that was only part one.

Knowing that Mr. Sutherland's daughter (a freshman at Indian Springs) was usually doing homework in the sitting area outside his office while she waited for him to drive her home, Carly made a final appointment to discuss her test results. At just the right moment, she turned to leave his office and drew the back of her hand roughly across her lips, smudging her lip gloss in the process. She quickly unbuttoned her blouse to below her bra, having worn an easy-access blouse that day for just that purpose. She assumed an expression of shock and surprise when she exited, as though caught totally off guard, while fumbling with her buttons and drawing a hand up to cover her lips. Carly got extra lucky that day. Mrs. Sutherland was in the waiting room with her daughter as Carly hurried past them, hanging her head in feigned disgrace.

All of this she shared with only Maggie and me. Jane was around less and less, drawn more to her drama friends than to the Kitty Committee those days.

"That's cold-blooded, Carly," Maggie said. But we laughed. It didn't seem possible Carly could have maneuvered the Sutherland situation exactly the way she claimed. She was prone to exaggeration, and the whole thing seemed absurd. But even if it was true, didn't he deserve it? He had bra-strap-groped Maggie. Maggie said he was a perv, and all the girls knew it. The part about not paying for the time Carly was shortchanged justified it in my mind.

The week before Christmas break, we all went to watch Jane in a production of *A Christmas Carol*. Jane had the role of the Ghost of Christmas Future. She was spellbinding up there on the stage, in possession of more charisma than I had ever suspected. I couldn't take my eyes from her, captivated as I was by her ethereal ghostlike beauty; I couldn't imagine she wasn't the focal point for everyone in the audience. Although she didn't speak, her gestures evoked more emotion than any of the other actors, even the actor who played Scrooge. And when she finally disappeared into a rumpled mess of bedsheets, I inhaled sharply, suddenly aware I'd been holding my breath. Carly laughed out loud.

"Carly," Maggie elbowed her. "Shut up; it's not supposed to be funny."

"I'm sorry." Carly wiped at her eyes. "She just looked ridiculous. It's such a sappy play."

"I think she likes that guy who plays Scrooge," Maggie

whispered.

And, just like that, the magic of Jane's performance was nothing but a joke. The dire warning of the consequences of an evil heart was just a bunch of words in a sappy play. Scrooge was just a guy Jane had a crush on.

Jane spent winter break at the Lake Tahoe home with her family. None of us were invited this time, although it was a skiing trip and, in fairness, Carly, Maggie, and I didn't ski. But two other kids were invited—Russell, the boy who played Scrooge to Jane's ghost, and a girl named Missy, a drama friend who was also in the play.

"Missy doesn't ski," Carly said one day over lunch at the mall. "So I'm not sure why she was invited and we weren't."

"My parents wouldn't have let me miss Christmas with the family even if she asked us," I said.

"My mom didn't care," Maggie said. "But I hate snow."

An enormous Christmas tree was resplendent in the atrium of the mall, shoppers taking turns posing for pictures under its magnificence. Tiny fairy lights were strung in every conceivable nook and cranny, which gave the impression of wandering through a giant snow cave glistening with ice crystals. Canned Christmas carols played tunelessly in the background while shoppers swarmed purposefully out of one store and into the next. It was an ideal place for people-watching or catching the Christmas spirit, at least the commercial side of it. For us, it was just our hangout transformed in a fun way for a different experience. My modest Christmas shopping was done, and even if it wasn't, I didn't have any money left—barely enough to pay for the hamburger and fries in front of me.

"I think you're both missing the point," Carly said. "Jane has abandoned us for a new group of friends. Probably even a boyfriend, if Maggie's right."

"Why shouldn't she have a boyfriend, Carly?" Maggie said. "It's not like we haven't in the past and won't in the future."

"There's nothing wrong with having a boyfriend. I never said that," Carly snapped.

I knew Maggie's reflexive wince by then. It was a subtle tightening of the muscles around her eyes, but it was unmistakable. To her credit, Maggie never hesitated to speak out against Carly when she disagreed, but Carly's rebukes caused her to cower like a dog that had been beaten too many times.

"I just mean," Carly lowered the tenor and tension in her voice, "she's not putting us first. Or even second or third at this point. So why is she even part of the Kitty Committee?"

"I don't know," I said, and I didn't. Why *was* she part of the Kitty Committee? Jane had clearly moved on, although it was apparent she wanted to maintain a friendship with Maggie. I twirled a French fry between my thumb and forefinger before plunging it into a puddle of ketchup.

"Maggie," Carly said as though just waking up from a profound dream. "Did Jane invite *you* to go with them?"

Maggie glanced evasively at a woman pushing a stroller with twins. It was obvious to me that she was unnerved by the question, but I don't think she had the ability to lie to Carly.

"Yeah," she said softly enough that I had to strain to hear above the cacophony of Muzak and random shreds of dialog trailing behind the shoppers who passed our table. "But I didn't want to go."

"That's what I figured," Carly said. "She's trying to break up our friendship. Don't worry, I don't blame you for hiding it from us. I just think it's really a crappy thing to do."

"I don't think she's trying to do that," Maggie said, but she offered nothing to back up her statement.

"Well I do," Carly said, and I had to agree. "You might

think the Kitty Committee is a silly thing, but when we drew up our rules, we were promising something really important to each other. We were promising to put our friendship above everything and to always have each other's backs. Call it what you will—the Kitty Committee was just a dumb name I came up with. But the fundamentals are what count. Who's going to look out for us? Parents, sure, but there's only so much we can share with them. I view our friendship as a lifelong commitment, but Jane doesn't see it that way, which really hurts me."

Carly was good. So good that I was moved to put my arm around her. So good, Maggie was moved to clutch Carly's hand and stroke it soothingly with her thumb. Tears sparkled in Carly's eyes, and I heard the unmistakable quaver in her voice that signified a monumental struggle to control uncontrollable emotions. I'm sure Maggie heard it too. Carly was on the verge of tears. This was real. This was almost earth-shattering. Carly had never before been vulnerable in front of us.

"Don't worry, Carly, you'll always have me," Maggie said. "I didn't want to go at all . . . I never even considered going."

"Maggie's right," I said. "You'll always have us." The power I derived from consoling Carly was nearly impossible to describe. For once, I was strong and Carly was weak. I felt such tenderness for her at that moment. I thought I knew how much it must have cost this girl, so supremely self-possessed and confident, to bare her weakness to us. It was a gift.

Fractured by the mall's sound system, a carol crackled and felt brittle in my ears. Twenty yards away, a tired-looking Santa stood in front of a bucket, incessantly ringing his bell for donations. This was my first Christmas in Indian Springs, and it had none of the warmth, love, or merriment to which I'd become accustomed. Images flashed through my mind—the Ghost of Christmas Past. A dead manzanita bush, its spare tropical beauty supporting our hand-made decorations. A tiny church filled with voices raised richly in devotion.

I felt the warmth of Carly's body, close to my own, and willed the peace of my memories into her soul.

"Let's wait until Jane gets back from vacation," Maggie said. "I promise I'll talk to her and see what she's thinking."

CHAPTER FIFTEEN

PROOF OF CARLY's act of fealty came shortly after school was back in session. One day, Carly was summoned to the principal's office where she was questioned about Mr. Sutherland. She was known to have been privately tutored by him, and Principal Page asked if she'd been satisfied with those sessions and whether there were any issues she wished to discuss.

"No," Carly assured them. He was a fine tutor, and she'd been quite happy with her SAT results. But she used long pauses, downcast eyes, and a nervous wringing of her hands to the best advantage, she later claimed to us. We had no way of knowing our junior year would be Mr. Sutherland's last year at Indian Springs High. We didn't know if Carly's charade had anything to do with his departure or even if the rumor mill about his inappropriate interest in female students was factual. Nevertheless, Carly claimed full credit after it happened; by then, she was grasping for anything which would redeem her as a champion of good over evil. Much later we learned that his wife divorced him and moved to another state, taking their daughter with her.

It was only left to Maggie to prove her loyalty. By then, none of us expected Jane would have anything to do with it. In our minds, Jane had been excommunicated from the Kitty Committee, but Maggie saw no reason to confront her with that fact.

"I'm still her friend," she said. "What difference does it make if she's officially in or out? She doesn't do anything with the group anymore, so it's obvious to everyone."

I missed Leann and privately mourned Jane's separation.

"Have it your way," Carly said. "I couldn't care less, to be honest."

We all knew Tim would be next on our list. Ostensibly he had wronged me, but it was Carly he had really wronged. Just by being a better, more formidable version of herself. But Tim had a weakness. He, like many others, was smitten with Jane. Locker time was a time when a goofier, less-guarded version of Tim appeared. He struggled for random bits of conversation and non sequiturs to hold onto Jane's physical presence for even one additional minute. His face betrayed his unrequited crush, flushing an outrageous shade of pink that I'd seen the few times I'd waited for Jane and Maggie. But Jane either didn't notice or ignored it. She was always kind to Tim, listening to his mind-less chatter and blessing him with her undivided attention the way she did with almost everyone. It was the only time I'd ever seen Tim's guard down—the only time he displayed vulnera-bility and appeared to be human.

Carly had connections through Rich Benson, who never gave up hope that one day he'd have the pleasure of sharing Carly's body again. Rich had connections with the local school druggie, who also doubled as the local school dealer of drugs. All Carly needed was enough weed for two joints. Rich even provided it free of charge, no doubt considering it an investment in his future. All that was left was for Jane to distract Tim long enough for Maggie to slip the joints into the back of his locker. And the best part, in Carly's mind, was that Jane performed this function unwittingly. She was complicit without being aware. It was a perfect trump card to hold out in the event Jane ever turned on us.

I didn't know all the details until weeks afterward.

Someone left a note on the car windshield of the young police officer who came to our school once a week to teach the D.A.R.E. (anti-drug) curriculum. The note claimed to be from a student concerned about Tim LeClerc, who had been getting high after school, offering to share his marijuana with others, including freshmen. It claimed knowledge of seeing said drugs in Tim's locker. The officer passed the note along to Principal Page, who found it impossible to believe but, nonetheless, conducted a search of Tim's locker with Tim present, all the while apologizing but saying he was legally obliged to follow up on the anonymous note. Tim was as cool as a cucumber, the talk around school went—either because he knew there were no drugs in his locker, or else because he thought Principal Page would conduct a cursory check without bothering to look in the back where the joints were stashed. Which version was told depended on who was doing the telling. Tim's friends never doubted the first version, but many people didn't like Tim, so they believed the second.

Carly always came to Tim's defense when the subject was brought up. Tim didn't do drugs of any sort—anyone who knew him knew that, she insisted. Maggie was mostly quiet about the whole thing, not offering an opinion one way or the other. The person who had written the note was most often judged to be one of a small group of religious freshmen who were unlikely to have ever interacted with either Tim or his friends. But the note had mentioned Tim offering the marijuana to freshman kids, and only a religious and totally uncool kid would refer to weed that way.

Maggie, who heard it from Jane, told me the way it went down. Tim was allowed to collect his books before receiving a two-day suspension. Being caught with drugs on campus would have meant a much harsher punishment another student, possibly even expulsion. But Mr. Sutherland and Principal Page couldn't believe it of Timothy, the shining star of the school. Probable National Merit finalist, 4.4 GPA, near-perfect SAT, Boys State, State Band finalist . . . If Tim LeClerc was guilty of bringing drugs onto campus, what did that say about Principal Page? One can imagine the superintendent breathing a sigh of relief when Tim's mother, a high-powered attorney, threatened a lawsuit if Tim suffered any negative consequences for what, she said, was obviously a plant. Nobody wanted Tim to have negative consequences—not in the long term—so the entire thing was eventually swept under the rug. In the meantime, though, Tim had his suspension, which began with a show of displeasure. According to those who were there, it was unlike any seen before in the hallways of Indian Springs High.

"If I ever find out who did this, they're going to be sorry," he yelled at no one in particular, slamming his locker shut. Anyone who didn't hear his outburst would certainly hear about it by the end of the day. Jane, standing next to him, was stunned. He didn't look at her or engage her in any way, but Jane felt the message was directed at her. And then she immediately thought of Maggie.

That day was a rare day because Carly didn't have an after-school activity, or she said she didn't. She offered to drive

Maggie and me home, so we went to Maggie's house to hang out and discuss the drama of the day's events. But we hadn't been there long before the doorbell rang—over and over again. Carly and I accompanied Maggie to the door, alarmed by the anger behind the repeated ringing. The door opened to a red-faced Jane, a sight that I never thought I'd see. Porcelain, yes. Serene, yes. But angry to the point of feverish cheeks and eyes raging a stark blue—that was unthinkable.

"Jane—" Maggie startled.

"Maggie, if I find out you had anything to do with this," Jane said, a fleck of spittle escaping from her mouth. "I swear to God, I'll turn you in." Then she focused her blazing eyes onto Carly. "*You* . . ." she said but left the sentence unfinished when she turned to me. "Grace, you should get out if you know what's good for you." Without another word, she turned to walk back to her car, her normally graceful lope transformed into a fearsome march.

Maggie closed the door and leaned against it to catch her breath. "Wow," she said before bursting into tears.

"I told you she couldn't be trusted." Carly wrapped her arm around Maggie's waist and led her back to the family room where she collapsed on the old sofa. "She's unhinged. I think there's something seriously psychologically wrong with Jane."

Maggie doubled over, hands covering her face. Her shoulders shuddered with sobs.

"C'mon, Maggie," Carly said. "Pull yourself together. We can't control the uncontrollable, and Jane is clearly a disturbed person."

I sat in stunned silence, still unaware of Maggie's role in Tim's suspension, but already beginning to have my own suspicions. I'd believed that Tim brought drugs to school, but I had suspected one of the boys in the locker room—one of Tim's past tormentors. I hadn't suspected Maggie until Jane's sudden appearance, but it was all starting to fall into place. I didn't have to ask what Jane was talking about. She hadn't spoken Tim's name, but I knew.

"It's just . . ." Maggie gulped, her voice muffled by her lap. "Jane's my friend. I didn't expect that from her."

"I know," Carly cooed. She rubbed her hand soothingly up and down Maggie's back. "I know that's how you feel, but *I'm* your friend. *Grace* is your friend. A true friend wouldn't talk to you that way, wouldn't say the things she did."

A vast uneasiness stirred within me. If Maggie did this thing, and Jane found out, would she really tell on us? Would I be implicated too, even though I hadn't been there? Would people find out what I'd done to Kerry?

"Is she right?" I asked. "Did you plant the weed in Tim's locker?" My heart thumped wildly. Kerry wasn't protected the way Tim was. Nobody cared about Kerry. But Tim had powerful allies and could bring the whole house of cards down upon us.

"You don't have to answer that," Carly said quickly.

Maggie sat up and dried the tears from her face with the sleeve of her shirt. "I don't want to talk about it," she said.

CHAPTER SIXTEEN

Just like the Sword of Damocles, Jane's threat loomed large, leaving the rest of us with a fractured peace of mind, at best. Would she be able to uncover Maggie's involvement? If she did, would she really tell or had she just said that in a moment of anger? Jane no longer sat with us at lunch, refusing even to make eye contact with any of us during class or in the halls. That day at Maggie's house was the last any of us had spoken to her. It had been one week.

"I'm tired of even having to think about this anymore," Carly announced. We were sitting in her car before school, waiting until the last minute to go in. "I just want to have it out with her. Biggest fucking mistake ever—accepting her into our group." She glanced accusingly at Maggie, who winced in the way that had become so familiar to me. "So if nobody else is going to do anything about it, I am."

"Like what?" I was horrified by the thought of a showdown between Carly and Jane.

"Like confront her and remind her that if she tells anyone about Maggie, we can always say that Jane distracted Tim while Maggie did it."

"That would be the worst idea ever," Maggie gasped. "First of all, we'd be admitting to her that I did it, and she doesn't have any proof of that. Second, why should we attack her if maybe she's gotten over it? Maybe she's cooled down and moved on."

Carly's less than well-thought-out plan was shocking. Carly was normally careful. Cautious, even. This seemed to me to be a reckless act of unnecessary aggression, and I was grateful Maggie said what was on my mind. "I agree with Maggie," I said.

"So this is how the two of you want to live?" she said at the exact moment Jane walked by our car with some friends. "Take a good look because there she is—the witch who'll control your destinies. You want to live in fear of her for the next year and a half—that one day she'll wake up in a bad mood and decide to turn us in? We could be expelled. Arrested. No college, no future. That's what you want? Well, not me."

"Let me talk to her," Maggie said. "I can see what she's thinking . . . reason with her. Even if she's mad at me, we have a bond. *Had* a bond."

"You always say that, but how well did that work out last time?" Carly said, her hands tightly gripping the steering wheel. "We're all invested in this, and we all have something to lose. Grace and I will let you do all the talking, but we want to be there."

"I don't care if I'm there," I said. It had taken fear to give me a backbone in the face of Carly, but I'd finally developed some semblance of one.

"Well, I do want to be there," she said.

"If Carly's going to be there, I want you there too, Grace. If that's okay with you."

How could I deny Maggie? I knew she needed me as a buffer—for emotional support. Carly alone was undoubtedly too scary a prospect.

We decided to do it that night. It was a Thursday night. Maggie would call ahead and let Jane know we wanted to talk.

We wouldn't admit anything, but it would be a way for us to judge Jane's emotional temperature. To convince her that nothing could be gained from picking a fight with us, that we should just part amicably and leave each other be. I can honestly say I felt a huge sense of relief. It would finally be over, and we could go on with our lives. I deeply regretted what I'd done to Kerry, but nothing like that would ever happen again. Carly was a flawed person, I could see that now. Maggie was flawed too. But the biggest revelation was how flawed I was. In that moment, I had an epiphany. I could be flawed but still loved by God, as my name implied. And even though I was on tenuous terms with God and religion in general, He would forgive me if I turned my back on negativity and evil—become a strong and good person like Luke. Like Jane. *The meek shall inherit the Earth*, I thought.

We piled out of the car and waited for Carly to collect her backpack from the trunk and lock up. I took a look around. The daffodils were already in full bloom. This was the time of year when I'd arrived in Indian Springs, and I remembered the optimism that had filled me those first moments on the day I had started school one year earlier. The nodding heads of those bright yellow blooms that lined the pathway leading to the entrance of the building—as though they were escorting me into a future where anything and everything was possible. I'd fallen short. But now was my chance to begin anew, this time with the confidence I had lacked back then. It was a new day, and like the saying goes, the first day of the rest of my life.

"Meet up at Maggie's tonight at six," Carly said. "I'll pick you up, Grace."

Once we were all at Maggie's, she made the call. Leann

answered and said Jane would be home in thirty minutes. She was at rehearsal. Maggie left word that she needed to talk and could Jane please call back.

"Let's just go wait for her," Carly said. "We don't want to talk over the phone, and we can't do it at her house with her family around. Let's catch her before she gets home."

It seemed like a reasonable plan. We could get near Jane's house in fifteen minutes and wait for her on the windy, narrow country road which led to her house. It was private. There were places to turn off and park. Places where we could sit in the car and hash everything out in private. Everything that required privacy for teens by necessity happened in cars, and we couldn't exactly persuade Jane to come to Maggie's house.

We got there quickly and pulled off onto the dirt shoulder. It was already quite dark at that hour in the winter, and a light drizzle was falling. Carly killed the headlights, and we admired the view of city lights from high up on that hill.

"I never realized how creepy it is up here," Maggie said. "So lonely."

"But it's beautiful in the day," I said. "And Leann gets to keep a horse."

"Hah! You and Leann," Carly said.

"What?"

"Nothing." She stretched back in her seat, but I resented the implication. Me and Leann what? Were lovers? Were little girls enthralled by a horse? I decided to drop it, but a bitter feeling overcame me, and I wondered if Carly wanted to deny me any pleasure that didn't have to do with her.

We waited in the dark on the side of that hill, the drizzle turning into pitter-patters of actual raindrops on our windshield. Thirty minutes went by. Forty-five. After an hour, Maggie and I complained of being cold, but Carly was low on gas so she didn't want to run the heater. I was also beginning to feel nervous and a tad skeptical of our plan.

"Here, warm up," Carly said, passing back the flask. I was happy to have it. It had the effect of both warming me and reassuring me. My optimism returned. Maggie must have felt the same way because she helped herself, as did Carly. By the time we saw car lights heading in our direction from the bottom of the hill, we had polished off the entire contents the flask.

"This has gotta be her," Carly said. "Let's get out and flag her down."

I was relieved it would soon be over.

"Be careful," Maggie pulled on the back of my jacket when I stepped into the street. "It's hard to see on this road."

"I'm here for you, Maggie," I said in a sudden feeling of goodwill. I put my arm around her shoulder. "We both are. Everything's gonna be alright." And I believed it with all my heart right at that moment.

"I know," Maggie said, as though surprised anyone would think otherwise. The crawling headlights inched their way up the hill, appearing and disappearing behind every turn in the road. "It's Jane," she finally announced once the car was close enough to identify. We were, all three of us, sopping wet by then.

With a stretch of only five or ten yards by the time her car rounded the turn where we waited on the shoulder, Carly lunged into the road, waving her arms wildly to flag Jane down. Maggie and I followed, and I remember being caught in the beam of her headlights, wondering, for one instant, if I'd just stepped into the path of my demise.

Everything tragic supposedly happens in slow motion—I read that some years later. Whether or not it's true, in this case it was, at least for me. Jane veered sharply to the left, surprised by our sudden and unexpected appearance. The road slick from rain. The dark night. The steep drop. Jane's car disappearing over the side of the hill. The sickening sound of crumpling steel. The unreality of what had just happened. My mind stalling while events raced ahead of me. Running to the edge of the road, looking down on the car. Upside down. Headlights pointing toward the lights of the city far below. Tires spinning in the air. Maggie's scream in my ears. Skuttling down the hillside on all fours, like a crab—muddy, cut by rocks. The driver's side window, smeared dark with what I knew was blood and not mud. And then someone grabbing me by the arm and pulling me back.

"We've gotta get out of here." Carly, yelling directly in my ear. Yanking me. Dragging me away. And me allowing it.

The drive back down the hill. Maggie's wailing and what I believe was my shock. Only Carly in control. Carly who assured us we'd be implicated if we stayed. We'd been drinking. Everyone knew Jane was mad at us. We had to save ourselves. Carly stopping at a gas station once we got into town. Calling the police from a pay phone to say she heard what might be an accident on Durham Road. Not identifying herself and hanging up quickly before they could ask.

"There's nothing we could have done," she correctly stated. "The police will be there soon." And indeed, we passed a police cruiser, lights flashing, speeding in the direction of the accident.

But Jane hadn't hesitated when I fell into the icy waters of Lake Tahoe. She hadn't given a second's thought to her own safety or whether anything could be done. Jane thought only of me and without her I would not be alive. *The meek shall inherit the Earth*, I thought again. *They already have. Not its glory and splendor. Just its problems and worries. The weight of it on their shoulders.* I was beyond redemption. I would never be a strong and good person. I would never be like Jane.

CHAPTER SEVENTEEN

It was reported that Jane had most likely swerved to avoid hitting a deer and plunged down the hill to her untimely death. Parents had talks with their children about deer in connection with the dangers of driving. They were plentiful in Indian Springs. Better to take one's chances hitting a deer head-on than to swerve off the road, it was thought. But this was only a guess, and nobody knew for sure. All that anyone really knew was that Jane was dead.

We all attended her memorial service—Maggie and Carly and I. Most of the school was there. We went separately with our families. Afterward, I waited to say something to Jane's family, but I only succeeded in catching Leann's eye. When she turned her back to me, I told my parents that I felt overwhelmed and needed to go home. It was the truth.

Carly's after-school activities occupied most of her free time. I was grateful for that because I had no desire to spend time with her anymore. We saw each other occasionally, mostly at Maggie's, where Carly would remind us we bore no legal responsibility, and nobody had any proof of our involvement.

"Leann knew I wanted to talk to her that night," Maggie said.

"And she knows you and Jane were having problems," I reminded her.

"It wasn't our fault," Carly repeated. "If anything, Jane was the instigator because she started the whole thing."

I got up and left. After that, Carly was careful what she said around me during the rare times we were together.

That summer, my mother suggested I get a job, and I jumped at the chance. I was only fifteen, but I was allowed to work less than full-time with a school-approved work permit. I got a job as a checkout clerk in the drugstore where Alice and I had once swooned over a made-up, grown-up version of Grace. It seemed another lifetime. I spent most of my spare time at home, and when my parents went to visit Luke in Sacramento, I always went along.

Mom and Dad fretted at the reclusive change in my nature since Jane's death. They encouraged me to return to church and throw myself into helping others. One Sunday, when I was sitting in the pew, only half paying attention to the sermon, I focused on the stained-glass image of Christ. A beam of sunlight hit the red robe at an angle which would normally have been breathtaking. Awe-inspiring. I thought about the driver's side window of Jane's car and the dark smear of blood that I knew was not mud. I got up and walked out of the church for the last time. My parents prayed for me every night, but I only wished I could tell them they were praying for the wrong person. I didn't deserve anyone's prayers.

I have very little memory of my senior year of high school. Generally, I recall that Dad improved dramatically. He'd taken a part-time job working in a local hardware store. He and Mom were already making plans to return to the field after my graduation. Mom and Dad didn't worry about me as much anymore. I'd become an expert at hiding what was inside. Only to Maggie did I let down my guard. Only with Maggie did I have any release. Maggie was my confessor, and I hers, although we could never absolve each other of our sins.

I'd fallen out of love with Carly, if that's what it ever really was. But Carly and I were, and would continue to be, inextricably linked like a divorced couple never able to be completely rid of each other because of their child. Our child—Carly's and mine—was our terrible secret.

As the year drew to an end, we learned that Tim LeClerc, who would graduate first in our class, had been accepted to Harvard. Carly, who would graduate second, would be attending Yale. I would be at the University of San Francisco. And Maggie was exhibiting the first symptoms of an eating disorder.

That year, when the daffodils were still in bloom but just on the cusp of wilting, we received our first letters. Carly, Maggie, and me. Handwritten in block letters. Postmarked from San Francisco.

"Will anyone cry when you die?"

SAN FRANCISCO

How QUICKLY IT seemed to happen that one year turned into two, and two turned into three, and then somehow fifteen. Fifteen years had passed since I followed Nathan back to San Francisco and rededicated myself to my studies, this time choosing a focus more in line with my past—an undergraduate degree in nursing and a master's in Public Health. Fifteen years of school and work. Fifteen letters, which had evolved into emails. Fifteen phone calls to Carly, whose reassurances I had become addicted to, divorced as they were from any troubling emotions. Even after I knew who she was. Even after I knew *what* she was. Fifteen years of obsessing over what kind of person would devote their lives to ruining ours, not that we didn't deserve it. Leann had the most realistic motive and justification, yet I couldn't imagine her penning that annual missive. Mr. Sutherland had been hurt. His wife. His daughter. Kerry and Timothy only superficially, relative to their lives as a whole. But one never knows who lurks hatefully on the borders of their consciousness. Sometimes I'd wake at night, panicked not only by what I'd done but by the realization someone out there was determined to make me pay for it. If time heals all wounds, the email was the means to reliably rip the scab from the wound in a predictable way. Never forget. And I never did.

Nathan and I rededicated ourselves to each other, and as long as we remained focused on school and work, things were close to wonderful between us. If I'd been with Nathan all along, I would never have felt that awkward tug of his life in a different direction. I probably would have gone there with him. But when I returned to San Francisco, we had to start all over again.

Fifteen years of school and work, the last ten bonded in

marriage.

Over the years, Nathan occasionally broached the forbidden topic of Carly, knowing all the while that it would inevitably lead to an argument between us. He couldn't help himself, perhaps hoping he'd eventually uncover the real me somewhere between hurt feelings and angry accusations. But we only picked around the edges of my relationship with Carly. If Nathan knew the full truth, he would be compelled to reject me. Wouldn't he?

"She sounds like a psychopath," he said one day after a grueling shift during his residency at Stanford. We'd taken an apartment halfway between Palo Alto and San Francisco, where I worked and continued to study. We sat at our small kitchen table, sharing a rare dinner together—cold pizza, salad, and beer.

A psychopath. This was before novices like us were using the more modern term of *sociopath* or the more appropriately medical term of *sociopathic personality disorder*. But I rejected that. It was impossible. I would have known. But a worm burrowed into my brain. If Carly was a psychopath, then maybe I was one too. After all, how was I any different from her? Wasn't I just her spiritual little sister without her courage?

"Well then, at least she must have had bad parenting," he said, knowing only that Carly was unkind, knowing nothing of the true depths of the darkness of her soul. So what was bad parenting? I knew very little about Carly's parents, but the little I did know, I didn't like. Her father raised the tiny hairs on the back of my neck when I was around him, and yet he had been one hundred percent supportive of Carly in all her endeavors. Her mother seemed absent. Vacant.

Nathan's parents were interested in every detail of his life, constantly breathing down his neck, making him crazy, causing him to doubt every decision he made, including marrying me.

My parents had left me to my own devices, Maggie's mom as well—and yet I never doubted their love for their children. But I was not my parents' priority. Their priority was their faith and their work. Each other. Would that reality make me a monster in Nathan's eyes? Unsuitable? Or did we reserve the label of bad parenting only for the children we didn't like?

As our careers took off, and our homes grew larger and larger, we grew further and further apart, sometimes spending an entire day without ever coming together in the same sprawling house.

Nathan began to suspect depression in me and suggested I'd inherited my father's tendency toward depression.

"My father's depression was situational," I corrected him in the middle of yet another argument.

"Depression can seem situational but be more deeply rooted. A person can be predisposed to depression. My grandfather survived the Holocaust but never lost his sunny disposition."

And just like that, the state of my happiness had been coopted as Nathan's weapon in our ongoing war.

Our arguments started out as theoretical, even existential. But after a while, they became practical. Nathan wanted kids. I didn't. At first, this wasn't a problem. We were young and never at home. We had work, studies. Money and time were tight, and Nathan didn't want to rely on his parents to tide us over financially. But there came a time when that was no longer a valid excuse. Nathan wanted kids, so I went on birth control and kept that fact from him.

"One or the other of us has an issue," Nathan said after nine months. "You definitely should be pregnant by now." We were both medical professionals. Who did I think I was fooling? "We need to see a fertility specialist," he added.

"It seems if it's meant to be, it'll happen."

Nathan looked at me curiously. "I can't believe you just said that. You're an OB/GYN nurse practitioner, for God's sake. Is this how you advise your patients?"

I tangled a piece of hair around my finger, pulling hard as I did. I couldn't bear to look Nathan in the eye and tell him the truth, but I couldn't bear to lie anymore. "I don't want kids," I blurted out. "I've been taking precautions."

At that moment, I saw all the love drain from Nathan's eyes. I don't think he ever looked at me the same way again, although he was an honorable and loyal man and would have stayed with me in spite of my deceit. "You might have mentioned that fact to me before we got married."

"You might have asked," I said.

"One assumes when one gets married." He looked out the window at our million-dollar view. Rolling hills, the color of caramel, dotted with dark-green oaks. Splashes of wild mustard still lingering, refusing to give up the ghost until summer. "I didn't realize we had to have that talk. I just assumed . . . silly me."

"I'm sorry," I said. "I should have told you. But I wasn't sure until you said it was time to have kids. Then I was sure."

"Grace." He turned to face me, his eyes rimmed with red. "I've tried every way I know to love you and make you love me. I've tried everything I could to make you happy. But it's never going to happen with us, is it?"

I didn't have to answer. We both knew we were done.

My separation was two weeks old, but it felt both older and newer. It seemed as though he'd been in my life forever, but then it seemed like he was never really there. My new apartment was small but felt safe. The close walls gave me less space to think. There were only two rooms I could travel to and from, unlike the house I shared with Nathan where I sometimes wandered from room to room looking for a misplaced object. Or a misplaced thought.

I pulled the blinds and the street opened beneath me. Cars and people going about their normal business completely oblivious of me and my life. The small market just across the street that sold overpriced essentials. Although my address was Nob Hill, the building was decrepit, and it seemed that even the most minor earthquake would bring everything down on top of me. The building was old, more than a hundred years. And yet, it had been through many earthquakes and still stood. What is or isn't resilient is sometimes surprising. I smoothed the sheets on my bed and shook out the light silk comforter dotted with bright yellow flowers. A quick snap before I released it to float down into place. I bought it for the pattern, the yellow flowers reminding me of a more innocent and hopeful time.

In such a small space, the scent of richly brewed coffee permeated every corner. I sat on the overstuffed sofa, which occupied every inch of square footage unclaimed by the coffee table, dresser, and bed. Day or night, the ancient radiator chugged out heat, requiring me to leave my window perpetually ajar. It was a typical San Francisco summer's day. Cool. Foggy. Nostalgic, as though somehow ghosts live more openly in this Land's End city.

With the mug of hot coffee in one hand, I perused the schedule of the conference I'd be attending in an hour: *The Crisis of Healthcare in our Inner City Localities.* The HMO that employed me required a representative, and with my background of nursing combined with public health, I was viewed as the natural attendee.

My gaze slid down the page, my pen poised to circle the various seminars I planned on attending that day—the ones I'd previously chosen from the website. But there was an addition not listed on the website, an early-morning option: *Silicon Valley Partners in Health*. The speaker, Timothy LeClerc, founder and CEO of CyberSmart, the most widely used security software in the world. Of course, I knew all about Tim and his massive success over the years. He inhabited the rare stratosphere of internet billionaires, which didn't surprise me. However, I hadn't realized he'd be speaking at this conference, as his presence hadn't been advertised and was only known through the materials distributed to actual paying attendees. It only took me a few seconds to decide. I'd have to hurry to make it in time.

Tim LeClerc, so inextricably linked to the path my life had taken. If it hadn't been for the way he had tricked me into giving the talk on herpes alone, I would have felt sympathy rather than revulsion when his shame was revealed outside the boys' locker room. If I hadn't felt that revulsion, I wouldn't have been quite as susceptible to Carly's unspoken promise of social and emotional protection. If I hadn't told Carly about Tim's ruse, she wouldn't have had an alternate excuse to go after him—one that didn't so clearly expose her own petty jealousies toward him. If it hadn't been for Carly's retribution, Jane would never have confronted Maggie, warned me away from the Kitty Committee, dismissed Carly with the hateful word *you* so disdainfully spat out, and then left us with a threat hanging over all our heads. If it hadn't been for the threat, we wouldn't have surprised Jane on that rainy evening. She would still be alive, undoubtedly a positive force in the world. I circled the seminar on my brochure along with the others I'd be attending that day.

I wasn't the same girl, in appearance, as the one who made her public speaking debut in health class at the age of thirteen, so why did I expect Tim would remain unchanged? He wasn't. To say he was handsome would be far too generous, but he'd finally grown into his natural self-confident arrogance—become worthy of it. One expected this from internet billionaires, after all. He was still tall but probably no taller than high school, so the rest of us had caught up a little. His acne was gone, his hair was appropriately cut and styled, his clothes were expensive and flattering. He spoke succinctly, knowledgeably, without inhibition or reticence. Aging had been kind to him, so he was Timothy, but he wasn't Tim. I listened to his talk, didn't ask any questions, and kept to the back shadows of the conference room. I saw what I came to see, and it did nothing to put my life into perspective or move my past out of my future. I felt slightly ashamed and disappointed that I'd missed a more relevant talk that would have been more worthwhile for my employer and myself.

In the foyer, I paused for a breakfast roll and a second cup of coffee. It normally took me three or four cups to make it through the day and I wasn't yet halfway there. I was reaching for the cream when I felt a hand come from behind and grasp my elbow.

"Well, if it isn't Grace Templeton," Tim said when I turned around. "How many years has it been?"

Our conversation bled over into the next time slot, and I couldn't help but be aware of the envious stares of other attendees standing at respectful distances, most likely wondering if it was permissible to approach the famous Timothy LeClerc once he was done speaking to me. After about ten minutes, Tim's young assistant moved to his side. "Sir," he said quietly. "We should be going. Your flight's scheduled to leave in less than an hour."

"This is Miss Grace Templeton," Tim said, eyeing my ring finger. "Who once accused me of nefariously setting her up to do my dirty work." He smirked. "Who has seen me at my lowest . . . and now at my highest. I ask you, Simon," he turned to his young assistant. "Which would you consider the priority? Lunch with Miss Templeton," he flashed a smile at me that I'd once seen him direct at Jane, "or make the flight that's scheduled to leave in less than an hour?"

Clearly this was a show put on for my benefit, and Simon understood his role. "Lunch with Miss Templeton?" he said with only a hint of a question at the end.

"Will you, Grace Templeton? Honor me with your company at lunch?"

It was one of those moments where fate takes you by the hand and shows you the way.

Arrangements were made to pick me up in his limo.

Tim brought a lightness into my life that had been sorely lacking for more than twenty years. He never probed, the way Nathan did. Tim didn't need to know who the real Grace Templeton was and what made her tick. He just wanted to keep things fun, and fun was everywhere to be had—a weekend away on his private jet at his private island in the Caribbean. A week at Lake Lugano in Switzerland. A sailboat cruise through the lesser-known Greek isles. He showered me with gifts until I asked him to stop.

"I'm not about gifts," I told him. "And if you want to spend time with me, you should at least know that."

But I wasn't above accepting the free travel and meals in restaurants where regular people had to make reservations a year in advance. Not Tim—a phone call from Simon, and Tim could be anywhere he wanted to be. Anywhere *I* wanted to be.

If I was completely honest with myself, which I often was, my desire to be with Tim went beyond a sudden and unexpected attraction to him. I had ulterior motives that didn't exactly make me proud, but which I couldn't resist. Being with Tim allowed me to unspool my life—go back to the time where I could be nice to Tim LeClerc instead of feeding him to the wolves. In addition, Tim was the founder and CEO of the world's largest internet security company. Didn't that give him resources others might not have? Couldn't he discover the identity of the person sending us the emails each spring? But I had to be sure of where I stood with him before I got to that point. And I wasn't confident I could ever be that sure.

Maggie came to see me in early December, sleeping on my sofa in the little apartment. It almost felt like we were girls again, staying up late watching movies and eating popcorn. Long walks in the rain around Golden Gate Park. Ordering in pizza. Catching up on gossip, mostly about Carly, who kept in regular touch with Maggie but only spoke briefly with me once a year. Carly was the first female manager of the most prestigious hedge fund in New York City. She had a lavish lifestyle, although it was nothing compared to Tim. She'd gone through a series of men but never settled on any one in particular. In that way, we were all alike. All of us losers in love. Maggie looked gaunt, and I worried about a recurrence of the eating disorder, but she said she was over that. She'd been okay for more than five years. But she was tired, she admitted. Tired of her life. Tired of Indian Springs. Tired of her parents watching over her like she was a child when she was almost forty.

"Can you believe how old we are, Grace?" she said. "I mean, we're seriously old."

"We're still young enough to eat stale pizza for breakfast," I joked before turning serious. "I've got something to tell you that I've been waiting to tell you in person because it's a hard thing to say."

"What?" Her eyes grew wide. "Are you okay?"

"Yeah, I'm fine," I said. "I mean, as fine as I can be." I took a deep breath. "I'm dating Tim LeClerc," I blurted out. "But don't tell Carly. I don't want her to know."

"Oh my God, how does that happen in this universe?" She shook her head in disbelief. "Tim LeClerc, no way! He's like famous . . . famous for something, right? Famously rich."

"He is that," I said. "And as to how it happened, it was just one of those flukes. I ran into him at a conference, and we clicked. Who would've thought?"

"It's like that fantasy where you get to go back and relive your high-school years with everything you've learned as an adult," Maggie said. "You're living that fantasy. So tell me everything. What's he like? Most importantly, what's he like in bed?" She laughed, and I remembered the effect it always had on me—hearing Maggie laugh.

And we talked about Tim like two giggling high-school girls. I filled her in without revealing my ulterior motives that weren't the only reason, but they couldn't be denied. Someday I'd be able to tell her. And someday, hopefully, I'd be able to trust Tim.

"Don't tell Carly," I reminded her. "I just . . . don't want her to know."

Maggie nodded soberly. "Don't worry," she said. "Your secret's safe with me. But Grace—don't tell Tim what I did to him. Please never *ever* let him know the truth about that."

"Look at us," I said. "All our secrets. We're pathetic, aren't we?"

"I mean it, Grace. Don't ever let him know. I'm so ashamed."

"I am too," I said. "Ashamed."

"But you never did anything to be ashamed of."

"Kerry," I said.

"What about Kerry? I mean, you just talked to her, that's no big deal."

"Are you serious?" I assumed Maggie knew all about what I'd done to Kerry, although I'd chosen to keep it to myself, pursuant to Carly's rules. Maggie had chosen to keep what she'd done to Tim to herself, and yet I'd found out everything. But it was Jane who had brought that on—maybe I'd never have otherwise known. "I did more than just talk to her. I—*Carly* took a necklace from the store where Kerry worked. She dropped it in my purse, and I shoplifted it. Then I mailed it back to the store with an anonymous note making it seem like Kerry had stolen it."

Maggie's feet were propped against the coffee table. Her toenails were painted a dusty rose. She looked down at the bare skin of her knees bulging through her tight ripped jeans and shook her head. "Wow," she said. "She really is a first-class bitch, isn't she?"

"Who?" I'd never heard Maggie say anything like that about Carly so, for a second, I thought she was referring to Kerry.

"Carly," she said, looking up at me. "She can really be an evil bitch."

I felt a breakthrough coming. First Tim. Now Maggie. Maybe things really could be different. Maybe it *was* possible to revisit high school with the knowledge I'd gained as an adult. Right my wrongs.

"But you have to know she did it because she loved us, Grace," Maggie said. "You really have to believe that."

It was a rare free Saturday when Tim joined me at my apartment for a home-cooked brunch. It was already February, and the weather was unusually warm. Simon kept the limo ready around the corner in the usual loading zone where he'd sometimes spend hours waiting to be summoned by Tim when he was visiting. I rarely spent time at Tim's mansion in Woodside. It was too far out of my comfort zone.

My spirits were high that day. Work was going well, and I'd just been promoted. I'd recently spent a week in Sacramento where Mom was visiting Luke. She'd brought Dad's ashes with her, exacting a promise from Luke to keep them until she was gone, at which point he was to comingle their ashes before scattering them at sea. The annual email hadn't arrived unless I had somehow missed it, which I doubted. I was hoping this year might be different. This might be the year that Carly always predicted, when the sender either tired of the emails or believed we'd suffered enough.

"Guess what time it is." Tim said.

I picked up my cell phone then laid it down. "12:38," I said.

"That too." Tim chuckled. "But what I meant was it's daffodil time in Indian Springs."

I knew that. I'd seen daffodils in the local flower shops—those bright harbingers of spring that always stirred warring emotions within me.

"Let's go see them," he said. "We'll clean up here, then I'll have Simon come get us. We could be there by two thirty, stop by and see my parents. Maybe an early dinner and then head home. What d'ya say?"

I was stunned by the suggestion. I'd never met his parents and wondered if this was a precursor to a formal commitment. I hadn't been back to Indian Springs since the day I had left to start college. After all those years, decades now, how would it feel? And if I ever wanted to move forward, wasn't this something I'd eventually have to do, and wouldn't it be easier with Tim by my side? I thought of the gorgeous daffodils, miniature suns against the clear blue sky of the day that would most certainly be even brighter and bluer in Indian Springs.

"That sounds nice," I said. "Bring the dishes in the kitchen. I'll wash."

"You cooked. I wash," he said, brushing his lips across the top of my head. I followed him into the kitchen, carrying stacks of dirty dishes. I took a seat at the tiny kitchen table, happy but nervous.

"How long's it been for you?" he asked, his long, bony arms flailing from side-to-side as he rinsed, scrubbed, and then rinsed again. "Since you've been home . . . or I guess not technically home for you."

"Ages," I said to his back. "My parents left the same time that I left for college. So there was never any reason to go back."

"Not even to see Maggie?" he asked.

"Maggie always comes here."

"Or Carly?"

My happiness took a detour at the mention of Carly's name, but still Tim faced away from me, not pausing from his dishwashing duties, so he couldn't read the distress in my eyes. I tried my best to disguise any sign of it in my voice.

"I don't really see Carly anymore," I said. "I've barely seen her in the last ten years. Maybe once or twice with Maggie. Briefly."

"That must have been a hard time for you," he said. "Losing your friend like that. Such a tragedy."

I knew he was no longer talking about Carly. "Jane?" I asked.

"Yeah, Jane. Must have been hard on you."

"It was . . . beyond hard," I said, clutching the salt shaker so tightly my fingernails still managed to find the opposing flesh of my palm. "You liked her, didn't you?"

I could see the muscles tense through the thin material of his expensive t-shirt. "Of course I liked her. She was a likeable girl."

"No, I mean you *liked* liked her."

The water in the kitchen sink ran uselessly down the drain, but it didn't seem the right moment to lecture Tim about California's drought and the need to conserve.

"Me and every other guy in school."

My insides clutched, and I didn't know which felt worse. My jealousy, or the fact that the object of my jealousy was a girl whom I'd killed.

"Every guy was in love with her?" I asked. I knew the answer—why wouldn't they be? I just had the perverse desire to hear Tim say it.

He picked up the bottle of dishwashing soap and squirted a dab onto the sponge. "Let's just say that Jane was the girl every guy wanted, but they thought she was too good for them. Carly was the girl every guy wanted, but they thought *she thought* she was too good for them. And Maggie was the girl every guy wanted and figured they had a reasonable chance of getting."

"That's a mean thing to say about Maggie," I said.

"Well it's the truth. Did you want me to sugarcoat it? Guys are pigs, especially in high school. Look what they did to me."

"And me?" I asked. "What was I? Invisible?"

"You were the cute kid sister," he said. He turned off the tap and put the sponge down. "Ready to go?"

"Gee, thanks," I said.

"Hey." He leaned back against the sink and looked at me through sympathetic eyes. "Look at you now. You're an absolutely stunning woman. You're gorgeous. A goddess. But you were a kid back then, and I didn't mean anything more than that."

"I know you didn't," I said, wondering how I had it in me to be so petty.

Tim and I had never talked much about high school except in the most abstract terms, but now I was plunging into the swamp of memories in the belief that I could slog through without being pulled under. I was wrong.

The conversation didn't end once we were in the back seat of the limo on our way to Indian Springs.

"Have you heard about Jane's sister, Leann?" Tim asked. "What she's doing now?"

"I read about it online. The center she founded where they use horses in conjunction with therapy for kids?"

"Yep. They have twenty-five acres now. Thirty horses. A state of the art residential treatment center on site. Families are charged only according to their ability to pay. Fully staffed with trained and licensed professionals. Pegasus, it's called. Nice name, don't you think?"

I thought I detected a note of proprietary pride in Tim's description. "It's a perfect name," I said, imagining the winged horse soaring high in the sky, children clinging to its silver mane and leaving their troubles far below. "Did you have anything to do with it?"

"Not me," Tim said. "My foundation. I'd love to swing by and say hi while we're there. Would you like that?"

"That'd be wonderful." I hoped he couldn't hear the absolute false note in my response. Who was I kidding? I was in no way prepared to return to Indian Springs. Meet Tim's parents. Stop by and say hi to Leann.

Tim went on his phone to check his email, and I waited a full fifteen minutes before speaking again. "I'm either carsick or coming down with something," I said at last. "Do you feel okay?" I put a hand to my forehead as if testing for a fever.

"I feel fine," he said.

"Well thank God it's not food poisoning then."

He looked me up and down as though checking for illness,

before bringing his free hand up to rub the back of my neck. He returned his attention to his phone and scrolling through emails.

"Tim, I'm sorry. I've got to go home. I think I'm going to throw up . . . or worse."

This time he put the phone down on the seat beside him. "Really?" he asked. He placed his palm on my forehead. "No fever." He clicked on the driver intercom button. "Change of plans, Simon. Grace is sick so we need to take her home." The disappointment I detected in his voice almost made me reconsider my decision. Almost.

A week later the email popped up in my inbox.

"Is God willing to prevent evil but not able? Then he is not omnipotent.

Is he able but not willing? Then he is malevolent.

Is he both able and willing? Then whence cometh evil?

Is he neither able nor willing? Then why call him God?"

Two weeks later Maggie called to say she'd been diagnosed with breast cancer.

Maggie's life became my life as her treatment options moved from theoretical to practical and finally to experimental, the latter of which took place at the University of California Medical Center under the supervision of the premier expert in his field. Doorways opened to Maggie that wouldn't have otherwise opened were it not for the interference by Tim. Deductibles and copays not covered by insurance were picked up by Tim. All of this at his insistence—and only revealed to her parents, never to Maggie, at Tim's request. And still it wasn't enough in the end. Money can't buy love. And it can't buy life.

Maggie hung on longer than anyone thought possible, considering the virulence of her cancer. When she wasn't strong enough to make the drive back and forth with her parents to Indian Springs, she stayed with me. My bedroom became hers, and even when she wasn't around, I continued to sleep on the couch. Carly made two trips to Indian Springs to see Maggie, each time staying only a few days. She didn't have the luxury of being a non-essential person at her firm. She was the firm.

"Tell me something . . . *anything*," Maggie said. I'd just walked in the door after a day at work. I'd had a patient that day whose child would be born medically fragile. I was concerned about this patient's ability to handle the inevitable devastation her unborn child would soon introduce to her world. For the first time in a long time, I was more concerned about someone other than Maggie. That changed the minute I saw her. Maggie was propped up in bed with the tiny TV on mute, an episode of *Friends* playing in the background. I knew she'd seen it a dozen times, most of them right from that bed.

I finally understood the term *painfully thin*—the painful part was having to witness it as an observer. Maggie had a scarf wrapped around her head, too embarrassed to let even me see her without hair. Her eyebrows were gone as well. Nothing was left to recognize Maggie except her eyes. And her laugh on the rare occasions it bubbled to the surface.

"What should I tell you, Maggie dear? A story?" I said in my usual light tone.

"Anything. I'm so bored, I could scream."

"Okay, but you have to eat something first. Did you take your pills?"

"Yes, Mommy," she said sullenly. I eyed the empty spot on the bedside table where I'd laid out her daily dose of medication, including pain meds. They were gone. The bottle of water was empty.

I went to the refrigerator to retrieve one of the variety of food items Maggie could manage to keep down. Applesauce. I sat on the edge of the bed and handed her the cup and a spoon.

"Well, I told you about the clinic where we lived in Guatemala. The one my mom used to work at."

"How it burned down last month?"

"Yeah. So you know they called Mom back to help with patients until they can rebuild. She'll just be helping out a doctor who works out of his house."

"Your mom's a saint." Maggie set the spoon down on the bed. "I don't know how she does it."

I picked up the spoon and scooped another mouthful, holding it up to her lips, which she parted reluctantly. "Anyway, Tim's lawyer called me today at work. Tim's foundation set up an irrevocable trust with Mom as the executor. And it's enough to rebuild a first-rate clinic. I mean—Mom's going to be . . . she's going to be so happy," I said while feeling slightly guilty about introducing the happy word in front of Maggie. But I needn't have.

"Tim's amazing," Maggie said. "Your mom's amazing. But you're the most amazing friend anyone could ever have," she said.

I shook my head and scooped another spoonful of applesauce.

"Grace," Maggie held my wrist before the spoon made it to her mouth. "I was just thinking about that day at the pool, the first time we met. You remember?"

I put the spoon and the cup of applesauce down on the small table by the side of her bed. "Sure," I said. "How could I ever forget?"

"I never thought . . . How could I have known you'd be

so . . . such an important person in my life? Maybe *the* most important person in my life, Grace. And I want to thank you for everything because . . ." Her voice was strangled, her eyes wet from tears. "Because I need you to know that before I die."

"You're not going to die, Maggie," I lied. "Because I can't live without having you around."

It was a lie she let me get away with that one last time. "Grace, I know about Tim paying for my medical expenses. My mom let it slip. Promise you'll never tell him what I did. Promise."

"I would never do that. You have my word."

"And Grace," she said. "I'm ready to die. I'm okay with it, and I want you to be okay with it too."

"How can I be okay with it, sweet Maggie?" I took her thin, bony hand in mine. "I could never be okay with it, but I'll try to help you get there, okay?"

She sighed deeply, and I gently laid her limp hand on the mattress beside her. "You know, Grace," she said. "We didn't kill Jane, but we should've helped her even if it was too late. And we should've told someone what happened. Somebody out there knows, or at least suspects, but we should have told our parents."

"We should've," I said. "But it's too late at this point. Too much time has gone by."

Maggie was tired from talking. Her lids were beginning to droop, and I knew the morphine tablet was taking hold. "We always say that," she said. "We said it after a day and then after a week. Then we said it after a year. And every year we keep saying it." Her lips were barely moving. Barely forming the words. "Maybe it's too late for me," she said. "But maybe it's not too late for you."

My greatest wish was to provide hospice care for Maggie until the moment she passed. I thought, as a nurse, I would know when the time was near and be able to stay home with her until it happened. Her outlook was for days and weeks. I was sure I'd be able to spot the transition to days and hours. But that conversation would prove to be our last. The following day, a fever raged while her parents sat at her bedside during the time I was at work. They panicked and called an ambulance that transported her to the hospital. On the way there, Maggie lost consciousness and never regained it. She existed in that state for a week before she left us. I thought I'd be ready when it happened—after all, I'd had a year to prepare, slowly descending from one stage into an ever more hopeless one—but nothing could have prepared me. It was like falling into the dark icy depths of Lake Tahoe all over again. Only this time, there was no Jane to pull me to the surface. In the end, I wasn't there in her final moments. But she wasn't there either.

Tim sent Simon to fetch me the minute he heard. He insisted that I take a few days off and stay with him for a while. My apartment was filled with too many reminders of Maggie's last days. We could deal with it together after some time had passed, he said.

A few days later, the email arrived just like clockwork.

"Vengeance is mine, I will repay, says the Lord."

I stepped into the private bedroom Tim kept for me at his house, although we always slept in his. I picked up the phone and called Carly.

"Are we really going to do this every year?" Carly concluded after our brief and bitter conversation. "How many years has it been? Twenty?"

"Maggie was better than you and me," I said before hanging up, grasping for the most destructive, spiteful thing I could say. I had a feeling it would be my last and best hope to hurt Carly the way I wanted to. "She proved it by dying."

Carly ended the call without another word, and I took a moment to compose myself, splashed some cold water on my face, and went out to join Tim in the game room.

"You okay?" He stood when I entered the room.

"Not really," I said. He led me to the plush love seat and folded me in his arms.

"It'll get better," he murmured into my hair. "You'll be alright. I'll take you out to a nice dinner tonight, okay?"

"I don't see how a nice dinner or anything else will ever make it better. I just don't see how that's possible."

"You did everything you could," he said, pulling me even closer. "You'll realize that as time passes, and it will bring you comfort. Your mom's coming in a few days. Simon will drive you to Luke's, and you can spend time with your family. That'll help too."

"I feel responsible," I said.

"Do you, Grace? Why would you feel responsible?"

"She was my friend?"

"That doesn't make you responsible," he said, lifting his voice into a near question at the end.

I realized how crazy it sounded, and yet it was true. It was how I felt.

"I'm going to lie down," I said. "In my room."

"You do that, sweetie. I'll come wake you for dinner."

Terms of endearment weren't normal for Tim. When they did come, they were almost jarring, as if I could sense the psychic energy he expended in saying them. I might have chuckled under my breath in different circumstances, hearing Tim call me sweetie—an old-fashioned expression he had perhaps heard his father use on his mother. But nothing seemed comical at that moment, and it was touching to hear it. I retreated to my room, closing the door behind me and lowering the blinds. I didn't exactly want to be alone with my thoughts,

I was just overcome with a fatigue so powerful that it seemed necessary to envelop myself in darkness. I passed into a deep and dreamless sleep.

I wasn't sure how much time had passed when I woke, aware that someone else was in the room with me. Without moving, I gave my eyes a few seconds to focus before surveying the dark recesses of the room. Tim was sitting in an armchair tucked into the tiny reading alcove next to the window. A thin sliver of light haloed the blinds, framing Tim's motionless figure. For a second, I thought he'd fallen asleep in the sitting position—I'd seen him do it before, in the most unlikely spots. But his eyes were open. He was watching over me. Or watching me.

"Have you had enough yet, Grace?" he asked so quietly that I questioned whether he'd spoken at all.

"Enough of what?" I propped myself up on one elbow.

"Enough of Carly . . . treating you like her lap dog, running to her, begging on your hands and knees for a scrap from her? Are you ready to join me now?"

"What are you talking about?" I sat up and swung my legs over the side of the bed, wondering how he knew about my call to Carly.

"I've been waiting for you to come around because it will be so much more fun if we join forces."

"Join forces?"

Nothing he said was making sense, and I wondered if I was still dreaming. Having an out-of-body experience. The old sleep paralysis—as if I looked down at myself, observing, but incapable of waking, from a dream so real as to be indistinguishable from life. I stared at him with a mixture of disbelief and fear while ideas shifted around inside my head. Disjointed thoughts.

Memories. Suspicions. Like ice floes coaxed by the tide to collide into each other until they formed a solid, unbroken surface—everything fell into place. Everything made perfect sense. The miasma of my brain crystallized and then shattered into a million pieces, finally revealing what I knew all along.

"It was you," I said. "All this time it was you."

"I figured at some point you'd be so mad at Carly that you'd want to join me." His mouth was a thin, hard line. How had I missed that hardness before? How had he so successfully hidden it? "And now it's time for you to decide. Are you finally ready? Have you finally had enough? Just say the word."

I slipped my feet into my sandals as though preparing to flee. It was an unconscious gesture that didn't go unnoticed by Tim. He reached over and clicked the lamp switch. A rosy glow spread across the white wool carpet.

"Do you realize what you've done? To me? To Maggie? You haven't done shit to Carly though." The pitch of my voice was rising, bordering on hysteria.

"I've given you the gift of a conscience," he said grimly. "Maggie too. I'm sorry if it cost Maggie her life, but consciences are tricky things. As for Carly, I never expected to impact her that way. I have other plans for Carly. This was my gift to you."

"Thanks for the gift, Tim." I was glued to my spot and he to his. Had he made a move toward me, I would have run. "Maybe you're a sociopath too—just like Carly."

"Maybe I am," he said. "Don't think I haven't thought that through and processed it. But sociopaths can be useful. Sometimes they can guide you out of a mess without the baggage of emotions."

I shook my head slowly. "You're no better than her."

"I *am* better. I'm smarter than Carly. And more patient. How about you, Grace? Why did you do it? Your parents had given you all the gifts they had available. They'd instilled you with decency and compassion, and yet you did those things anyway. How are you better than us—Carly and me?"

"I wanted to belong," I said. "Carly made me feel like I belonged."

"Ah, there you go. Belonging is one of the most fundamental human drives—even more than procreating. It ranks just below hunger. I think you might have had the teeniest little crush on her too. No?"

"What do you know?" I asked.

"What do I know? I know that Maggie put drugs in my locker. I know that Carly, and therefore you and Maggie, had something to do with Jane's accident. I know that Jane was furious with you for what you did to me, that Carly had such incredible jealousy toward Jane—a person whose shadow she wasn't worthy to step on—that she couldn't contain it. All this, I learned initially from Leann and had confirmed over the years through your unprotected emails and texts. I also know my old mentor, Mr. Sutherland, suffered the loss of his family because his wife suspected him of inappropriate sexual behavior with Carly. Granted, there were others, and probably at least some of the rumors were true, but Carly was the tipping point. I know other things too, Grace, but we can stop at that, can't we?"

All that time, I thought. *All those wasted years. The victim had become the victimizer.*

"You're probably wondering what happened to my compassion, or maybe you're not because you've already figured that part out. Compassion is a Christian virtue and yet the Old Testament preaches an eye for an eye. You know about Christian virtues, don't you, Grace? To err is human, to forgive is divine. But I'm not divine, Grace. I'll leave the forgiveness part up to the divinity, if there is one. Who said "Vengeance is mine?" Oh yes, it was the Lord. But sometimes he might need a little help, don't you think?"

"You're crazy," I said, but still I couldn't resist. "And how did I fit into your insane plan?"

"Have you ever heard of swatting?" Tim leaned forward, his bony elbows resting on his knees. He seemed twenty years younger. Alert. Enthusiastic. "Have some fun with it. Call the NYPD anonymous crime reporting number. I'll give you a phone that can never be traced. Tell the police you're the house-keeper and accidentally came across five kilos of cocaine hidden in the back of Carly's closet. Give them specific details so they can't ignore it. I can provide very specific details of the house. They'll figure it out sooner or later, but in the meantime, it's guaranteed to mess with Carly's head."

"How do you know details about Carly's house?" I asked. "And wouldn't the housekeeper lose her job or worse once Carly found out? Don't you at least care about the housekeeper?"

"That's child's play," Tim said. "For a child." A chill ran up my spine. I was the kid sister, Tim had said. Was this the desig-nated role he'd planned for the kid sister? "Carly's housekeeper is on my payroll, although she doesn't know it's me. I give her more in a month than she'd earn in ten years of working for Carly."

"So that's your big plan?" I asked. "Carly will brush that off once it's straightened out. It won't even phase her."

"No, that's not my big plan," he said. "That's my little plan for you, if you want to join forces. Just to give you a taste. My *big* plan has been methodically put together over many years. I've documented every wrongdoing—every instance of insider trading, every Securities & Exchange violation, every time Carly's taken a shit in the wrong bathroom."

"And you've done that how?"

"Please, Grace, don't embarrass yourself. My company's the largest cyber security network in the world. We provide cyber security for the NSA. I'm a passionate man. A driven man. I don't ever stop until I've gotten what I want. And what I want is to destroy Carly. But I want to do it right, so I bide my time."

I stood up and reached for my purse that was hanging over the bedpost. "Destroy her?" I said. "You should marry her."

Tim didn't move to stop me. He pulled his phone from his pocket and smiled. "That's something I hadn't considered," he said. "Might not be a bad idea."

"Goodbye, Tim," I said. "Please don't ever try to contact me again. And please take your money for the clinic in Guatemala and shove it up your ass."

"Can't do that, Grace," he said. "It's an irrevocable trust." His phone was at his ear, ringing for someone. "Simon," he said. "Can you please take Miss Templeton home?"

"Did you do it?" I asked, pausing at the door. "Set me up for the herpes talk in health class?"

"Of course." He smirked.

"Why me?"

"You were the only one gullible enough to fall for it."

"And the others? The guys who shoved you out of the locker room? Why just single us out?"

"I dealt with them years ago." Timothy winced, but his eyes remained hard. "They're ants. Not like Carly. No one's like Carly."

"I won't ask what you did," I said. "I don't even want to know."

"That's good because I didn't plan on telling you." His phone beeped with an incoming text, and he glanced at the screen. "Simon's waiting for you," he said. "Goodbye, Grace."

The following day, I drove to Sacramento where Mom was visiting for two weeks. After that, she'd be moving to Guatemala to supervise the rebuilding of the clinic that had burned down in an electrical fire—the reconstruction completely funded by Tim's irrevocable trust. Anything I had to say to Mom, I had to say now. And Luke—waiting for answers from me for most of my life. He was confused by me, by my inability to hold onto happiness the way he could. I sensed that I was his biggest frustration. His failure to locate the thing inside of me that was broken and fix me was his biggest disappointment. But he never stopped trying.

I drove in silence with no music to distract me, only Maggie was by my side.

It was too late, wasn't it? I'd asked her.

Maybe not for you, she'd said.

I had to answer that question before Maggie could rest in peace.

Mom cooked, and I cleaned up from dinner. Although her voice and step were as youthful as ever, Mom was getting old. That realization was hard to face. Mom always being around was a given, until that night when it wasn't anymore—too much had happened in the past year. My nephews were both out of the house, busy forging new identities as independent young college men. Soon they'd have families of their own. Linda was involved with a late-in-life career as a financial planner; Luke, nearly fully gray-haired but handsome as ever, was getting closer and closer to the time when he could retire with a pension. Life was coming full circle.

Once the dishes were done, Mom and I joined Luke and Linda in the family room. Bob the cat had been gone for three or four years. He'd lived to be a very old cat and I missed him.

Linda poured wine for us, Mom at first refusing and then agreeing. "I don't usually," she said. "But in Grace's honor tonight." She took a sip and then placed it on the coffee table where it would remain untouched.

I took a deep breath and steeled myself. It was my time now. I knew I had the stage if I wanted it.

"I have something to tell you," I said. "Maggie died."

"No, Grace!" Linda got up and came to where I was sitting. She hugged me and pressed her cheek against mine. "I'm so, so sorry. I know she was your best friend."

"Why didn't you say something earlier?" Mom asked. "I'm awfully sorry, Honey." She scooted closer to me on the sofa and took my hand. Hers was as soft as an old glove. Pale. Nearly translucent.

Luke looked at me and then inclined his head toward the ground. I think he sensed more was coming and was waiting to see what it would be.

"Maggie was my best friend," I went on. "But we had a terrible secret . . . and I just don't want it to be a secret anymore. Maggie didn't want that either."

Luke raised his eyes level with mine. Linda left my side and perched on the arm of his chair.

"A secret?" It wasn't the moment Mom had been hoping to share with her children that night. It wasn't the moment any mother would want for her child. "What kind of secret?"

And so I told the entire story. Carly. Jane. The inevitable power struggle between the two titans, and how Maggie and I, caught in the middle, vacillated first one way and then the other. The weak ones who allowed Carly to thrive. I told of the awful thing I'd done to Kerry and implied, without telling, that Carly and Maggie had similar misdeeds. I told of the night we waited on the side of the road so Carly could have it out with Jane. How we'd been drinking. How we'd startled Jane and caused the accident that led to her death. How I'd scrambled down the hill, seen the blood on the window, and allowed Carly to pull me back to her car, how we had stopped at a pay phone to alert the police. I explained how this terrible secret had eaten away at my soul—rendering happiness an impossibility in my life. How I was afraid that no matter what I did going forward, I could never honestly consider myself to be a good and decent person. I would never be worthy of the family I'd been given, I explained. I'd always known that.

I told them almost everything, leaving out the prurient details of my brief sexual encounter with Carly and my misguided feelings of love—Mom could never understand that if she lived another two lifetimes. I left out the annual letters, later annual emails. I left out everything about Tim's involvement. And I couldn't bring myself to tell them the name of our sisterhood—the Kitty Committee—such an innocent and silly name for the incubator of such evil thoughts and deeds.

"We should never have left you at such a young age," Mom said once I'd reached the end of my confession, punctuated by several minutes of heavy group silence. "We shouldn't have skipped you ahead. You were too young. You didn't know what you were doing. It was all my fault." Tears drizzled down the thin, wrinkled skin of her cheeks, but I just shook my head, over and over again for every excuse she made on my behalf. I stood up abruptly, as though sitting was somehow complicit in lessening my guilt. Let them see me for who I really was. Let them open their eyes to a reality none of us in the room wanted to admit.

"No, Mom. It was me. I made these decisions. I did these things." And then I told them the story of how Jane had jumped into the ice-cold water of Lake Tahoe to save my life without a thought to her own safety. "Don't you see? Don't you get it? Jane was only a kid herself, but she did this thing for me. For *me*, Mom. Not because she was older, but because she was good."

Mom covered her face with both hands, as though willing

the vision from her mind. Luke rose from his chair and stood facing me. He put two steady hands on my shoulders to ground me to Earth.

"You did a terrible thing, Grace. Jane didn't deserve that, even if you couldn't save her. But your past doesn't define your future unless you choose to let that happen. I see that in my job every day. People who come out of jail and turn their lives around. It happens."

I looked helplessly up at him. My cheeks were wet, but I didn't remember crying. "Maybe I should've gone to jail. Maybe that would've helped me to move on."

"That was never going to happen," he said. "No DA would have charged you, let alone tried you as adults. Especially not back then. What was the crime? You were kids. It wasn't intentional. You left the scene of an accident, but you stopped and called for help." He ducked his head so I couldn't help but look right at him. "You want my advice?" he asked.

I nodded yes. I'd never wanted anyone's advice so much in my life.

"Move past it," he said. "Forge ahead until you break through the other side. You can choose the rotten beams for the foundation of the house you build," said the man who'd built a cabin in the woods with his own hands. "Or you can decide to choose the strong ones instead."

EPILOGUE
MONTE VERDE, GUATEMALA

It's been two years since I moved out here with Mom. I'm the midwife, also known as the crazy dog lady by the locals. I have my own dog Tramp, a rescue from the streets. Tramp's been neutered, vaccinated, and undergoes regular flea treatments. He sleeps at the foot of my bed. I started my own unofficial rescue operation, funded by my earnings. At any given time, I feed and care for up to ten dogs who all get the same medical treatment and food as Tramp.

There's a hand-painted sign that hangs over the front door of the tiny cottage I call my home—Jane & Maggie's Dog Rescue. The locals know to bring the most pitiful of the street mutts to me. Whenever someone asks who Jane and Maggie are, I tell them they were two ladies who had a soft spot for cats but wouldn't hesitate to help a dog in need. If they ask *where* they are, I tell them they're in Heaven with the angels because that's what most people around here would want to believe.

En el cielo con los ángeles.

Mom lives down the street, and we see each other every day at work and at home. The clinic was built with enough money left over to build a new school. Occasionally, I fill in as a substitute teacher. I keep a copy of *The Wizard of Oz* by my bedside because it reminds me, like Dorothy, that grace wasn't something I had to seek—it was there all along. All I had to do was believe in its power, in *my* power to forgive and to love, myself as well as others.

A few weeks ago, Luke sent a newspaper clipping about Carly's arrest by the FBI. How her lawyer claimed she had been set up, and none of the charges were true. How they would fight it every step of the way and eventually prevail. How they knew things about illegal wiretapping and who was behind it. I threw the article in the garbage and emailed Luke, asking him to never send me news about Carly or her case again.

Sometimes I miss California and think that one day I might like to return. But then I look at my life and wonder if I could ever find anything to complete me in the same way my life completes me now.

But I miss the long walks through Golden Gate Park when the fog moves in and a stillness descends that seeps straight to the heart. I miss standing at Land's End and watching the waves crash against giant boulders while huge freight ships glide by as silently as cats on velvet paws. I miss the daffodils springing forth from the anonymity of winter, their improbable sudden appearance alight with the vibrancy of life. Reminders of the eternal and unfathomable optimism that resides somewhere within us all.

ACKNOWLEDGMENTS

First and foremost, thank you to my husband, George Berla, who keeps me writing through his expectations, love, and belief in me. In marriage, I won the lottery.

My family is the bedrock from which I launch all endeavors. Jeremy, Lucas, Corey, Samantha, and Nishita, thank you for your support, feedback, glitch-fixing, and general superior abilities.

Eternal gratitude to Amberjack Publishing. Dayna, Kayla, Cherrita, and Cassandra. I couldn't ask for a more hardworking and talented group behind me.

Macy, your insights are thought-provoking and motivating. Thank you for caring about *The Kitty Committee* and for summarizing it in four words. Vicky, thanks for being there for *The Kitty Committee* and all its book siblings.

To Orange Dog. We are in awe <3

ABOUT THE AUTHOR

KATHRYN BERLA LIKES to write in a variety of genres including light fantasy, contemporary literary fiction, and even horror. She is the author of the young adult novels: *12 Hours in Paradise*, *Dream Me*, *The House at 758*, and *Going Places*.

The Kitty Committee is her first novel written for adult readers.

Kathryn grew up in India, Syria, Europe, and Africa. Her love for experiencing new cultures runs deep, and she gives into it whenever she can. She has been an avid movie buff since childhood, and often sees the movie in her head before she writes the book.

Kathryn graduated from the University of California in Berkeley with a degree in English. She currently resides in the San Francisco Bay Area.